Noble Heart

The Nobility Series, Book Two

by

Linda J. Parisi

Noble Heart: The Nobility Series, Book Two

COPYRIGHT © 2009 by Linda J. Parisi, LLC

Cover Art by *Tamra Westberry*

The Wild Rose Press
PO Box 708
Adams Basin, NY 14410-0706
Visit us at www.thewildrosepress.com

Publishing History
First Black Rose Edition, 2010
Print ISBN 1-60154-734-X

Published in the United States of America

Dedication

To the two halves of my Heart:
my husband John, and my son Christopher.
I love you both very much.

What was he driving at?

All of a sudden, Elena looked at him. She saw the torch light dance in the midnight of his hair. She saw the tiny laugh lines around eyes that told her how much he truly valued life, in spite of his careless attitude.

Against her will, her head moved closer to his. The sounds of the party faded. Her heartbeat sped up, racing wild as the wind. She could smell the spicy tang of the desert mixed with his scent and a warm glow grew in her belly.

Was this desire? True desire? If so, no words could ever describe the sensation.

This was how a man teased a woman. But shouldn't she be trying to seduce him?

Did she dare?

How far could this go before one of them stepped too close to the fire?

His gaze caught and held hers. She'd never made love before.

They started walking. As soon as they were far enough away, Elena whirled and threw her arms around his neck. Alexi's mouth opened in surprise and she took advantage. He groaned and his arms tightened about her like two steel bands. His mouth engulfed hers. His tongue ravaged the inside of her mouth sending shivers up and down her spine.

All of a sudden, he tore his mouth away from hers. "I'm not a toy," he reiterated, his anger like daggers.

Tears flooded her eyes. She'd insulted him again. With a heavy heart, Elena realized she couldn't learn everything from books. They certainly hadn't prepared her for a man's wounded pride. Or for a Noble pride. With a hollow feeling in the pit of her stomach, Elena knew the truth.

It was time to leave.

Chapter One

Alexi Valentin stood in the center of the darkened stage alone in the silence. A single spotlight illuminated his face giving his features an ethereal glow. She couldn't see his eyes but could feel the power emanating from his body, the power of the Sun, as a Noble, the source of his strength.

He held up his hand to the audience. In supplication? No, that would never be his style. As a God, perhaps, with all the natural arrogance his race demanded. They called themselves the Nobility yet they were not as noble as they would have others think.

Single notes of music filled the theater. She didn't recognize the song but found the music strangely haunting. All of a sudden a thousand butterflies flew from his upraised palm. A magical voice sang of them spreading their wings and flying away as they dispersed through the theater. Their wings caught the rays of the spotlight as they swirled and floated through the air. They became stars dancing in the darkness.

The audience gasped and sighed.

A fool's trick, she scoffed.

A fool's desire, the tiny voice inside her head answered.

Instead of growing strong, the Houses, the families of the Nobility, fought amongst themselves. They had not destroyed the Ancient one; they'd only succeeded in making him angrier. Now the Nobility would need her help, for the evil they'd unleashed was going to make them pay, especially the

Valentins, for their part in his last defeat.

She had no right to ask him but Elena Kyrinova refused to feel guilty. Would Alexi agree to her bargain and give her the child she so desperately craved—the child that could be the savior of her race? She sighed, hating herself for stooping to this level to get what she wanted.

Without a word, an assistant joined Alexi on the stage. Together they performed magic, giving the people inside the theater a chance to escape for a few brief moments. Perhaps this was how the Nobility stayed hidden. They used tricks that dazzled the eye and were meant to deceive. But tricks wouldn't save them now that the sleeping evil had reawakened. There would be no escape if the evil that threatened them all was not destroyed.

Pyrotechnics shot out from the stage surrounding him, bringing her out of her thoughts with a start. Darkness surrounded him once again only this time she could make out the shape of a large square vault of some kind being wheeled on stage. An announcer told the audience that Alexi would now be handcuffed, placed in a straitjacket, chained, and hung upside down inside. He had only three minutes of air inside the chamber, a digital timer appeared in the background above the vault, so the audience could count down the time. Then a single spotlight highlighted him and the door of the vault before it swung closed.

Elena nearly laughed out loud as the digital timer counted out the seconds. She knew how fake the threat was. She knew that as a Noble, Alexi could hold his breath much longer than the numbers counting down on the stage. She could sense his every move even from inside the steel safe. Hanging upside down, muscles straining to lift his body and reach the clip to release his feet. Only something was wrong. His heartbeat sped up as his fingers worked feverishly at the metal. The clip holding his ankle cuff was jammed.

Even he couldn't make his muscles do more than they were intended. He had to let go, rest a few seconds, then try again. She surmised that normally he would be standing, waiting for the door to open by now.

Should she? She had the ability. But the cost might prove too great. Elena bit her lip. Just as she was about to focus, train her power on the object of contention, he broke the clip free, grabbed the chain, and lowered himself to the ground. He drew in deep breaths to calm himself and opened the door just before the timer reached zero.

A magician. A fake. A fool.

She would never understand why he took such risk, she thought, as the show ended. She struggled to rise, a young man came forward to help her, but she waved away his kindness. What the young man didn't know was that as a human, he was both the bane of her existence, and the ultimate joy. She breathed his every breath, knew his every heartbeat, and could hear the rush of blood flow through his veins. A simple cut on his finger burned inside her like fire. So did a thousand others.

No, he would never know. He wasn't supposed to. That was her gift. And her curse.

While the rest of the audience filed out of the theater to go to their rooms or back to the casino, Elena followed the man she'd braved humanity to find. Strange, she mused, not quite sure what caused their personal connection. He had the reputation from what she could gather, as a playboy, as a man who had no desire for responsibility. What would he say to her...request?

Down a long hallway, she came to a bank of dressing rooms. She didn't knock. She simply opened the door to find the man of her thoughts slumped over his dressing room table.

"I thought I said—," he barked.

She closed the door with a gentle nudge.

"You're on the wrong side," he continued, without looking up. "Get out." The fingers threaded through his gleaming black hair trembled ever so slightly.

"You cut your act quite close tonight."

"This is a private dressing room."

As if she cared. "Prince of Darkness." Her voice dripped disdain.

His head lifted in slow motion. "You—you're not human." Curiosity swirled in his blazing gray gaze as he stared at her in the mirror.

"No," she replied, thankful for the hood that hid her from his search. "And you're not a very good performer."

He inclined his head. "Thank you for that most uninvited review," he bit out, his tone taut with anger. "Now remove your presence before I do it for you."

She laughed. "Macho, macho, man," she sung softly.

He flew out of his seat. "Who the hell are you? What House?"

"No House," she replied, her contempt easy to recognize.

"Your name?"

"Unimportant for the moment. May I?" She began to move very slowly towards him.

His expression changed three times in the space of as many seconds. First angry, then confused, then contrite. "My God," he whispered as he watched her struggle to approach.

"I ask no pity."

"I never said I'd give any."

Elena smiled. *Touché.*

Funny, but the constant agony of being inside a

city surrounded by so many humans, eased a little as she drew closer to him. He gestured for her to sit. She held her body straight and proud as she did.

"Why are you here?" he asked.

He sat and swung his legs around to face her. Their knees nearly touched. "The one you thought destroyed was not destroyed."

He frowned. "And your point is?"

"His revenge will be the life of the child your sister-in-law now carries. I fear the child will die before it takes its first breath."

All of a sudden he held a vice-like grip on her upper arms. The shock of the contact rocked her to her core. Sweet blessings of relief. *Oh, do not let go. Never let go.*

"The hell you say!" he cried.

"The Ancient one is beyond revenge. His hate is a festering wound that will never close. He will not rest until his agony is your agony."

Alexi Valentin tossed her aside and tears formed in her eyes. *Just a few more seconds. Please.* His chair crashed to the floor as he drove himself upwards to his feet. "How do you know this?" His tone held all the emotions she knew he'd feel: disbelief, anger, and an overwhelming fear that she might be right.

"I don't have time to explain. You must take me to your brother and sister-in-law. Now."

"For all I know," he turned, stopping his pacing in the small space. "You could be one of his emissaries."

"Mr. Valentin—Alexi," she began. "Nothing in this world, except the direst of circumstances would get me to endure this—" She swept her hand across her body, the suffering in her tone real and hopefully convincing. "Believe me."

He started pacing again, righting the chair, then throwing himself into it to face her again.

Touch me, she begged. *One touch.*

"All right, you have my attention. Now start talking. Who are you?"

"Elena Kyrinova."

"What House?"

"My own, I suppose. We do not have Houses, as you call them."

"Where do you come from?"

"My village is in Alberta, Canada."

"I know of no Noble village in Alberta. Explain."

She shook her head. "We're wasting time." When she saw he was adamant she added, "I'm not a Noble but I'm not human either. I'm a healer."

"How do you know about us? Tara? The baby. Not babies? I don't understand. All of our first born children are twins."

Elena shook her head again. "She called to me in a dream. Several dreams."

"Since I seem to have no choice, I'll accept that for now. How do you know the baby is the target?"

"I just do."

He let go of a frustrated sigh. "You only spoke about the baby. What about Tara? Can you save both of them?"

She nodded. "That is my intent."

"Why come to me? Why didn't you just continue on to my brother?"

Here was the sticky part. "Because I need a favor in return."

His face fell. "I should have known." His voice grew colder than the winters she knew at home. "How much?"

"Money? Oh no, I have no need for your money."

"Then what do you want?"

How was she going to put this delicately? Politely? With discretion. "Your seed."

"My what?" he choked out.

"Your sperm. I want you to make me pregnant."

He laughed. He looked at her for a few seconds and laughed even harder. "And how, madam, do you think I'm going to be able to—" He paused, growing sober. "Get it up?"

She had to admit he had a point. "As soon as I get away from here, I'll be able to move, to perform."

He threw her a look. "I think you missed the gist of what I was saying. Even in your present condition." He stopped to inspect her from all sides. "The act could be accomplished. My question was how do you expect me to get aroused? You know, in the mood? Ready?"

His question startled her. She didn't know. Having never initiated sexual advances before, she had absolutely no idea. But she did know she had one ace up her sleeve. Lifting her twisted, gnarled hands to the sides of her hood, Elena threw the material back away from her face and off her head.

"Oh," he whispered.

Alexi found the painting of the Madonna to be much less beautiful than the historical raves it garnered. The present rock star Madonna, he found to be less than interesting. Yet the word and all its connotations kept pounding inside his brain. Flawless. Flawlessly beautiful. The woman seated before him was a true Madonna.

Yet her features were not what reached inside his heart. Innocence. Pure, unadulterated innocence. Indeed, with her coloring she reminded him of a newly born fawn with auburn hair and huge liquid brown eyes.

To his Wolf.

In the span of time taken to draw in his next breath and restart his heart, Alexi knew he was in deep trouble. He shuddered, clamping down hard on his control. She gave him a quick smile. She knew the consequences of her well-timed salvo.

"If I'm not mistaken," she replied, her gaze

smug. "That should no longer be a problem."

She reached back to put the hood over her head and he caught her hand. The least she could do was let him look. "Don't."

An electric shock ran up his arm, catching him by surprise. "Why?" she asked.

He had absolutely no idea except that he felt an inordinate need to drink in her beauty. "I'm enjoying the view."

He sat down, as nonchalant as possible considering he was feeling anything but.

Her gaze darted to the doorway. "I—I'm hard to explain."

"Indeed," he agreed. "And if I don't believe a word you're saying?"

She looked as if she hadn't considered this possibility. "There's so much that I need to tell you, but we waste precious time here. Please," she begged. "Take me to them."

"Not so fast." He shrugged, using his body language to tell her that her pleas didn't move him in the least. "I'm not in the least convinced. We have some pretty good practical jokers around here."

Her shoulders fell. A strange sadness filled her gaze. "What do I have to do to convince you?"

He smiled, not liking himself for having to test her. Alexi rose and she blanched, rearing back away from him. For a moment she seemed to believe he would take her up on her offer right now. Although perfectly capable from a physical aspect, sex was the farthest thing from his mind. He opened the door to his dressing room and a few seconds later one of the stagehands walked by. "Andy. Is Sheila still here? With Eric?"

The elder man nodded, trying to peek into his dressing room. "Got something goin' on, Mr. Prince?"

Alexi's stomach turned. Dirty old bastard. "Go find them. *Both* of them, and bring them to my dressing room." The look on his face must have scared the old coot because he hurried off.

He turned and dropped his gaze, unable to take the incredible sadness in hers for more than a second. "This woman? She is special to you?"

He nodded. "Her son's eleven. Leukemia. Terminal." He couldn't help the anger in his tone as he bit out the words. "She's had a hard life. The only being on this earth that has ever mattered to her has been that boy. Now he's going to die." Alexi looked up and caught her gaze, the anguish in his matching the sadness in hers. "Prove you are who you are. Save the boy."

"Not your own niece or nephew?"

"Are you telling me I have to make that choice?"

"If you did?"

Did he believe in God? That had always been a question for him. His usual answer a joke; change the subject, run away from the problem. But his guts screamed at him that he was making the right choice. "I would stick with my decision."

She nodded. Was that a hint of respect in her face? She went to replace the hood and once again his hand stayed hers. Such beauty, such innocence, all contradicting the incredible weight of the sins of the world. She bore them with quiet dignity.

Without knowing why, his thumb slid down her cheek. She closed her eyes at his touch. In revulsion? No, that would make her plan rather difficult. Rather like ecstasy but not sexual, more spiritual, as if his touch healed her.

All of a sudden she whirled away and threw her hood over her head. A knock on the dressing room door followed a second later. He watched as she moved to a darkened corner of the room. She seemed to want to stay hidden and he wondered why. But that question would have to wait.

Opening the door he said, "Hi, Sheila. Eric, my

man." He performed their ritual handshake, knuckle to knuckle, top hand to bottom; fingers interlocked tight, then a small bump of the shoulders. Eric looked tired tonight, pale, wan, and listless. He looked like the fight had been beaten out of him. "How's it going?"

"The usual," Sheila replied for her son.

"Doctor says I can have a week off from my treatments," Eric added, his tone sounding as excited as the boy could make it under the circumstances. "You gonna show me that trick you promised?"

"Sure, kiddo, just not right now."

He turned and caught Sheila's elbow in his hand, guiding her through the door and out into the hallway. "Listen, Sheila. I have a friend in there that says she can help Eric. You trust me, don't you?"

The door closed behind him with a faint click.

"What?" she replied, her tone derisive. "A healer?"

More than you'll ever know, he said to himself. And yet, did he truly believe? "If I said yes?"

She let go of a shaky laugh. "Been there, done that."

"Sheila, listen to me. I don't propose to know everything, okay? But you've always kept the faith, right? You've earned your break."

A wave of power hit him, so incredible and with such force that he swayed and reached out to hold onto the wall for support. He didn't have time to react as a second, even more powerful wave, hit him again. Then the air around him seemed to implode.

Alexi staggered. At first he couldn't breathe. He slumped against the wall and for a moment the world went black. When ho came to, Sheila was standing next to him with concern written all over her face.

"Alexi?"

He struggled to remain upright. Every cell in his body felt drained of energy. "I'm, I'm all right. Just give me a sec."

The click of the door opening made him whirl his head around. Bad move as the walls began to spin out of control. Sheila cried out and he tried to focus. He saw her run into the room and gathered himself to follow. He found Sheila on the floor of his dressing room crying and holding Eric as if she would never let go.

Alexi kneeled down beside the boy, gently nudged Sheila aside, and gathered him up, ready to take the child to a hospital or wherever they needed to go. Eric radiated heat, incredible heat, like a nuclear afterglow. Or the afterglow of a morning feed.

With all the strength he had left, Alexi lifted Eric into his arms. The boy nearly scared him to death when he said, "Put me down, Alexi. I can walk."

He let the boy's legs slide to the floor. "Eric?"

"I'm okay." He looked over and caught concern warring with hope in Sheila's gaze. Could it be?

"Eric?" He looked straight down at the boy. "Can you tell me what happened?"

"I saw an angel."

That made sense. Elena would look like an angel to an eleven-year-old boy. "Did the angel hurt you?"

"Nah. She was cool. I mean, not cool 'cause I got really hot for a few minutes, but really neat."

Alexi was terrified to ask the question. "How do you feel now?"

The boy paused for a moment. "Hungry. Mom?" he asked, turning to Sheila. "Can we go get something to eat? Like maybe pancakes or French toast? I'm starving."

Alexi caught Sheila's gaze. Eric hadn't been hungry in weeks, not since the chemotherapy started. "Have faith," he told her, reaching out to squeeze her hand. "Take him to your doctor. I think you'll find he's cured."

Her breath caught as hope flared in her face. "Alexi?"

"No questions. Just go."

He watched them walk away and tears formed in his eyes. He turned and stepped further into the dressing room, to beg Elena's forgiveness for not believing her. At first, he couldn't find her. She sat huddled in the deepest, darkest corner of the room. A tiny whimper escaped her lips, as if she were in great pain.

He ran to her and knelt down on the floor. He reached out and she cried, "No. Do not touch me."

After what she did? After the way he behaved? He would grovel at her feet in remorse. He reached out and gathered her into his arms. Pain the likes of which he never wanted to experience again, shot up his body. He cried out but clamped his teeth together and held on.

When the pain subsided a bit he turned her over. Her hood fell back and he gasped. Her face bubbled with what looked like leprosy. Like something out of his worst nightmares. He closed his eyes to blot out the image.

The vision would never leave him but it didn't matter. He drew her into his body, cradled her, rocked her, trying to ease the misery. How long they stayed that way he would never know. Just when he was ready to open his eyes, a shriek tore through his mind, cutting right through his heart and into his soul.

Tara.

Chapter Two

Already weak. No rest. Just mocking laughter. The Ancient one wouldn't fight fair. Had she expected any less? "Hold me," Elena begged, his touch cooling the burning disease ravaging her body.

"Never let you go," he whispered over and over again.

Such solace in his words. Such strength in his touch. She had no idea why, couldn't begin to question the miracle of his presence. The boy had a terminal disease, one that would normally take her days to recover from. Instead, she stretched and attempted to push away in just a few minutes. "Thank you."

He stared at her. "Your—your face. It's normal."

She caught the awe in his tone. "I—" She choked in surprise. Normal? How could that be? It usually took her days to recover or at least hours, not minutes. "Eventually I regain my powers." Was this possible with all Nobles? Would they all have this kind of effect? Or only Alexi? The magician.

"Eric is going to live. I don't understand how, but he's going to live."

"Yes." She tried to struggle out of his grasp. He wouldn't let her go. "You must let me get up. The boy will now live a long and normal human life, but Tara and her child will not survive if we do not hurry."

He nodded, setting her away from him. She struggled to rise, not in any pain but still rather weak. He rose first then helped her to her feet. The heat from her body had invaded his and he tore off his sweat-soaked shirt, changing into a fresh one. He put on a light jacket and grimaced. "I have nothing for you to wear."

"I'll be fine. I'm used to this. Please, we must go."

Alexi led her to his BMW. He helped her get in. The leather was so fine, she was almost afraid to sit. Her hand ran lightly over the leather seat almost of its own volition.

"You like the car?" he asked getting in and closing the door.

"I have never been in one like this," she breathed. She settled deep into the seat. So soft. The chair made her think of the owner. Soft of heart yet strong as steel.

"We have wealth accumulated throughout the ages. You don't?"

"My people have simple needs. We live alone. We travel only when we have to. Wealth is not a necessity."

She watched him shake his head. "Sorry, I don't get it. We're the Nobility. We're so far above them. You, your people, could have anything you want and then some. Why don't you?"

She sighed. Now she knew why these people, these Nobles as they called themselves, irked her so. They were so far from the true definition of the word noble. "Your words speak of physical domination, intellectual manipulation, and plain old greed. Don't you know the meaning of the word "give?" Don't you know the price that must sometimes be paid?"

He was silent for a long time. "I didn't. Not before. Now I'm not so sure." He paused again. "What you did tonight. These are your powers?"

"Yes."

He let out a shaky laugh. "What *are* you?"

"You know the word empathy?"

"Of course."

"I am empathic. A true empath, to use a

derivative of the word."

"I don't quite understand."

"Total. Full. Every cell in my body absorbs the ills of the world around me. I come from a race of healers."

"Ills?"

"I have no other way to describe pain, suffering, disease, do you?"

"No, I guess not. That's why you walk the way you do, why your hands look the way they do?"

"Yes."

He was silent again. "From all living things?"

"No. Mostly humans, although I have felt the pain of some of the creatures who live with us." She frowned, still puzzled by her connection to these people. "I can feel Tara, your sister-in-law, and the baby with every breath I take. That's why I braved the city and came in search of you."

"Not the only reason."

She blushed; glad he couldn't see in the dark of the car. Or could he? "I must admit your request was—" She paused. "I did not expect that you would—"

"And I didn't believe a word you said. I'm sorry." He flipped her a quick glance. "I'm still not quite sure of your request either."

"I know." She hated to ask again but needed his power badly. "Would you, would you touch me again, please?"

"Can't get enough of my body?"

"You tease to hide your fear. Fear well, Alexi Valentin. Even with your help, I may not be strong enough to fight him."

"My choice."

"Yes. And one not made lightly. I know."

"Sheila was dying. Right along with the boy. I couldn't let that happen."

Elena smiled to herself. Soft of heart. "And

15

that's why I agreed. And why I need your strength now. Your touch. I don't know how to explain. Your touch heals me."

"Indeed. Well, then, if that's the case." He lifted his arm and invited her to lean against him. "Does that help?"

"Yes," she sighed. Sweet, blessed, relief.

"Good. Stay there and rest. But the hood has to go." He released his arm and waited for her to pull the material back from her face.

Confused, she wondered at his need. She'd lived a totally sheltered life. She wasn't used to her beauty being admired by a man. Wasn't once enough?

She didn't dare ask. Instead she leaned back into him, closed her eyes, and drank like a greedy child. All of a sudden the car swerved.

"Sorry," he apologized. "I felt a bit sleepy."

"No," she replied, removing his arm. "I'm the one who must apologize. I took that which I should not have."

"Don't worry; take as much as you need. I'll revive with the morning feed."

"Morning feed?"

"The difference between our races, I believe. My people feed off the sun. It's our lifeblood. Oh, we eat food. For fuel just as you do. But the sun feeds our power."

"The sun," she repeated. "Fascinating." No wonder he had so much energy, she thought to herself.

"I'm not sure how to explain," he continued. "I didn't pay attention to science that much in school. But the Nobility gathers their power from the sun. We're stronger than ordinary humans, we have enhanced senses like sight and smell, and we have increased psychic abilities, especially amongst ourselves. And you, it seems."

Elena nodded. Then another thought occurred to her. Why had her people not joined with these Nobles long ago? If their power could give her such strength, help her regenerate—

A terrifying shriek tore through her mind. He shivered against her. "Did you feel that?" she asked.

His response was to stomp on the gas pedal. The car shot forward throwing her back into her seat. "Drive, Alexi. For the love of all you know, hurry."

He complied. Feeling the car speed up, Elena opened her mind. She reached out to this woman who haunted her dreams. She felt the incredible bond the woman carried for her mate and the special place in her heart reserved for Alexi. Elena's blood ran cold at the fear Tara felt. Would she be strong enough to save both mother and child? *Hold on.*

Elena was out of the car before the tires finished screeching to a halt. She ran, sensing Alexi on her heels and found comfort in his presence. Just as Alexi was about to unlock the portal, the front door swung open. And elderly gentleman greeted them. "Sergei. Where's my brother?"

"Up here," came a voice, deeper than Alexi's and filled with worry.

Elena followed Alexi as he ran up a long staircase. A man identical in looks walked out of a room and into the hallway. "My name is Elena," she told Nicholai, greeting the man with the traditional bow of her people.

Another shriek tore through the house. "Let her in," Tara cried.

"It's all right," Alexi added from behind her. "I'll explain." She watched as he deftly steered his brother out of the room. She was grateful; she had no time for explanations.

Tara writhed in agony on the bed. Too much pain, Elena thought. And not her own but demon made. A pall hung over the room and death greeted her every breath. *Hold on.*

First she looked at the African-American woman sitting on the bed. "You are Jeri. I saw you comfort Tara in one of her dreams."

Then she looked over at the elderly gentleman who had followed them up the stairs. "You are—"

He bowed. "Sergei. Steward of this House."

She returned his bow, throwing back her hood. Jeri gasped and Sergei simply stared. "I will need both of you before the night is over."

Jeri nodded in answer as Sergei replied, "I am at your service, lady."

"Good." She turned to her patient and smiled. "Do you remember me?"

She watched Tara nod. "Elena."

Elena removed her cloak. She placed her hand on Tara's and closed her eyes. Most of the evil she sensed swirled in the air of the room like a viscous cloud. She opened her mouth and breathed in the evil, allowing the cells in her body to transform the decay into water. When she breathed out, she expelled a harmless mist back into the air.

"The Ancient one is here."

"Yes, lady."

"What can we do?" Jeri asked, the fear in her tone belonging to them all.

"Fight him. With every breath you take. Believe in goodness, that evil can and will be defeated, help me save them both."

"How?" Jeri asked.

She turned to Sergei. "Gather your people. Use their strength."

"Already done, lady."

She turned back to Jeri. "Isn't she the daughter you never had?"

Jeri nodded even as her gaze asked how Elena knew. "Love her as you would your own. Love is still the best weapon we have against evil."

"Tara," she called, laying a hand on the woman's forehead.

Her patient quieted immediately. "I'll protect you as best I can, but I need you to fight with me. Do you understand?"

The door flew open. "Who are you?" Nicholai Valentin demanded to know.

"A friend."

Nicholai walked back over towards Tara. Elena could feel his focus on his mate, his terror at the thought of losing her, his relief as he saw that Tara seemed more at ease. Tara was breathing easier, there was more color in her cheeks, and she even managed to give the man a half smile as he approached. A streak of envy tore through her at the obvious love they shared. "Alexi has told me a... fairy tale. Now I ask you, Noble to Noble—"

"I'm not a Noble, Nicholai Valentin," she interrupted.

He seemed to reserve judgment on her remark. "Can you save them?"

She read the helplessness in his gaze but refused to lie to him. "I'm not God, either."

He didn't answer. Instead he lifted one of Tara's hands in his own and placed a kiss on her palm. She averted her gaze. The moment was too private to intrude upon. "We will win with love," he reassured his mate.

Then he turned to her and caught her gaze. "Alexi tells me you work miracles. If I do as he asks, I'm putting my life in your hands. No, more than my life."

"I'm no miracle worker, either."

He bowed. "Forgive my distrust. The very air we breathe breeds foul thoughts and deeds."

She bowed in return. "Already forgiven."

"Then tell me, for I sense that you're not human. And yet, I also feel a kinship with you. Who are you?

What are your people?"

"A simple woman born to a simple people, with a great gift and a terrible burden," she answered. "Something you would relate to, I think."

He smiled. So alike yet so different than her magician. "Indeed. We are the Nobility, Elena. We are a strong race, so much more powerful than humans. We try to coexist and not take advantage as you seem to think. But sometimes we do. Perhaps that makes you believe that in doing what you were born to do, in healing, that makes you more noble."

She smiled in return. "Perhaps."

"The air seems clearer," he commented.

"For now, I have absorbed most of his essence. But the result will only be temporary."

Tara moaned and Nicholai focused on his mate. "Come, Tara. You must still go through the act of childbirth. Don't work against the pain," Elena advised, then added to Nicholai, "Now we must wait."

****

Alexi paced in the solar next to Nicholai's room. When he thought he'd had just about enough, he reached out and threw the door open, determined to find out what was going on. Instead, he found Elena blocking the doorway. "Have patience, magician."

He had none. "I wish. If I did, if I were, I'd make this whole mess disappear."

"That, no one can do."

"But she's in pain."

A corner of her mouth lifted in a sardonic smile. "It's called childbirth."

"But I thought—."

"You *think?*"

He deserved that. Or did he? "And you have a sharp tongue when you wish."

She sighed. "I'm afraid so."

He silently noted she looked tired. "The sun

rises soon."

"There will be no sunrise in this House."

"I don't understand."

"Yes, you do."

He didn't want to, but he did. "In the beginning there were two; one good, one evil, created by a meteorite infused pool of water. The Nobility are direct descendents from the good twin. The Ancient one is the other half of the Nobility, the evil twin that never perished."

She nodded. "Tara and Nicholai fought against him. I recognized that from Tara's dreams."

"We thought we'd destroyed him once and for all."

He watched her stop, could almost hear her brain churn as she processed. "I think they changed him, changed his essence. As the antithesis of the Nobility, he feared the Sun. He doesn't any longer. He wants revenge."

That wasn't good, not good at all. Revenge was a word the Nobility understood all too well. They'd been using it on themselves since their race began.

Alexi projected a picture to Elena. At the dawn of time, a cavewoman carrying twins went to draw water from a pool nearby. Inside rested a glowing blue rock. Once she touched the rock, she was changed. And so were her children. She knew she had to destroy the evil twin and took him out into the unprotected wilderness to die. But he didn't. He rested under the frozen earth. And waited.

No one knew exactly what set him free. It might have been a change in climate due to the passage of time. Whatever it was, revenge became part of the Ancient one's plan to destroy them. He'd created circumstances so that the Houses would constantly fight each other. Once weakened, they would fall easily. "The first go round, he used the old divide and conquer method. Any idea what he's got up his sleeve this time?"

"I don't know. I'm a healer, not a fighter."

And he was being selfish thinking she could cure the ills of his world. The thought of something happening to Tara or the baby froze his heart. "I know. And only here to fulfill a bargain."

He stepped aside, allowing her into the room, and turned towards one of the windows to stare out at darkness. But the darkness didn't feel right; it felt oily, dank and old. "The bargain I ask for myself. The Ancient one must be destroyed or he will destroy your people and mine," she replied.

"Why?" he asked, genuinely confused. "Why your people?"

"Because hatred is hatred and his revenge has no boundaries. He'll destroy you first, then my people, then the humans."

He shrugged not quite understanding yet, in a sense, understanding far more than she ever would. The Houses had been more than happy to try to kill each other off and help the Ancient one in his plot to destroy them. "I suppose the sins of a race catch up with them sooner or later. This shouldn't be anyone else's fight but ours."

When she didn't reply, he turned, reached out, took her hand, and placed her fingers between his. After a minute he let go. Her fingers looked nearly normal, almost straight. She lifted her hand and flexed her fingers. "Feel good?" he asked.

"Yes," she sighed with contented satisfaction. "I have touched others of your race. They don't have the effect that you do."

"Then sit back and enjoy the ride. Stop questioning why and accept what is."

She didn't answer right away. "I can't. There's too much at stake."

"I keep trying to come to terms with the job you've been given."

"If—if I can't save Tara or the baby, I release you from your promise."

So strong, yet so small. He was impressed by her integrity. "A bargain is a bargain. Besides, I might like taking you up on your offer. You never know."

Although she seemed to wince at his words, she said, "Thank you for your faith. I can only hope I live up to it."

He put his finger on her lips. "Shh. Don't."

They stood in silence for a moment, then a short while later; she made to slip out of the room. He let her go, a mixture of hope and dread roiling in his belly. "Go with God, Elena."

She bowed. "Thank you. And Alexi?"

"Yes?"

"No matter what happens or what you see, when the struggle begins?"

"Yes?"

"Don't try to help me."

****

The room had gone cold hours ago. She'd become used to the dark stench permeating the air, but wasn't sure she'd ever get used to the cloak-like oppression. Still, she took heart in the unflagging faith of those around her. Not the least of which came from her magician.

Alexi Valentin. Her unlikely hero.

Elena hovered over her patient but with each contraction, Tara's strength waned. Soon she would be forced to take the baby, willing or no. Alexi seemed to chafe at the delay, throwing a questioning glance her way every now and then as if to ask why she hadn't done what she'd come here to do.

A valid question. And she had a simple answer. She was waiting for her enemy to make his next move.

Reaching down, Elena placed her hand on Tara's forehead. Her hand turned red, redder, then nearly black. A bubbling began under the skin coming to an intense boil. The pain was like fire burning out of control, as if someone injected hot acid into her hand. Still she didn't remove her palm until she was certain she'd taken *all* the disease out of her patient.

Alexi rushed over and reached out to take her hand between his. His touch cooled the fire instantly. Yet each time she tried to stave off the inevitable, it took longer for her to recover and Alexi was growing weaker. She could see the weariness in his gaze, the strain around his lips.

"Sergei."

"Yes, lady?"

"Do you have a samovar?"

"Yes, as a matter of fact, we do."

Elena had been saving the leaves for the last moment. "Take this pouch and brew the strongest tea you can." She could still hear her mother scolding her for her sweet tooth. "And some sugar, please."

"Right away."

The leaves came from a plant unique to her home and her race, named for the woman who found their power, Lorraine. They wouldn't grow anywhere but near the lake where she lived in Canada. They gave strength when there was none left. Like Alexi. The magician.

She couldn't understand his ability and why they connected in this way. But she did know she couldn't ask him to do any more. "Alexi," she said, her tone gentle. "You're tired."

"So are you."

"Our enemy has tested us. Now he prepares for battle."

Genuine surprise lit his face. "You mean, this hasn't been the battle?"

She shook her head. "Simply the beginning of the game."

Funny, she hadn't expected him to last this long. She'd expected him to cut and run a long time ago. Yet each time she'd looked, she'd find him standing in the same spot with a stoic look on his face and fear in his gaze. "You care for her, don't you?"

"She saved my life."

Ahhh, she thought. That was the answer. She'd wondered, sensing the connection between Tara and Alexi went deeper than simple familial ties. "Now you're returning the favor."

Sergei entered and placed a beautiful, antique, silver samovar on a table near the bed. He poured cups of the tea for all of them. "This is a tea made from a plant of my people. The brew will refresh us. Nicholai, try to get Tara to sip some. She needs the strength the leaves will give her. So does the babe."

Elena drank hers in one gulp.

Fresh energy flooded her veins, giving her a swell of invincibility. As the power of the leaves ran through her system she straightened, able to stand tall for a few moments and free of pain. The pall in the room disappeared, as once again, she absorbed his evil.

Yet he was far from finished.

As soon as the liquid touched Tara's lips, she began to hiss and sputter, like a snake caught in the grass. "All of it, Nicholai. Hurry."

Tara choked and coughed but Nicholai kept forcing the liquid down his mate's throat, a dribble at a time.

Elena ran to Tara and began to chant in the ancient tongue of her people. She closed her eyes and passed her hands over Tara's body, back and forth, never stopping her chant.

Soon, Sergei's voice joined hers.

Then Nicholai's.

And of course, the magician's. Funny how she held onto his voice most of all.

Then she made the mistake of opening her eyes. Instead of her hands she saw nothing but hundreds of writhing snakes where her hands and arms should have been.

Chapter Three

Jeri gasped as she saw snakes where Elena's hands should have been.

"*I love games, don't you?*"

Jeri had heard this voice before when she walked through the shadows of the Ancient one's mind. She had heard his laughter too. Her last encounter with him had nearly proven fatal. A cold dread seeped into her bones. He'd taken hold of her mind and she had a really bad feeling he wouldn't let go.

"*You won't win,*" she answered

"*Oh come now,*" he drawled, still chuckling. The echo of his laughter set her teeth on edge. She would never understand how anything so evil could laugh. "*Do you really believe this healer can stop me?*"

Jeri looked around the room. Nicholai was still trying to feed Tara the tea. Elena stood transfixed, staring down at her hands. Sergei and Alexi had turned their backs to the bed and were pouring more tea into cups by the samovar. No one knew of her predicament. A sharp shaft of fear pierced her.

"*Evil will never triumph.*"

"*Brave words. Spoken like a true friend.*"

"*I'm her friend,*" she replied, her heart swelling with pride.

The last time they'd met, Jeri hadn't seen the Ancient one because of her blindness. But the power from the casket and the Water of Change cured her. She could see him in her mind now. Tara told her he'd been able to conjure a human form, made all the more terrible because of his physical beauty. But

27

this form wasn't physical; it was without shape, vague and ephemeral. Jeri was pretty sure his form, or lack of one, wasn't because they'd weakened him. But she could hope.

"Why don't you believe I'll win?"

"I refuse to," she answered, terrorized by his nonchalant tone.

"I'm stronger than all of you put together."

"If you are, then what are you waiting for?" she challenged.

His voice shuddered through her. *"I told you, I love games. Over and done with is so...boring, so...final."*

She shook her head. *"That's not the way I see it. You're just a charlatan, and a lousy one at that, playing with parlor tricks."*

He tskked. *"Is that so? You don't have to get personal, you know. I thought we were having a lovely little chat."*

"Bite your—" The next thing Jeri knew, her tongue was between her teeth and her jaws were being forced together against her will. She fought with every ounce of strength she had yet she still tasted blood.

"You were saying?"

The pressure eased and she swallowed several times. Her abused tongue felt ten times its size. Still, she refused to give in. She rolled the organ in her mouth and swallowed slowly to mask the damage he'd caused.

"You'll never know, you'll never understand."

"And what great gem of wisdom is that?"

She smiled. *"It's driving you mad."*

She could hear him becoming annoyed in spite of his temperate tone. "What is?"

"Love. Honor. Trust. I know your story. You can't put a heart into a solid block of ice. How cold you must feel."

The pity in her voice hit its intended mark with a vengeance. Anger washed over her in waves, and that made her wonder. Why was he holding back?

"Good question," he answered, reading her thoughts. *"You're wondering what is he doing? What game is he playing this time? Haven't you figured out the plan yet?"*

What scared her the most was that she wasn't sure. His ultimate goal was the baby's destruction. But she didn't understand the purpose behind the game. *"No matter what you do to me, to any of us, you still won't win. That's what you haven't figured out yet."*

"Death, mayhem, destruction. They're all a gas."

Jeri felt truly sorry for him. *"None of those things will ever bring you the one thing you crave beyond all else. That one thing you see all around you but will never feel."*

In her mind, she watched as the nebulous energy of his being become harder, sharper. *"What thing?"*

"Love. Caring. You'll never know the warmth of another. You'll never feel the embrace; bask in the security, know intimate knowledge. Looking at Tara and Nicholai is killing you."

"Not me," he replied with a smile in his tone.

"What goes around comes around," she warned. *"I'm not sure why you were never given the choice, but I do know that everything you do, every step you take, every decision you make will come back to you. It will push you farther and farther from the very thing you covet until the goal is so out of reach you'll have forgotten you ever wanted it. When that happens you'll be lost forever."*

He burst out laughing but Jeri heard his pain. Her words had pierced his soul with a truth he didn't want to contemplate.

"So be it. Now you have sealed your own fate."

Her heart sped up and she swallowed hard. God, please give me strength, she prayed. Help me be brave. Help me protect my friends. *"Do your worst."*

Her inner calm stopped him. *"I will, my dear. I will."*

For one split second she wanted to cry out, rail against the unfairness of it all, then the world went black. This time she knew it would stay that way.

****

The snakes disappeared and Elena breathed a sigh of relief. One of her greatest fears was that she might be forced to fight him by herself, which would take her away from Tara and the baby.

All of a sudden, she lifted her head. The air she'd inhaled held an all too familiar stench. Why hadn't she known her nemesis focused on another? But whom?

Tara moaned and Elena knew her priorities. "Good, Tara. Push with the contraction."

Nicholai stood by Tara's head, holding her hand tight, giving her his strength. Alexi stayed at arm's length in case she needed his touch. Jeri stepped closer and Elena caught the faintest hint of their enemy's unique redolence. "The battle begins," Elena announced.

Alexi moved closer. Elena waved him back. She needed her senses unfettered by his proximity. How was the Ancient one going to attack? Which of them was he using to do his dirty work?

"Nicholai. You must help your mate now. In between contractions, she must pant. When they stop, she must relax. As much as possible. Now, help me move her to the end of the bed."

Elena would have felt better if Tara could walk in between contractions but Tara didn't have enough strength to stand. "That's it," she encouraged them both. "Jeri, help me with this sheet." They grabbed both ends and shook the material out. Again, Elena caught a whiff of the acrid stench of their nemesis.

Elena turned her head towards Jeri. She couldn't grasp anything more than the unease sitting in the pit of her stomach. And that frightened her even more. Had Jeri been chosen as the pawn to carry out the Ancient one's game?

Tara moaned and Elena focused on her patient again. After draping both ends over Tara's legs for modesty, Elena checked the baby's progress. She was fully dilated. Elena rose and walked up to stand by Tara's head. "Soon," she told her. Tara's gaze told Elena she did not have much reserve left. "Be strong, Tara. For your mate. For your child."

Elena moved back to the foot of the bed as Tara went through contraction after contraction. Only once did she cry out.

"Pant, my love. Breathe. Yes, keep going. That is it," Nicholai encouraged.

Elena checked the baby's progress again to find the head beginning to crown. She looked up. Sweat poured off of Tara's face. "Sergei. The people. We need them. *Now.*"

Sergei left the room and soon Elena heard the chant of the Nobility. The air seemed to lighten a bit and she took a deep breath. "The babe is ready, Tara. With each contraction, you must push down as hard as you can."

Tara nodded and Elena watched the woman steel herself for the final stretch.

Elena watched as Nicholai placed a gentle finger under Tara's chin and brought her gaze to his. "With love we will win," he reminded Tara.

With love, Elena thought, trying not to be envious. For a half a second she wondered what that must feel like. Then she knew emptiness, darker and colder than anything she ever imagined. For a moment she almost felt sorry for her enemy. How terrible to exist without anything but malice and revenge. At least she had her gift, the love of her family, and the respect of her people. How empty and alone he must feel.

Tara cried out again and Elena used what was left of her powers. She threw a protective mental cloak over the baby then touched the child's head. Sparks flew from her fingertips and intense heat ran up her arms. But the baby's heartbeat rang strong and true in Elena's ears. "Push, Tara. Again."

The next contraction cleared the child's head, but Elena could not get a firm grip on the shoulders to help Tara push the baby out. "With the next contraction. Use all your might."

This time Tara really let out a scream. The sound was the sweetest music Elena had ever heard. If Tara could scream like that, she had strength to survive.

One shoulder popped free and this allowed Elena just enough leverage to twist the other shoulder loose. "Last one, I promise. Again. As hard as you can."

Tara did as she was asked and the baby slid into Elena's hands. "You have a beautiful baby girl," she announced.

Silence. No one moved. No one smiled. Even the baby was silent.

She freed the child's airway and tapped the baby on the back of the leg. A tiny whimper was all she got but sound enough to make her realize the room was still silent.

Looking up, she read consternation, bewilderment, and horror on Nicholai's face. With a shrug, she resumed her tasks. Once the afterbirth was taken care of, she cut the cord, tied it off, then placed the infant in a warm blanket.

No one moved. "You have a beautiful, healthy, baby girl. What is wrong with all of you?"

Tara looked completely lost. She looked over to

find Alexi unable to meet her gaze. "What's going on?"

"True blood to true blood." She heard Alexi's pain as she watched him look everywhere but at the baby. All of a sudden Jeri began to laugh. Elena knew that laughter, crushed the baby to her body, and jumped away.

"I love it when a plan comes together."

The baby began to cry and Elena loosened her hold. "I don't understand."

"True blood to true blood, healer," the Ancient one cackled through Jeri's mouth. "The first born children of all true Nobles are twin boys. As it was in the beginning. As I was once a twin."

His terrible laughter filled the room. "Fight him, Jeri," she cried.

"There is no need, healer. Blind she was before you all tried to kill me; blind she will be again when I leave. No amount of love will fix that."

"You bastard," she hissed.

"No," he replied, his bitterness overwhelming. "As legitimate as those you see in this room. So is the child. And so will every child after her. A bit trickier to accomplish but just the same. Healthy. All the fingers, all the toes."

Jeri struggled against him but he forced her to lift her hand and hold up her fingers and count.

"With one tiny little exception."

"And that is?" she bit out, hating to have to play his game.

He made Jeri shrug and throw up her hands. "Human. Forever."

Nicholai exploded, his cry of rage reverberating throughout the room. "I am going to stop this insanity once and for all."

Alexi jumped on his brother. "No, you can't defeat him."

There's a terrible strength in anger, Alexi

realized as Nicholai shrugged him off. Nicholai tackled Jeri and he watched Elena skitter out of harm's way, shielding the baby with her body.

With a roar, Alexi grabbed Nicholai and tried to drag him off the prone woman. "You can't win, brother."

Nicholai would not be denied. In spite of Alexi's best efforts, Nicholai's fingers wrapped themselves around Jeri's throat. "Come out of there demon and fight. Fight like a Noble."

Jeri's eyes began to bulge. Her face turned dark, then darker.

"Don't you understand?" Alexi cried, desperately trying to pry Nicholai's hands loose. "You'll kill Jeri."

Deep laughter reverberated throughout the room as a cloak of darkness descended on them. "Tighten your fingers, Noble. That's it. Let your feelings go."

"Nicholai," Tara begged, her voice weak. "Don't do this. Revenge solves nothing."

"Listen to your mate, Nico. Please," Alexi added.

Alexi watched as slowly, fighting himself every inch of the way, Nicholai released his grip. His brother stood, heaving for breath, quivering with the need to kill. "Come out and fight me, coward."

"No," Elena cried.

"No," Alexi seconded. He moved to his brother's side. "We stand together."

Nicholai flashed Alexi a look, first of surprise, then of gratitude. It seemed his brother still couldn't quite trust him to stand by his side. "Your fight is with me, demon. Not him. Not them. Me," his brother cried.

"You pitiful, chivalrous beings. First the woman, now the man, then the friend. You people just don't quit, do you?"

"No," Alexi and Nicholai cried out in unison.

Out of the corner of his eye, Alexi caught Elena

moving towards the head of the bed to stand beside Tara. Out of harm's way, he hoped.

All of a sudden the Ancient one appeared, terrible in his cold beauty. Jeri gasped and choked. She was alive and if they were all lucky, would remain that way. Then he realized something was terribly amiss. Why would the evil one, so bent on revenge, having been foiled once before, quit now?

"You're right to ask, magician."

"You read minds? So do I. Every night. In my act."

"This is no act, buffoon. Just the beginning of the end."

Alexi's blood ran cold. "What are you talking about?"

"I know. I know. I should just kill all of you now and be done with it. But let's just say there's a method to my madness."

"The same method as before? No new true Noble births?" Nicholai sneered. "Without true Noble births we mingle our blood with humans until we become human?"

"Exactly."

Alexi shook his head. "And your point is? We will still exist. You never will."

"Beep. Wrong answer. Mine will be the only True Noble blood left."

Blood, Alexi wondered? What blood? How can something with a block of ice for a heart understand blood? Yet as he looked at his brother he knew all about blood, the ties it gave him, the pride that needed no words.

And the knowledge that something terrible was about to happen. Later, Alexi would wonder if it wasn't just Nicholai's stubborn sense of duty that made him snap. Or maybe it was the natural arrogance of one so proud of his race and his heritage. Perhaps the thought of this being...this thing as the last representative of all that was good, true, yes...Noble about them.

Whatever the cause, Nicholai let out a keening cry of agony and bolted forward before Alexi could stop him.

I love you, my brother.

Chapter Four

Darkness had fallen hours ago, not the darkness they'd suffered but the natural black of night. Elena tried to reconcile the beauty of the stars with the sadness of the house she walked through. Few would meet her gaze, those that did, held hope in theirs until she shook her head, then tears filled their eyes. Nicholai rested comfortably, sound in body but lost in his own mind, in a coma of his own making.

Had she ever seen such a magnificent yet futile fight? Even fueled by his righteous anger, Nicholai was no match for the Ancient one. They grappled but the more strength Nicholai used the more the Ancient one absorbed. Nicholai wrapped his hands around the man's throat, his muscles bulging from the strain, and the evil one simply smiled. Until Nicholai had no more strength left. Until he'd been drained so much that Nicholai had fallen to his knees and finally collapsed.

Elena was not one to accept failure. She fought with every cell in her body but she could not find Nicholai. At first Alexi stood by her side, his need to believe in her carrying her through paths she'd rather not tread. Then even he lost hope and quit the room without a word. Of them all, only Tara remained hopeful. She held onto the baby not allowing anyone to see her inner pain. She remained steadfast, thanking Elena with and without words for all that she had done.

Eventually, however, even Elena had to accept the truth. Until Nicholai wanted to be found, he would stay in the coma. Her greatest challenge now was to make Alexi accept that truth.

She found Alexi in the solar, the light of the stars overhead just enough for her to make out his form in one of the chairs. As she drew nearer, she smelled the distinct fragrance of alcohol. "Drink will not bring your brother back to you."

"I knew I could count on you for just the right platitude."

That stung. "What would you have me say?"

"Oh, I don't know. Something like, your brother is well and resting comfortably. Your niece is a True Noble just like you. Everything is as it was a few hours ago without the threat of death hanging over everyone. Something simple like that."

"You know I can't."

He took a long pull on his drink. "Kinda thought you couldn't."

"Just for your information, I have a brother too. I know what you're going through."

She knew Alexi was frustrated and angry. But nothing prepared her for the explosion that came as he cried, "No you don't."

Shocked, Elena didn't respond right away. She bit back her own anger and frustration and replied, "There has to be a way to reach him. I just don't know what it is yet."

"You saved Eric. I thought you could heal anyone."

That barb hurt worse than the first. But she understood where his emotions were coming from, so she tried to be patient and explain. "Only those that wish to be healed. Your brother doesn't want to be found yet. And your drinking is the same wish as your brother's."

"Well, well, well. A lecture from the perfect one. Excuse me for being...wow...it just hit me—human."

"There's no shame in acknowledging your feelings."

"Really? You sure you want to go there? Because I have a lot of them stored up."

Elena shrugged. Perhaps talking out his pain would be cathartic. "Go ahead."

He snorted when he realized she was calling his bluff. But the alcohol loosened his tongue. "Goddamned idiots, each and every one of them."

"What do you mean?" she encouraged.

"This whole Nobility thing. You can't live on pride."

Secretly she agreed. "It's a part of your race, though."

That much she had learned from Nicholai and Tara.

"Just so stupid. There's only one being that everyone needs to take care of. Just one. Themselves. That's it. No more. No less."

"So Nicholai should never have fought to save the woman and child he loves."

Alexi's laugh dripped with derision. "You think that's why he attacked? Because of Tara and the baby?"

"Of course."

"Then you're just as much of a fool as they are."

"What else would have pushed him to attack? The people he had sworn to protect, the ones he loved the most, were being...still are being threatened."

Alexi simply shook his head. "I see he snowed you too." She watched as Alexi struggled to get up, wove a bit, righted himself then walked a few steps to a small bar.

"Haven't you had enough?" she asked.

"Nope, not yet. Not until I pass out. Then the sun will burn it all away and all will be right as rain. At least, I will."

His words struck her. "I know you care, magician. You just cannot, no, let me rephrase that,

39

will not let the pain inside. I sympathize."

He rounded on her with a roar. "I don't want your damned sympathy. Don't you get it? Nicholai attacked because he couldn't stand to see us demeaned to the point of being human. Noble to the core. That's my brother. And look where it got him."

She didn't believe Alexi. "He was trying to protect them."

Alexi started laughing. She heard the raw anger behind the forced merriment. He imitated the sound of a buzzer. Just as the Ancient one had earlier. The sound sent a shiver down her spine. "Wrong answer. *Noblesse Oblige.* Death for one's race. Honor. Duty. Forget the people you love. Who love you..." His voice trailed off and Elena's heart cracked.

"Are you any different from your brother? Aren't you both proud? Doesn't this pride you both carry stem from who and what you are?"

Even in the dark she could see the belligerence on his countenance. "At least *I* have my priorities straight. Take care of *numero uno* first."

Elena had no desire to deliver a lecture, but he'd asked for it. "And that accomplishes what? Does it help Tara cope with her loss? Her mate lies in a coma." She drew in several deep breaths as Alexi's attitude got under her skin. "Does it change your niece into the nephews you prize so highly so that all is right in your Noble world?"

When he didn't answer, she kept on going. "You have a healthy baby, a precious commodity, given to you. Does your attitude protect your niece from this God-only-knows-what that wants to destroy her?"

"Tara can take care of herself better than I ever could. The baby isn't a target anymore. She's what this thing wants her to be—human."

"And Nicholai?" Elena had to ask. She had to make him see that trying not to care wasn't going to ease the pain.

"I—I can't help him," Alexi choked as pure anguish poured from his soul.

"Neither can I."

The arrow he aimed was true to its mark. "How does it feel?"

Hadn't she asked herself that very same question before walking into this room? "I'm not a failure, Alexi."

"I didn't say you were."

"Your brother chooses not to be found."

"That's bull and you know it. Man. Talk about a snow job. I mean, I thought I was good. You're better."

Elena didn't appreciate the compliment. "I came here to save Tara and the baby. As I was meant to do. They're alive and well." In fact, she was tired of being abused. "Just because events and fate have not gone the way you want them doesn't mean I'm at fault."

"You're the one who rode in here on your white horse, madam savior."

Had she? And yet she'd done what she was meant to do. Now it was his turn. "We still have a bargain and you still owe me. Without my help, neither one of them would be alive. Pay up."

What the hell? Did she know what she was asking for? "Now? Right this minute?"

"Why not? I have read that alcohol is a great equalizer in relationships between men and women."

"Read? As in books?"

"Of course. You can learn anything you need to know from a book."

Dear God in Heaven, not only was she innocent, she had no freaking clue what she was talking about. "You can't learn about someone's emotions from a book."

She moved to stand in a star beam coming from the sky. Why did she have to look so innocent, so goddamn beautiful? "Perhaps not. But you can learn to examine them. For a magician, you're terribly easy to read."

Oh really? Little did she know. She thought there was some goodness inside him. Some sort of redeeming quality to him. Innocent little fool. "What am I thinking right now?"

"You are wondering whether or not to take me up on my demand. But you also want me to hurt. As you do. Because you believe I've failed. So go ahead."

Ahhh, man, she was daring him now. She really didn't think he would hurt her. "Hurt you? You have no idea."

"I wouldn't be standing before you if I believed such a thing. You seem to want to scare me away. Or else push me away. Neither will work. I won't release you from your bargain."

Alexi leaned back in the chair he was sitting in, lost his balance, and fell forward. He rubbed his hands over his face. "You're right. I do owe you. You saved Eric. No doubt about that." He deliberately left out what had transpired here. "But right now I just want to be left alone."

She walked up to him without an ounce of trepidation, threw her arms around his neck, and sat down on his lap. This time she imitated the buzzer. "Wrong answer."

No, no, no, no, no. What was wrong was his response to her. Or was it? Why should he be concerned over her feelings? If she wanted to get screwed, he was more than willing to oblige. He was real good at getting it on.

Her arms snaked around his neck and he caught just a hint of the Lorraine leaves on her breath. Man, she was teasing his earlobe with her nose, her short staccato little breaths tickling the sensitive skin of his neck. "Elena."

"Hmmm?"

She knew what she was doing all right. Only something was wrong. "Get off me."

She lifted back. In doing so, her bottom wiggled around on top of his erection. "Why?"

Because I'm not an experiment. "Because I just don't want to."

"Really?" She cocked her head to look at him.

He read the amusement in her gaze. And the disbelief. Then it hit him. Even through his alcoholic fog. This was out of some book she'd read. She was playing out some kind of game with him. That's why nothing felt right. "Really."

She tried another salvo, nuzzling her face against his. Pressing light kisses down his cheek to his jaw. But Alexi wasn't buying into her ploy. Or should he say her drama. Funny, but she might just have a point about that pride of his.

She must have sensed that he was serious because she said, "You made a bargain."

For some reason that struck him as terribly humorous. He wasn't known for being a man of honor. Wrong brother. "I'll stick to it."

She lifted her head and sounded genuinely puzzled. "I don't understand."

"My time and place, sweetheart. Not yours. I'm not a stud-muffin. Now get off of me."

She rose, and he could tell she was completely befuddled. So was he and not just from drinking. But if he was going to become a stud-muffin he was going to become a stud-muffin on his own terms, not hers.

****

Even Elena was amazed as she visited her patient the next morning. Tara was nearly healed from the birth. The baby thrived. "I must leave, Elena," Tara told her as she fed her daughter.

"I wondered if you'd want to. But I'll never understand why."

"We are who we are," Tara answered as she

kissed her daughter's head. "The Nobility have always lived in structure. Sort of like an Arthurian novel. Pride and race are ingrained in our cells." Elena watched Tara's tender gaze turn to rest on her mate's face. "And some of us try to kill ourselves with nobility." Funny, of them all, Tara seemed to understand best. And forgive the most.

"Will you be safe?"

Tara snorted. "As safe as anywhere, I suppose." The woman, now her sister for what they had shared, sighed from the depths of her being. "I want to go home. I want to smell the ocean."

"You live by the sea? I have never seen the ocean. Is it beautiful?"

Tara smiled. "I asked Nicholai if we could share homes, fearing I would come to hate the desert. I find I love both. But the shore is my home. It's where I grew up. I have a business that will keep me busy there. There's little I can do now except make Nico comfortable."

"You can do that here."

"I won't be a burden to this House. Besides, Alexi deserves..."

The door to the room opened. Tara quickly turned her back as Elena looked up to see why. Alexi stood in the doorway, true to his word, unaffected by the night's overindulgence, a scowl on his face.

"A knock would have been polite," Elena chided.

"A thousand pardons," he sneered back at her. In response, she moved to shield Tara from his gaze.

"Tara?" His tone softened with the name, so much different than before. "Is it true? What the people say?"

"What do the people say?" Tara asked him, her shoulders slumping.

"That you'll leave for New Jersey tonight."

Elena watched Tara's shoulders rise and lock. She admired the woman's strength. "I fought this thing with all my might. It has either changed or destroyed all that I love. I need to go home, where I belong."

"You can't let the people of this House dictate your life."

Elena looked down at Tara and watched with envy as she nuzzled the baby in her arms. "I'm not."

"So you're just going to go? Give up?"

Elena stiffened. "How can you be so selfish? Her priorities rest in this room. I don't call that giving up."

"No one asked you."

"Alexi," Tara admonished. "That was uncalled for. I leave because it's what's best for both of us. I need to try and find a way to bring Nicholai back to me. You need to take over the House of Valentin."

"I don't want the House of Valentin."

After fixing her clothing, Elena watched Tara lift the baby to her shoulder and pat the babe gently. "I haven't named my daughter yet. Do you know why?"

Alexi hung his head. "Yes." Even Elena knew. The baby was outcast. She was completely human.

"Try to understand," Tara begged.

"I am. I have." Alexi moved closer and Elena stepped away. His hand reached out to touch the baby. "I can't do this on my own. I need you."

"I know." Tara gave him a sad, understanding smile. "But you have priorities." As Tara said that, her gaze flicked to Elena. Was Tara trying to tell her she was one of Alexi's priorities? Not by their last conversation. "There's safety in strength."

"What do you mean?" Alexi asked.

Elena understood right away. Working together could become their best defense. "The Houses must join together. For the first time in your history, the Nobility will have to become one House."

He blanched. "Wait a minute. Are you thinking

what I think you're thinking?"

Both women nodded. However, Tara's gaze was full of pride whereas Elena wondered if they were all simply doomed.

"By right and by the laws of this House," Tara began, "you are now the Head of the House of Valentin. Nicholai must forfeit all claims. Our daughter will never have any."

Tara hesitated to continue. Perhaps the sadness of her own words finally sank in. So Elena took up the reins for her with just the right touch of irony in her tone. "As Head of the House of Valentin, it will be your task to pull them all together. Welcome to reality, Alexi. I hope you're happy now."

Chapter Five

Head of the House of Valentin.
Alexi ran as if the Ancient one was one step behind.
Head of the House of Valentin.
He ran until his only thought was the next breath and the next stride he took.
Steward? Member of the High Council?
Alexi shuddered to a stop. Bent over, gasping for breath, he should have been sick to his stomach. Determined to be honest with himself, just once in his life, Alexi remembered all the times he secretly coveted his brother's position as Head of the House. He hated being the 'second' son.

Time now to be brutally honest. Nicholai thought he was going to be the next Steward to the High Council, a stepping stone to the High Council itself. Nico'd been groomed for the position for years. And told to wait. Be patient. Just another year or two. Again and again. The Council kept on dangling the carrot in front of his brother's nose. Nicholai never admitted it was a carrot. He kept working. Harder and harder. And all Alexi could do was try to tell his brother he was being used.

When Nico wouldn't listen, Alexi turned away. He thumbed his nose at responsibility because he'd lost respect for the people who wielded the power. What Nico refused to acknowledge, Alexi saw in one glance: for whatever reason, the Council was never going to let Nicholai be Steward or sit on the High Council.

Then Tara became the unwitting player in the

Ancient one's revenge. In the eighteenth century, a casket had been created to protect the Chalice holding the water from the pool the meteorite fell into-the Water of Change as they commonly referred to it. As a result it gained the power of the water. When Tara unwittingly touched the casket, she was changed into a True Noble. The change gave her amnesia. Her ensuing amnesia forced Nicholai to help her find out who she was, leading them to an ugly truth. Both of them had been used by the High Council as expendable pawns, chess pieces the High Council had been willing to sacrifice to save the Nobility. Her family had been destroyed and her brother, Morgan, was permanently brain damaged. And for that, the High Council deserved what they were getting right now.

But what about the people?

Had their race become so arrogant that they deserved extinction?

Alexi fell to his knees. "I didn't want it like this!" he cried to the scrub and desert grasses, arms akimbo. "I didn't want it like this," he whispered again, bent over in a ball.

Ahhh hell, Nico. Why did you have to go and fight 'til the very end? You had it all, everything you'd ever wanted. You always have.

Such bitterness, Alexi, he chided himself.

All right, then, let's cut to the chase. Nico was always the chosen one. Alexi was the backup. Did that make him any less loved? He'd rip out his heart first than even think he was less loved. His mother, Sylvana, was gypsy born of the House of Konin. She didn't care a damn about Council's or politics. But his father? Now Mikhail and Nico were like two peas in a pod, stern, duty bound and bred. That was why, in a small way, he understood what pushed Nico over the edge.

Which brought him right back to kneeling in the

sand and not a clue as to what to do. Rising to his feet, Alexi brushed the sand off his legs and started walking towards the house.

He had no business being in this position. First and foremost, he told himself, he was a magician. A master of deception. A Las Vegas star. All glitz and glitter. No one to worry about except himself. Life was so much easier that way.

What am I supposed to do now?

Poof, you're a leader.

He started laughing. Didn't anyone understand? Couldn't they see how ridiculous that thought was?

"I'm not certain I find much humor in this situation."

Alexi looked around, focused, and realized he wasn't far from the house. Of all the people on this earth, she was the last one he wanted to see. "I really don't want to talk to you right now."

She started and he wondered why. Was she expecting daffodils and sunshine? "I only came to tell you Tara is gone."

Why was it that he always got caught running away? "I told you to leave me alone."

"I will. As soon as I do one more thing."

Not exactly certain what that was, Alexi felt the need to justify his actions well up from deep inside. "She saved my life," he answered.

"So you told me."

"She's the first true friend I've ever had."

By her tone he recognized she was beginning to understand. But that didn't stop her from saying, "Perhaps, if you'd stop pushing people away, you'd find more."

He came to a complete halt and turned, rounding on her. "Quit lecturing me, Okay? What makes you so much better than the rest of us, huh?"

He watched as she drew herself upright, a light of pride blazing in her gaze. "I'm not better, Alexi. I don't believe anyone has the right to believe that. Being a Noble doesn't mean you have to give up your humanity. Neither does being a magician." She fumbled in her pocket, holding her hand out to him. "Here. Tara asked me to give you this."

Alexi stared down at the box in his hand wondering if he could feel any more miserable. Opening the lid, he smiled as tears welled in his eyes. A sterling silver magician's wand overlaid a black magician's top hat made of onyx. The charm was attached to a silver chain.

A gift. From a friend. Something he'd forgotten how to be.

"Wait," he yelled as he realized she was walking away.

She didn't stop. "Wait a minute, will you?" He ran to catch up with her.

She still didn't stop. "I'm sorry, all right?" She slowed down a bit but he still had to reach out and grab her arm to get her to stop. "I said, I'm sorry."

"I'm not the one you owe the apology to."

She was right. He owed one to Tara big time. "Agreed."

"You also have a great deal to learn about people."

"You're right. I'm an ass."

She finally came to a complete halt and turned to face him. "Why?"

"Because being what people expect me to be comes naturally."

"You thought Tara expected you to run away?"

"Yes."

For the first time, Alexi watched her smile. Truly smile. "You're an ass, then."

He grinned back. "Thanks."

She cocked her head to study him. "You're welcome."

He began walking again, and this time, she

joined him. What made him open up to her? He wasn't used to telling anyone the truth. Even himself. "You're not going to make this easy are you?" he told her.

She shook her head. But he could tell she wasn't so angry with him any more. "I've never met anyone like you before. I only know one way to live. I always try to be honest. I've always tried to live my life with integrity. You seem not to know how to tell the truth."

This time he laughed. "Ouch."

Instead of answering, she reached out and took the box from his hand. She lifted the chain from the box and placed it around his neck. As the clasp clicked shut, he felt a weight lift from his shoulders. "Be yourself, Alexi. Believe in yourself."

"I'm not sure I can."

"Why?" When he didn't answer right away, she continued. "You keep trying to convince everyone you don't care. I think you care too much."

He snorted in disbelief. "That's not how the magic works."

"Why not? What's stopping you?"

"Too much shadow."

"I don't understand."

They approached the gardens that surrounded the house and Alexi blanched. "Uh-oh."

"What's wrong?"

"The people. They've gathered."

"So?"

"They're looking for a savior."

"No, Alexi. They're looking for a leader."

He gave her a wry smile. "I don't know how. I only know how to be a magician."

"Then you must work your magic. Have faith." He felt her hand squeeze his shoulder.

He walked up the steps to the patio where most of his House awaited his arrival. Were they really his he wondered? All of a sudden he realized Elena no longer stood by his side and a shard of panic sliced through his belly. A quick glance at her standing in the shadows reassured him that she hadn't abandoned him to his unwanted fate.

"What say you, House of Valentin?"

"Do you accept the role you are given?" another voice in the crowd called out.

"My brother lies in a coma. I have a niece punished for simply being."

Sergei was next. "Do what must be done, Alexi Valentin."

"We have an enemy determined to destroy us all," he warned.

"We can't fight him without you," came a feminine voice from far back.

"You don't need me, you need a miracle."

Sergei called out again. "The High Council—."

"Is just as scared as you are," he cut his mentor off. As I am, he said to himself.

"They've brought us through every human tragedy and we have survived," Sergei shot back.

"The terror we face isn't human. He is us. Of our own making, from our very beginning," Alexi answered. "He's powerful and bent on our destruction. So what say you? Should we succumb to fear?"

"NO!" came a rousing chorus of voices.

"Do we kneel before this thing and give up our very lives or do we fight for our survival?"

"We fight!" they answered.

"Then I accept my duty as my blood demands. True blood to true blood."

And while his heart ran with adrenaline from the belief of his people, Alexi knew the truth. All he had at the moment was the illusion of reality. And that illusion was really smoke and mirrors.

****

Now that he'd accepted the responsibility of taking care of his people, would he remember their bargain? Elena wondered as she watched him.

"The Ancient one wants to make us pay, toy with us before he attacks. He'll try to hurt us. Those of you who sensed his presence before his arrival must now become our watch guards. If you even imagine that you sense him, I must know immediately."

"Will he come after our families?" someone wanted to know.

"He might. There's no telling how he'll get his revenge. But I think something simpler with more devastating consequences."

"The horses," he breathed.

"My lord," came a shout. Elena couldn't see from whom. "You must come quickly. Hurry!"

She watched as a young man skidded to a stop before Alexi, gasping for breath.

"What is it?"

"Noble Pride..."

"What about Noble Pride?" Alexi asked. Elena could hear the terror in his voice.

"He's collapsed. He won't get up."

An agonized cry ran through the crowd. Everyone started to rush towards the pasture. "Hold!" Alexi cried.

Good for you, Alexi, Elena thought to herself.

"All of you can't help," Alexi called out. "Sergei, take Andre back to the pasture. Make the stallion as comfortable as you can. The rest of you wait here or go back to your duties. Please. We won't know if this is an attempt by the Ancient one to hurt us until we examine Noble Pride."

Alexi turned to her. She read the terror in his gaze. "I'm going to need your help. Noble Pride is the most magnificent animal we've ever produced. He's fathered many of the colts you see in the pasture.

Our House lives for our work with these horses, and though these animals provide income to the many who live here, they're more than just horses. They're like our children."

Alexi paused before continuing. "Our name resides among the elite of the show horse world. Noble Pride is the best we've ever had. Can you at least look at him?"

"I'll try." Elena replied, hoping to ease Alexi's fears. But she'd failed his family once before. She wasn't thrilled with finding herself in the same position again.

Alexi shuddered with relief. "Thank you."

He hurried down the steps and she tried to keep up with him as the whispers followed. Would she prevail this time?

He slowed down to her pace, coming to a halt as they reached a pasture high upon a hill. What a magnificent animal, she thought. Aptly named.

The horse's eyes rolled with fear as it tried to move and found it couldn't. Elena knelt down to touch the soft, shiny coat. Gently, she reached out with her mind. Most animals had no sense of the human language, they learned by repetition. Tone and force with the same sound inflection meant a command to them. So she used a calming, warm influence to quiet the animal. Once she was able to settle him down, Elena ran her hands over his body trying to sense what evil had been done to him.

How strange, she thought, sitting back on her heels.

"What's wrong?" Alexi asked. She could hear his concern in every syllable.

"I don't know. But the horse is paralyzed."

"Is it the Ancient one?" She looked at Alexi and found him grimacing. "It would be just like the bastard to play this kind of game. Keep the horse alive but damaged to hurt us."

She sighed, well aware that this was just the type of punishment their nemesis would use. "I'm not sure. Give me a moment."

Elena took a deep breath then placed her hand over the brow of the animal. She reached into its mind but again found no hint of the evil that had befallen them. "Sergei. The tea. Is there any left?"

"Yes, I believe there is." She watched Sergei turn, she assumed to send someone for the samovar, only to find Alexi on his feet and running towards the house.

While they waited for Alexi to return, Elena told both men the truth. "I didn't want to worry Alexi but I think he's right. I'm not certain of the how yet."

The young man Alexi called Andre kept stroking the horse while Sergei simply looked grim. "I wondered how his revenge would begin," Sergei said.

She sighed. "I find it very hard to understand such hatred."

"Would you believe me if I told you I'm having a hard time also?"

Elena studied the proud old gentleman and saw the pain he bore at the loss of his prized pupil, perhaps more of a son to him than his own, she thought. Then she watched the light of pride fill his gaze as Alexi returned from his mission. "Thank you," she said, hoping that the tea would work on a horse the same as it did on them.

"You're welcome," he replied in between deep breaths.

"Andre, turn his head. If he is so frozen, I'll have to pour some of this down his throat."

A look of horror crossed the young man's face. "He'll choke to death."

"Do you have a better plan?"

Andre nodded and ran to a nearby barn. He returned with a funnel and a tube. With great care, he slid the tube down the horse's throat while Elena made sure the horse knew they were not trying to hurt it. "You love him."

Andre nodded. "I'm studying to be a veterinarian."

She dribbled some of the tea into the funnel, paused, then dribbled some more and waited for the leaves to work their magic. "Take care," she warned them all. "If he starts to move, back up. I'm fairly certain he'll want to kick out."

When Noble Pride didn't move, Elena ran her hands over the horse's body one last time. Just when she thought she might have failed for a second time in just as many days, she felt the notch in the horse's spine. Although not positive of the cause, it was very possible their enemy had forced the bones to shift, causing the paralysis. She smiled, breathing a huge sigh of relief.

"It's difficult to explain but the problem is physical, probably demon made but perhaps not. There's a bone in his spine that's out of place."

"But lady, I checked him," Andre cried in defense of his abilities.

"So you did. But you wouldn't have found this."

He gave her a skeptical look. "I'm going lull him into a dream state first." Elena bent down and covered his brow again. Once she was certain the animal would not panic, she used her telekinetic abilities to move the bones back to their correct placement. "I'm not an expert on equine physiology but the bones seem to be in order now. I would hazard a guess and say that riding him wouldn't be in his best interest but perhaps in time. He'll continue to live a long life, however, and hopefully create many more foals."

She motioned them all to stand back then set the horse's mind free. Noble Pride struggled to his feet then shook himself and she heard Alexi laugh. The horse walked over to her slowly and nuzzled her with his nose. She stroked his neck and whispered words of goodness in her own tongue. He neighed and lifted his head in pride before trotting off to survey his kingdom.

Alexi came rushing over, lifted her in his arms, and twirled her around before setting her down on the ground. "Thank you," he said over and over again. Her reward, though, was his smile. The one that was all Alexi, not the one he gave the rest of the world because he thought he had to.

Sergei bowed. "My lady, you have saved us yet again."

"No, Sergei. I simply did what I'm meant to do. Heal that which is broken."

"Keep an eye on him, Andre," she called to the young man as he started after the horse. "He might be a bit woozy for a little while."

"I will, my lady. Thank you."

Elena turned to head back to the house and Alexi began to follow. All of a sudden she realized Alexi wasn't next to her. She stopped and turned to see why. As she did, she watched Sergei hand Alexi a ring. His fist closed about the metal so tight she knew his hand had to hurt. In his gaze she found a pain so raw and so deep, she almost looked away. In fact, she would have but her gaze was caught by the determination growing on his countenance. Alexi nodded then turned to join her. "Are you all right?"

"I will be. Once this goes back where it belongs." He opened his hand and she saw a ring bearing the crest of the House of Valentin.

"For now, it rests where it belongs."

With that, she slid the ring onto his finger. "You are the Head of the House of Valentin."

Chapter Six

The ring weighed so little yet gave those who wore it great power. "Temporarily," Alexi insisted as he stared at the signet on his hand.

"I assume there's a ceremony that goes with this honor," she answered, her thumb rubbing the back of his hand.

"There is," he choked out, not sure which scared him more, the touch of the cold metal or the touch of her finger.

"One you want but don't want. True?"

"Yes," he answered. Being honest with himself, yes to both. He'd always coveted the ring. He shouldn't have. Now he coveted the woman in front of him. Again, knowing he shouldn't. "But I'd rather have earned the right."

"All things happen with purpose, Alexi Valentin. For whatever reason, you've been chosen. You must walk in your own footsteps now."

"My own footsteps," he repeated with a bitter laugh. "I don't have any. I step and they disappear. I'm a magician. Or have you forgotten?"

"No, I haven't forgotten. Anything."

"What do you mean?" he asked, sensing something behind her words, something he was sure he wasn't going to like.

She sighed. "Unless I'm mistaken we still have a bargain, don't we?"

Just when Alexi thought his heart could go no lower, it managed to find a subterranean level. "Yes. And no."

"What do you mean?"

"That I have priorities, obligations that have changed the rules of the game."

Between the look on his face and the words he spoke, she must have realized something was wrong. "I don't understand."

They'd begun walking towards the house. As he saw all the familiar scenes, the way the scrub looked against the blanket of green pastures in the distance, the way the sky looked so bright and blue overhead, Alexi wondered how the earth could be crashing down all around him. He didn't answer right away; instead, he led her to a small garden next to the patio and pool behind the house. "This was my mother's most favorite spot on earth."

"You're stalling," she told him in no uncertain terms.

"What I'm about to.... well, it's difficult to explain."

"I prefer the truth."

"Of course," he concurred. "I know that. I would never lie to you. It's just that...well, this isn't something I normally talk about."

God, if the circumstances hadn't been so bad, he'd have laughed. The great Alexi Valentin. Prince of the Vegas Strip. Embarrassed. And making more of a mess than he'd ever thought possible.

Alexi started pacing causing several emotions to cross her face. They ended with simple confusion. "Why don't you just tell me and let me be the judge."

"Uh, Houston, I think we have a problem."

"I'm getting the feeling that whatever you say, I won't like."

Wasn't that the truth? But he couldn't get the words out. She was expecting integrity and he was about to give her Masters and Johnson. If the situation hadn't gone so far south that it was already irretrievable, he'd laugh.

"All right," he said, taking a deep breath.

"Here's the way it is." He exhaled again. "You want my seed to strengthen your race. Maybe the mixing of our bloodlines will stop the agony you live with. Maybe it won't. I don't know that and neither do you."

"It's the chance I take. Coupling with humans is an excruciating task."

Wow, he told himself. He'd never thought of *that*. "Sorry, but this is where you're wrong. Now it's the chance we both take."

"You owe me no obligation. Just a flesh and blood baby."

He shook his head. "Not so fast. I'm the Head of the House of Valentin now."

"And I repeat—you owe me no obligation. I'll take the baby and go back home where I belong."

"Aside from the fact that your thought process doesn't go very far—"

"I beg your pardon," she interrupted, obviously miffed.

"Well, it doesn't. As in, we would be creating my child too."

"But I thought...," her voice trailed off. "I never thought the child would interest you."

"First of all, that could be plural as in twins. It's kind of genetic you know. Second," and this time he stared hard at her. "You thought wrong."

Her brow scrunched as she realized he cared. And he did. "I apologize."

"Accepted. But you're still missing the point."

"There's more?"

Oh brother, was there. "The obligation isn't my status. Being Head of the House changes my obligation to my people. I will now have to marry a True Noble. But that can be dealt with. A child, children, would certainly be an obligation, but one I would willingly accept. One I accepted before all this went down."

"Then what *is* the problem?"

"Once I give you my seed, we're mated for life."

"Mated?" Bewildered, she asked, "As in the way your brother and Tara are mated?"

"Sort of. Only they love each other so much it hurts to look at them."

Elena totally agreed. "I don't understand your use of the word. Do you mean, connected? Physically? Some sort of psychic connection? Explain."

He sighed. "I'm not sure I can. I won't really know your thoughts unless you allow me to. But as you can see by Nico and Tara, it is possible."

"That's a relief," she told him. "I'm a private person."

"I know."

Now what was that supposed to mean? "Go on."

"I'll know when you're hurt. I'll sense your emotions. They'll never leave me."

She sensed many of his emotions now. That was easy. But then she was born to sense these things. Perhaps he wasn't. "I understand."

"I'll want you until the day of my death."

"Want me?" she asked, again uncertain of the meaning of his words.

"I'll physically desire you. Something to do with pro-creation, I guess. You know, continuation of the race. But it is something I'll never be able to get away from no matter how far apart we are."

Good God, she thought. "I had no idea. And you were willing to do this anyway?"

"I had nothing to lose. No ties. It didn't seem to matter where or when I was bound, or to whom. Not if you could save Tara."

Elena held up her hand and shook her head. "A moment. Please. I need to sort all this out." She swallowed. "What you're saying is that if you have sex with me, you will be mated to me. But as Head of the House, you will be forced to marry someone else."

"Umm, just so you know everything, I can have sex with you anytime I want. Complete with orgasm. Just not..."

Was he blushing? If she hadn't been so intent on his statements, she would have enjoyed his discomfort. "I believe the word is ejaculation," she told him in a droll tone.

"Yes."

"But if you're mated to me, how can you mate to anyone else? I mean, the entire reason you would marry is to create more True Nobles, isn't it?"

His face tightened and she realized she'd pricked his...well the only word she had for it was his Nobility. "You're right. But it has happened. Rarely, but it has."

"And the outcome?"

"I would want both of you, one to a lesser degree but nonetheless. The bond, once forged, will never be broken. Not until one or the other mate dies."

He paused, she thought, to allow her to digest his words. "You'll want me as much as I want you," he continued. "In that case, I'd be more than happy to make conjugal visits upon occasion."

Affronted, she exclaimed, "I will not."

He snorted, rounding on her. "I assure you, madam, this isn't a game. If you decide on this course of action, you'll become a bitch in heat. I'll become a male animal. I won't be able to resist the pull of you; you won't be able to resist me."

"Even if you're mated to someone else?"

"They'll understand. It's the way of our people. I'd have no choice but to satisfy the bond."

Elena sat back and tried to digest all the information he'd given her. "But I'm not a Noble. How do you know this will happen to the two of us?"

"I don't. I can only explain the way my

physiology, my morphology, my psycho-biology, jeez, my mojo works."

Elena didn't know how to respond. None of the books she'd ever read covered anything like this. "I have much to consider."

"I think we both do. In the meantime, I'd be honored if you would join us for a celebration tonight. Noble Pride is like the heart and soul of the people. What you did to save him can never be repaid."

Elena rose, pain shooting through her. Then again, perhaps her heart had something to do with this hurt as well. "Only the people, magician?"

She turned and left him there, presumably staring after her. In all the words, all the statements, all the discussion, Alexi had never answered the most important question of all. *Do you care, Alexi?*

****

Lanterns and torches gave brightness to the night sky. The desert didn't sleep, Elena noticed, enjoying the background symphony of the evening. Funny how she missed her home with it's huge trees and dense forests, yet had come to love the spacious expanse and peacefulness of the desert.

"Good evening, my lady," Sergei greeted her with a bow.

"A good evening to you also," she replied, returning the bow with respect.

"The clothing of our people suits you."

She inclined her head. The red tunic with the V-neck collar was wonderfully spacious yet warm against the slight chill in the air. And the embroidery. No one in her village could match such excellent stitch work. "I'm honored by the workmanship."

"As we are here tonight to honor yours. Come." Sergei led her out onto the patio where everyone had gathered.

Too many people, too many heartbeats, she thought in panic. Then she caught sight of Alexi. His tunic was royal blue, the embroidery white, red and black, setting off the swirling gray of his gaze. Which at the moment seemed to beam with pride. At her. Elena's heart swelled.

He held out his hand and she placed her fingers against his. His grip was strong and true like his heart. He didn't know how to believe that, but it was.

He helped her up onto a dais to stand next to him. The crowd quickly quieted. "We gather tonight to honor a guest of our House. Great evil has befallen us, yet from a most unlikely source, we have been saved. Perhaps not the way we envisioned, but Nicholai and Noble Pride could both be dead. Instead of tragedy, we have hope. Let's all celebrate that hope and thank our guest for her help and intervention."

A rousing cheer ran through the crowd then musicians started to play and people began to dance. "I did nothing, Alexi, except that which I have been born to do."

"So you keep saying. But they need this celebration. So do you. Come."

He turned, leading her towards the middle of the dais and a table gaily set for celebration. "Just the two of us?"

"Would you prefer more?"

"I don't know."

He laughed and she found the sound music to her ears. Not many laughed with true enjoyment. "After our last conversation, I thought for sure your next greeting would be a slap in the face."

"Why would I do that?" she asked, genuinely puzzled. "You told me the truth. You gave me the consequences. Many wouldn't."

He threw her a pained look. "You don't think too highly of others, do you?"

"No," she replied without guilt. "Don't misunderstand me. I don't set false expectations. Thus, I'm surprised when another goes above and beyond them. Even pleased."

He grinned. "Are you pleased now?"

"Very. I've never been honored so."

"Only that?"

What was he driving at? All of a sudden, Elena looked at him. Not as a baby maker or a necessity or even a godsend. She simply looked at him. She saw the torch light dance in the midnight black of his hair. She saw the tiny laugh lines around his eyes that told her how much he truly valued life, in spite of the careless attitude he showed so often. She saw the deepening gray of his gaze that became a trap she might never get out of.

Against her will, her head moved closer to his. The sounds of the party faded. Her heartbeat sped up, racing wild as the wind. She could smell the spicy tang of the desert mixed with his scent and a warm glow grew in her belly.

Was this desire? True desire? If so, no words could ever describe the sensation. "No," she replied.

He seemed to know exactly what he was doing, for just as she was about to cross a point of no return, he reared back and began to clap to the music.

Was this how a man teases a woman, she wondered? Shouldn't she be trying to seduce him?

Did she dare?

How far could this go before one of them stepped too close to the fire?

Great platters of food were brought out and Elena found her appetite skewed in favor of sensation. Funny how he seemed to understand what he did to her. He grinned as he piled her plate high. "You must taste this duck. Amelie makes a sauce that comes very close to heaven."

"I've never eaten duck before. We have geese at home, but we rarely eat them. Only on special occasions."

"Then consider this one of those occasions, for this is one delight you'll truly not want to miss."

Unsure, Elena let him tease her with a small bite. As she tasted a tiny bit, the sauce exploded into a combination of cherry, orange, and lemon. Growing bolder, she opened her mouth and took the rest of the meat from the fork. The taste was very much like that of a goose, but lighter. But the— combination—Alexi was right. The dish was heavenly. "How wonderful!" she exclaimed.

Alexi smiled. "Amelie will be pleased. She feels we take her cooking for granted."

"She's an artist. And this bread." She reached out and tore off a piece to taste. "The bread is so light and crispy. I consider myself a decent baker, but my creations can't compare."

His gaze caught and held hers. "You have other talents."

His words went straight to her core. Did she? That was a question as yet unanswered. She'd never made love before.

Her feet began to tap in time to the music and Alexi asked, "Would you like to dance?"

She threw him a look. Even though she walked without distress, dancing was out of the question. "Perhaps a walk. I need to move."

"Come on." He helped her up and they walked away from the patio towards the pastures.

"I have never known such peace before."

"The desert has that effect."

Elena wondered about her effect on him. As soon as she was sure they were far enough away, she whirled and threw her arms around his neck. His mouth opened in surprise and she planted her lips on top of his. His arms hung at his sides as if he was struggling with himself, but Elena kept on trying. He finally caved in when her tongue outlined his upper lip. He groaned and his arms tightened about her like two steel bands. His mouth engulfed hers, and she realized her kiss was mere child's play in relation to his. His tongue ravaged the inside of her mouth sending shivers up and down her spine.

All of a sudden, he tore his mouth away from hers. He gasped, drawing deep breaths of air. It seemed he wanted this experiment as much as she did. Then again, maybe he didn't. "Why, Elena? Are you playing with me? Trying to force my hand?"

"No, I—" She didn't have an answer. Was she playing with him? Any more than she was playing with herself?

"I'm not a toy," he reiterated, his anger like daggers.

"I know. I didn't mean to—."

"If you force me into this, it'll be on my terms."

"Of course it will."

He threw her away from him. "Make sure you understand that."

He turned in the direction they'd just come and stormed off.

Tears flooded her eyes. She'd insulted him again. For whatever reason, she'd done it all wrong and had no idea why. She didn't understand when to start, where to go, or when to stop. With a heavy heart, Elena turned to follow. It seemed you couldn't learn everything from books. They certainly hadn't prepared her for a man's wounded pride. Or for a Noble's pride. With a hollow feeling in the pit of her stomach, Elena knew the truth.

It was time to leave.

Chapter Seven

The rays of the Sun sizzled through his body. No matter how bad or wrong events from the night before were, Alexi could always count on the Sun to set things right. Power surged through his body as he lifted his face to the sky. Invincible. No one could hurt him. Especially not a five foot nothing gnome who couldn't make up her mind what she wanted.

Alexi flexed his fingers, his skin crackling with energy. He'd worn only his boxers to catch every ray. Like the jolt of a thousand cups of coffee, the Sun made Alexi want to run a ten-mile race. He left the solar and went to his father's study.

He watched Sergei lift a brow at his state of near undress but by God, if Elena wanted a baby maker, then she was going to get very familiar with his body very quickly. "Where is she?"

Both brows went up. "I assume you're speaking of the lady, Elena?"

"No, I was talking about Marilyn Monroe."

He watched Sergei's face fall in disapproval. Been there, done that, he thought to himself. Sergei reached into a closet and threw a shirt at him. "I told your father many times that you needed more discipline. Once again you've proven me right."

"Yeah, well, that's just Alexi for ya. Always a disappointment. Never quite as studious as his brother, never quite as fast, as sharp, as..."

"Enough!" Sergei rapped out. "How dare you! You have no time for self-pity. You have a House to protect. To run. To save."

Alexi chuckled. "Now there's a picture. Alexi

Valentin. Court jester. All decked out like a knight in shining armor. More like a Woody Allen movie if you want to know the truth."

"If you see yourself as such, then you are a disappointment, Alexi. I don't expect you to be Nicholai. I don't expect you to be your father either. I expect you to be...you."

"Some bargain," he answered, bitterness riding his tone.

Sergei walked over to him and put a comforting hand on his shoulder. "The people love you."

"They love the facade. I put on a great magic act."

Sergei shook his head. "Do you really think they're so shallow? That they can't see beneath the stage presence? They know. They see. You. The real you. The strong, stalwart, independent man who is bendable. Approachable. As your brother was not. Nicholai knew only one way to lead. By authority. But there are other ways. One is called democracy. It seems to work rather well in this country."

"So what you're telling me is... it's okay to ask for help."

"Now I understand," the elder man said, half to Alexi, half to himself. "You believe Nicholai never did." Alexi watched him shake his head. "I can't tell you how many times. Right here in this very room."

Now that was interesting. "I thought he just, well, you know, knew."

"Because it wasn't in his nature to let anyone see indecision."

"And he listened?"

Sergei snorted in amusement. "Now that's another story. I would like to believe we discussed many problems and that he listened to my advice about certain courses of action. However, I'm sure that more often than not I was simply a sounding board."

"I wish he would have come to me."

Sergei sighed and Alexi read a deep sadness in his gaze. "Would you have dealt with him honestly? Would you have answered his questions with the thought and consideration they deserved? You acted the child more often than not. You still do."

That hurt. But Sergei was right. "Bad Catch-22. I thought Nicholai didn't want to include me. He thought I didn't want to be included. I pushed him away so it became harder for him to approach."

"If you understand that, then you've grown much in the last few days, young one."

Alexi looked down at his hands and wondered whom they belonged to. No surprise there. He didn't know who he was anymore. "I'm not cut out for this, Sergei."

"How do you know until you try?"

He thought about that for a long moment. "I guess I don't."

He sighed, long and loud. "So. Where is she?"

"I assume you mean the lady, Elena."

"We're not gonna start that again, are we?"

"No," Sergei replied, moving about the room to straighten up. If Alexi didn't know better, he'd say Sergei was hiding something from him. "But I'm not really sure at the moment."

"I guess I'd better explain why I'm asking," he told his mentor as he put the shirt on.

"Explain?"

"I...ummm, sort of, well, made this bargain with her."

"Bargain?" Sergei frowned at him. "What kind of bargain?"

"If she saved Tara and the baby," he said in a rush hoping that by getting the words out faster they might get him into less trouble, "I would make her pregnant."

It didn't take long for Sergei, judging by his

facial expressions, to figure out all the consequences of that remark. "I see. I think."

"You gotta understand," Alexi felt the words tumble out of his mouth. "It was before I knew anything would happen to Nico. I had no ties, no obligations. And a damn good reason for making the bargain."

"Hmmm. There's only one flaw in your statement. Now you do."

Alexi hung his head. "Yeah, I know."

"You have a penchant for predicaments," Sergei muttered in reply.

"Tell me about it."

Alexi looked up to see indecision cross Sergei's face. "Then I guess you had best know the rest."

"What do you mean?"

"The lady Elena left this morning. Before sunrise."

"Left? What do you mean, left? As in gone? Good-bye? *Kaput?*"

"Yes."

Stunned, Alexi asked, "Did she say why?"

Sergei's stern gaze tore through him. "Did she have to?"

Oh no, he'd done it again. Screwed things up royally. "She kept making me feel like some kind of boy-toy. Stud-muffin."

Sergei clucked his tongue at him in disgust. "A woman who feels so compelled that she braves the agony she does wasn't looking at you as anything *but* a savior. Did you ever take into consideration the sacrifices she's made? Here she seems almost normal."

Alexi thought back to how she'd looked the first time he met her. He remembered the first time she touched him and the look on her face. "No," he mumbled.

"Albeit that you owe the woman an apology,"

Sergei began, stressing his last word. "You also owe her your honor. You have no choice but to fulfill your bargain."

"What about the House?"

Sergei took a deep breath and let the air out slowly. "Much has changed these last few months, Alexi. I fear we will go through more change before this terror is over. But if we change who we are, if we compromise our principles, give up our integrity, and forgo our honor, we are nothing. I still believe we call ourselves the Nobility for a reason."

Alexi chewed on Sergei's words for a long moment. As much as he might joke and show disdain, he believed everything Sergei said. "Do you have any idea where she went?"

"She mentioned she wanted to see Tara."

"Then you'd better call the airport. I'll need a flight out to Newark right away."

Alexi turned to leave the room. As he did, the study door flew open nearly hitting him. Standing in the opening young Andre gasped, trying to catch his breath. Tears streamed down the young man's face. "Noble Pride is dead."

****

Alexi knew the stench that surrounded the horse well. He could feel the wetness on his cheeks. His fist clenched so hard the ring bit into his finger yet he felt no pain. "What happened, Andre?"

"After the Lady of the Lake…"

"The who?" Alexi cut him off.

"We call her the Lady of the Lake, my lord."

"Go on."

"After she healed Noble Pride, he was like a young stallion again."

"The tea," Alexi muttered.

"He wouldn't be denied. Since we had two mares in season, I decided to take the opportunity. We took him to the breeding shed. He was magnificent. Both mares...I'm positive both will foal."

Alexi reached out to touch the lifeless animal. So beautiful. So much lost. Then Andre's words reached through his anger. "Then the most amazing thing happened. Noble Pride was ready for more. So I had his semen gathered to be frozen."

"Continue."

"Naturally, I expected him to be very tired. I thought he was still asleep. I thought he was still asleep," the young man repeated, then broke into sobs. "The lady can't save him, can she?"

"Not this time, Andre. The stench of the Ancient one still lingers. A parting gift to us all." Alexi rose from his crouch.

"Yet we have hope. One or both of the mares will foal. I'm sure of it. Perhaps another Noble Pride will be born to us."

Alexi watched Andre wipe at his eyes, eyes now filled with hope. "Yes, yes. I must believe that."

"We must all believe that."

Alexi reached out and clasped Andre's shoulder in commiseration. "Ready a pyre. Noble Pride will depart this earth as he lived in it. As a king."

Alexi strode into the house. He went to his bedroom and pulled out a garment bag, tore some clothes off hangers, threw them in. Then he picked up his cell phone for the tenth time. He sighed in relief when he heard her voice at the other end. "Tara?"

"Alexi. Hi."

"How's Nico?"

"The same."

"Is she there?"

"Is who here?"

"You know damned well. Quit razzing me."

"No."

"I need a favor." He raked a hand through his hair. "No, wait a minute. Let me do something right for a change." He started pacing. "Thank you for the gift. I'm sorry I wasn't there for you to give it to me personally."

"I understand. You were being a maroon."

He smiled. "Doesn't make up for my behavior now does it?"

"No, it doesn't, nerd-brain," she replied. He could hear her grin all the way across the country. "But if it helps any, I really do understand."

"You're the best."

"I am. I also know better."

Sometimes he wondered how everyone around him seemed to know him better than he did. "Can you keep Elena there for me? She's on her way to visit you."

"I'll try."

His tone turned grave. "You'd better keep on your toes too. Noble Pride is dead. A parting gift from our friend."

"Oh no!" He could hear her tears. "But I spoke with Sergei. I thought..."

"She did," he replied, his heart heavy. "The Ancient one wasn't through with us yet."

"That piece of..."

"Don't," Alexi cried, cutting her off again. "Don't stoop to his level."

"You're right. But one day there's going to be a reckoning."

"I'll be right there with you."

"I know you will. And you know something else? You'd give your brother a run for his money."

Stunned by the compliment, Alexi didn't reply at first. "Thanks."

"Just so you know, I've named the baby. I can only take so much of this stuff too."

"You go, girl. So, c'mon. Give."

"Sylvana."

His heart melted. "My mother would have loved

that. Thank you."

****

Elena shook her head and watched Tara's face fall. "Forgive me, Tara. Nicholai treads just beyond reach. It's almost as if he's waiting for something."

"I wish I knew what."

"Myself as well. There seems to be some piece, a part of a puzzle that I haven't grasped yet. When I do, I'll know. Until then, have hope."

"That's hard to do sometimes."

Elena couldn't understand. Was it wrong to want everything right? "You have that which I crave beyond life, Tara. You must think of your daughter as well."

Tara smiled, her smile tender yet sad. "You don't understand the bond yet."

"Yes, Alexi explained this to me."

Tara simply shook her head. "He wouldn't understand. But I'll try to explain. My heart beats with every beat of Nicholai's heart. We share the same breath. We are each other."

"Beautiful words to be sure."

"Not just words. But that's why I knew you wouldn't understand. Perhaps someday you'll be lucky enough to find out."

"Perhaps. But I have a quest to complete."

Elena watched Tara pick up the baby as she started to fuss. The infant quieted immediately. Then Tara grinned and handed the baby to her with a diaper for her shoulder. "Here. You might as well get some practice."

Elena looked down at the angelic face of the babe in her arms, swallowed hard, then started rocking as if she were born to nurture. "What's that you're humming?" Tara asked, an amused expression on her face.

"What? Oh. Just a lullaby."

"So when are you going to stop running long

enough to get Alexi in bed?"

Elena whipped her head up to stare. "That won't be possible."

Tara raised both brows. "Really?"

Elena shrugged. "Every time I remind him of our bargain..."

"Bargain?"

Elena sighed. "I didn't tell anyone. The bargain was between Alexi and myself. I was called to save your life. Yours and Sylvana's. I would have done so no matter what. But I could think of no other way to get pregnant. My people are dying, Tara. I need your blood, your strength. I told Alexi I needed his sperm."

Tara burst out laughing. "I'd have paid money to witness that conversation." Then her friend sobered. "But I understand, now, about your desperation. Forgive me, I wasn't laughing at your need."

"I know. But every time I try to, well, this is so difficult. I have no knowledge of men and women. Not really. I don't understand why he gets so angry. I don't consider him a stud-muffin."

"Is that what he said?" Tara chuckled again then shook her head. "Listen girlfriend. Men have egos that are like delicate china. They're fragile. A part of him understands his obligation to you, but men have to be male around a female. Macho. Take charge. The initiator."

Bewildered, Elena considered this. "So, he's angry because I haven't let him instigate the process."

"Honey, you'd better quit calling it a process or you're going be in for the shock of your life," Tara warned.

"I don't understand."

"Got that. So let's start with Relationship 101. You didn't understand what he needed and he felt he couldn't give you what you needed. Now, try to put yourself in his shoes for a second. He wants to do the right thing, but thinks he can't," Tara paused a moment. "Umm, not to get personal, but he is attracted to you, isn't he?"

Elena blushed. "Yes."

"So every time he reacts to you, he gets angry with himself."

Horrified, Elena whispered, "I didn't mean to hurt him."

"I know. But you do have a way to remedy that. Seduce him."

"I don't know how. I think...I thought I tried. He pushed me away."

"So? Try again."

"I'm not so sure I'll be able to."

Confused, Tara stared at her. "Okay, you lost me. Why?"

"Because I've already found another stud-muffin."

Chapter Eight

Somehow it didn't seem right, standing outside a door and eavesdropping. He sent silent thanks one more time to Tara for her understanding. She didn't have to help him. But she knew what was inside him, probably better than he did himself.

He'd followed Elena to New York City. The apartment building made him want to take a shower. The smell was a combination of stale, moldy, and old. Paint peeled from the walls in between the graffiti. And he certainly didn't need his sensitive hearing. The walls were already paper-thin.

Concentrating on her, he sensed her distaste with her surroundings. But worse than having put her into this position, he sensed an inner sadness. Had he done that to her as well? Or was she feeling the weight of her duty as he had?

"I need you to make me pregnant."

Pure laughter reached him and from a source that set his teeth on edge. "You're kidding, right?"

"I assure you, I'm not joking."

Couldn't the bastard understand her dignity? The cost of her request? Then he slammed himself. Had *he*? "Who sent you here?"

"No one. I came of my own accord."

There was that laughter again. Alexi felt his blood begin to boil. "I'm sure you did. But this is either a really great joke or you're serious. Let's go with serious for a moment. Who are you? What are you? And here's the really important one, why me?"

"I'm not a Noble if that's what you are asking."

"Works for me, but then I kinda figured that."

Alexi heard the bed creak. Was this creep trying to take advantage of her already? "So, if you're not a Noble, what are you?" There was a pause that made Alexi think the man beyond the door was raking Elena with his gaze. "Cause honey, you certainly ain't human."

"I'm like you but not quite. Whereas your powers are like humans, only enhanced, I'm empathic."

"Em-what?"

Alexi nearly laughed. Charles Rhys-Jones was not nearly as bright as he thought he was. "Empathic. I'm attuned to the human race. Their sickness is my sickness, I absorb their diseases, their pain, in a sense, I'm a total healer."

"Impressive. Is that why you move the way you do? You really seem stiff."

"Yes. So as you can tell, mating with a human is excruciatingly difficult."

"Yeah, I guess so." There was a pause again. He could almost hear the wheels inside Rhys-Jones' head grinding. "So you're looking for a Noble to make you pregnant. Why'd you just up and decide to choose me?"

"Because Alexi Valentin refused my first offer."

Alexi shook his head. God, sometimes she had the tact of a bull elephant. But a huge grin split his face. He could just picture the scowl on Charles' face. "Now that's what I call a real sales pitch. Besides the fact that I'm not real fond of the Valentins, you just up and tell me I'm second best to boot? Lady, you're a piece of work."

Obviously Elena saw she'd made an error with her honesty. "I didn't mean it that way," she backtracked. "I was thinking more in terms of what you'd call a business deal. I would prefer to do this without emotional involvement."

That was cold. But Alexi had forced her to this

way of thinking. Again, there was a pause. "You're aware of the bond?"

"I am. However, I'd like to keep this as close to a business arrangement as I can. I need your sperm. What would you like in return?"

Without hesitation he heard the answer. "Money."

Of course, that was no surprise. But her reply was. "Very well. How much?"

"Ten."

"Thousand?"

That garnered a short bark of laughter. "Nope. Million."

"Hmmm." Her turn to pause. "That will take a bit of time."

"You're serious?"

"Yes, of course I am. You're not? Because that much money will take a good deal of effort to gather."

"You mean you can? Legally? I don't want to end up in jail."

"That depends on your definition of legal. Let's just say that from a human standpoint, you'd have nothing to fear."

He could hear Rhys-Jones salivate from here. "When can you deliver? As you can tell, my status isn't the best. I'd like to get out of this hell-hole as soon as I can."

She answered honestly as only Elena could. "I'll have to get you installments. I don't know how much I'll be able to garner but the first take will be the largest."

Alexi could just imagine Charles pumping his fist in triumph. "So now my only problem is to get it up."

"Only problem?" He heard her puzzlement. "The connection between us won't bother you?"

This whole fiasco was really getting on Alexi's

last nerve. The thought of Charles Rhys-Jones becoming the father of a new race made him sick to his stomach. "Hey, for ten million I can live with anything. Even screw anything."

That was enough. Damn bastard needed some serious lessons on how to treat a lady. He was just about to open the door when Charles yelled, "Don't break it, Alexi. Just come in. It isn't locked."

So Chuck knew he was there. Okay. So what?

"What are you doing here?" Elena cried, turning to watch him enter the room. Her gaze couldn't have been colder.

"Trying to save you from a really big mistake. He's nothing more than a giant slime ball."

"Your opinion isn't welcome." Nor was the frost in her tone.

"Too bad," Alexi replied. "Did he tell you he was banished? That this is why he's alone and without a House? Why he's living in this dump?"

"No." She looked between both men then focused on Charles. "Explain."

"Well, nymphet, it's like this. His big brother and I..."

"Nicholai?"

"Yeah. Him. We weren't seeing eye to eye. So I figured I'd get rid of him."

"Get rid of him?"

"That's what we do, nymphet. Try to kill each other. Blood feuds. Things like that."

Alexi watched Elena shudder. "Barbaric."

"Whatever. Anyway, his woman got in the way."

"Tara?"

"He almost killed her," Alexi confirmed.

"Would you have told me this?" she asked Charles.

"Nope. No reason to. The past is the past. Besides, I made amends. I saved her life."

"Only because you wanted reinstatement."

"Actually, I kind of like her. She's a tough cookie."

Alexi wanted to puke. "You make me sick."

"Both of you stop. This instant," Elena cried. "Charles, you're not a scrupulous man and I don't like being manipulated." Then she turned to Alexi. "By anyone."

Alexi had had enough. "Elena, let's just get out of here." He swallowed a little ball of pride and added, "Please?"

She turned to Rhys-Jones. "Are you all like this?" Her disgust was more than evident.

He shrugged and smiled. "Welcome to the wonderful world of the Nobility. Not very Noble, are we?"

She dismissed the man's words with a wave of her hand. "I'll consider your offer. The money's not a problem. However, I want no ties. If you must have sex with me upon occasion, it will be on my terms. The connection dies there."

Charles looked straight at him and grinned. "You have yourself a deal."

"I don't think so."

Elena simply stared at Alexi. He'd followed her. But she had no idea what that meant. Or didn't mean. Did he care? "You have no say in this matter anymore. Nor do you have any right to be here. Leave."

"Yeah, magic man. Poof. Disappear."

"Look, *Chuck*. You're beginning to get on my nerves. Butt out."

"No can do. The lady here and I have just made a deal that's going to get me out of this dump. So I believe it's your move. *Sayonara.*"

Elena flicked her gaze from one man to the other. But it ended up staying with Alexi. She'd thought there was a connection between them. Or maybe she'd wanted a connection between them.

What she hadn't counted on was that his behavior would hurt so much.

"You think I'm going to let you touch anything decent?" Alexi asked, ignoring her outburst completely.

Rhys-Jones merely smiled. "I think that's up to her."

Of course, she'd made this impersonal so she shouldn't expect more. But being a "her" didn't sit well with her insides at all. "I'm sorry, Alexi. You need to leave."

"That's right and you're coming with me."

Elena frowned. Alexi had certainly picked a bad time to begin ordering her around. "I don't think so."

He sighed. "What you're doing right now is ten times worse than whatever you think I deserve. So I give. You win."

"I win nothing, Alexi. You forced me into this, you refused my offer. He hasn't. All I want is a baby. I really don't care who gives it to me anymore." Of course, she was starting to realize deep down what a lie that really was.

"But you see, that's where you're wrong, Elena. You can't let him... Oh God, just saying the words." She watched Alexi shudder. "Touch you."

Charles laughed. He'd been watching the two of them argue with a smug smile on his face. Now he held up his hands. "Hey, these are clean. I even wash under my fingernails."

Elena decided to ignore Charles. She caught Alexi's gaze with hers. When they'd first met he'd been guarded but approachable. Now Elena had no idea how he felt about her. He wouldn't let her in. "Do you care, Alexi?"

"Of course I care."

"Enough to give up your obligations?"

Alexi hesitated. As long as the hesitation existed, Elena would never ask him to give them up.

"I can't."

"I know."

Charles started clapping as he swung his legs over the bed. "My, my. That was really touching. What a performance. Beautiful. See?" the man asked, bringing a finger to his eye. "I'm even going to cry."

Elena reached out just in time to stop Alexi's arm from swinging. His muscles quivered beneath her fingertips. "I have my obligations too, Alexi."

"Don't do this, Elena," Alexi pleaded. "You're making a big mistake. He'll end up using you somehow. He has no honor. He'll tell you anything now but wait. Give him the money, any money, and he'll find a way to renege on the bargain."

"Is that a fact?" Charles asked, a rather hurt look on his face.

She looked at both men before continuing. "What makes either of you so different then?"

Alexi's face turned to stone. He threw her hand off his arm. "Nothing," he whispered.

She watched Alexi turn away and thought her heart would break. She didn't want to hurt Alexi but what couldn't be just couldn't be. She knew that now. He had the Nobility. She had her people. End of story.

"Hey, Valentin. Don't let the door hit you..." Charles stopped speaking in mid-sentence as a man stood in the now open doorway.

"Dmitri?" Alexi asked, perplexed. "What are you doing here?"

"You are summoned by the High Council." Elena watched the man throw a look of pure distaste at Charles. "Even you."

****

Every mile that took them further from New York enabled Elena to breathe and sit easier. They followed the Hudson River and she lost herself in the beauty of the woods against the cliffs. Once they'd reached the Palisades, she'd been able to see the majesty of the greatest city in the world from the outside looking in. What an incredible sight.

Yet no more incredible than, she could not describe the building other than to call it a castle, their destination. High stone walls, magnificent arched windows, a massive wood door trimmed in what looked to be real gold. Amazing.

Would she ever understand the Nobility? So many contrasts. Petty in their insults yet gallant and dignified in their world. Hierarchy, order, loyalty all conflicted with jealousy, greed, and aggression.

Yet she knew such beauty from them. Not the beauty that surrounded her. The tapestries and artifacts were indeed beyond belief. But the smile of a young man when his beloved animal rose to his feet and nudged his pocket for a treat.

Elena, Alexi, and Charles were ushered into a huge hall. Their footsteps echoed in the empty chamber. They walked to stand just before a raised platform that held a plain wooden table and three high-backed wooden chairs. None were occupied.

Instead, a man with snow-white hair, and a lady with long jet-black hair walked into the room and greeted them. "Thank you, Dmitri for helping bring our guest," the gentleman began.

Dmitri bowed and said, "My pleasure, Stefano."

"Allow me to introduce myself. My name is Stefano Benedetti. This is Ariel Gold. We are members of the High Council."

Elena bowed in the manner of her people as best she could. Pain was her constant companion, although here in this building, she felt a bit more ease. "You honor me with your welcome."

The lady, beautiful and probably old enough to be her mother, smiled. "As you do with yours. Allow me to finish the introductions. Behind you is Dmitri Konin. We asked him to find you. All of you."

"You have found me."

"Yes, but I ask your indulgence a moment." She turned to Alexi. "Welcome, Alexi. My heart is with you and your family. How is Nicholai?"

"He'll come out of it," Alexi answered with conviction. Elena hoped that would be true.

"And Tara?"

"Her strength is my strength," he added. "Though where it comes from, I don't know."

"Indeed. Our prayers are with you."

Alexi snorted. "From you, Ariel, I accept that statement. From him? Never."

She watched Stefano stiffen. "You lack respect, young one. Especially now. I love Nicholai as I would my own son."

"Love," Alexi replied with derision. "Is that what you call it these days?"

"Alexi," Ariel cautioned.

"No," he cried. "I won't stop. You dangled a carrot in front of my brother's nose and look what it's gotten him…"

What carrot, she wondered? A moment later she found out. "Your brother was not ready to become Steward."

"Says you, Stefano. Who died and left you all-knowing, all-powerful?"

"What we do, we do for the good of all," Stefano replied, a hint of anger riding his tone. "But if that is not enough answer, isn't the real answer in where your brother rests at this moment? He couldn't control his emotions."

"Bullshit."

"That's enough!" Ariel cried. "This bickering serves no purpose. But to your point, we may have made a mistake where your brother was concerned."

"Tell *him* that," came Alexi's bitter reply.

"Someday I hope to be able to." Elena heard the pain in those words. The lady cared about Nicholai; very much it would seem.

"One of the ways to compound a mistake, Ms. Kyrinova, is to ignore it. Isn't that correct?"

"Yes, it is. But call me Elena, please."

"Thank you." She watched Ariel turn to Alexi. "Ignorance isn't always bliss, is it?"

She watched Alexi break his gaze away first. Good for you, lady Ariel, she thought. "No, it's not."

Ariel turned to her and said, "I'm very pleased to finally meet you. The High Council has known of your people for a very long time. Yet we never deemed it appropriate to make contact. An omission that may very well have cost us all."

"Sad, but true, my lady. The Ancient one knows no bounds."

"Yes, and I fear he'll try to destroy you and your people as well."

A shudder ran through Elena. Hearing the words spoken out loud scared her to death even though she'd known them to be true for a long time. "It's difficult to understand such hatred. I fear as well."

"But I'm also curious," Ariel continued. "We have no idea how you, your people came about. Have you been told of our beginning?"

"Not exactly."

"And we have no knowledge of yours. Perhaps you would share your past with us? And we will do the same."

"I'd be glad to."

Chapter Nine

"I do not want to swim today, Lorraine. The lake will be cold."

"Just a quick swim, Isobel. Please."

A stiff breeze blew her hair into her eyes and she pulled the strands out of the way. "It is cold. I am cold."

"You will warm up once you swim. I promise."

Isobel had no desire to go near the cold water. She tried another tact. "Maman will be angry."

Loraine laughed. Nothing scared her sister. For which she was very proud but at the same time, she worried. No one should be fearless. "Maman will be angry if I go in alone. You know what she said."

Isobel sighed. Why did Lorraine always have to be right? And force her into doing things she did not want to do? For as sure as there were clouds in the sky, Lorraine would swim with or without her. "Very well."

Loraine turned and hugged her. "You are the very best sister."

Isobel smiled but rolled her eyes. She was always the very best sister when Loraine got her way. They picked a path through the rocky shore to a small, flat, patch of grass and sand. From here they could get into the water without walking over too many sharp stones.

The icy water numbed her toes, but as the waves lapped at her feet, Isobel became bolder and bolder. The shock of the water as she finally submerged herself was not nearly the hardship she'd imagined. Indeed, she felt quite refreshed.

A race of sorts ensued. But Isobel was nowhere near the swimmer her sister was. They frolicked for a while and just when Isobel thought they should begin to go home, Lorraine stopped playing. She turned and noticed Loraine swimming farther and farther from shore. "Isobel. Come. Look. Do you see?"

At first, Isobel was concerned. She did not like that her sister was swimming so far from safety. But when she realized that Lorraine was not listening to her, all Isobel saw was danger. Her sister was headstrong and had no fear. "See what Loraine? I see that if you do not return this instant, we are going to be in great trouble."

"No, no. The rocks. The shiny blue rocks."

Isobel couldn't see anything because she was trying to keep up with her sister. "Loraine. Please. If we do not stop now, we will not be able to get back to shore."

With a great spurt, Isobel lunged. She caught hold of her sister's ankle, but Loraine kicked free. "No. I must get closer. Closer."

All Isobel could see was her mother's face and the promise she'd made. The one where she would keep Loraine safe from harm. "Ma soeur. Please. You must stop."

"I cannot. I must touch them. Hold them. They are so blue. So beautiful."

Isobel swam harder because their lives depended upon her strength. She caught up to Loraine again and grabbed onto her sister's arm. "Look where we are, Loraine. We must float. Come, lie back. We will float and paddle so we can reach the shore. We will let the currents take us."

Loraine's answer was to shrug free and dive down into the dark water. Isobel, her heart in her throat, followed. Down, down, pulling ever closer to the murky depths of the bottom of the lake. Then she saw them. The rocks. So very blue as Loraine had described. But more. Alive. Pulsing with a power she did not want to know.

Terror clawed at her belly. The rocks were too beautiful, too blue; they were cold and bright, they would cut and slice, they were dangerous.

A moment later, Isobel reached out to grab onto her sister once again. At the same time, Loraine picked up a rock or a handful of them, Isobel would never know. She blacked out for a moment then instinct kicked in. She had to pull them both up to the surface. Her lungs burned, her limbs dragged like lead weights, yet she kicked and clawed. Ever upwards.

Isobel broke the surface and gulped huge draughts of air. Then she pulled Loraine up. She tried slapping at her sister's face but there was no response. "Cher. Loraine. Please. You must breathe."

A slight sputter was her answer. And though Loraine showed little sign of life, Isobel was determined to save her. Then she looked around. Dismay nearly crushed her. They were near a grotto, but the walls were solid rock. There was no place to lift her sister and pull her out of the water. She would have to get them both back to the shore they came from.

Shaking with fear, Isobel lay on her back and pulled her sister's body so she would rest above her. She half floated, half swam, always trying to keep to the direction in which they'd come. Fighting dizziness, fighting the cold lethargy that began to seep into her bones, Isobel kept plodding along. Soon the sky overhead began to darken. Yet the shore seemed no nearer.

Despair filled her heart. She should never have let Loraine talk her into this. She should have forced her sister to listen. She should have...

Her arms hung like they were attached to lead weights. Her legs barely moved. Her teeth chattered from the cold. Inside her mind, she sought the warmth of her bed. Sleepy. So sleepy.

A loud sound startled her. The sound of water against rock. Somehow God had seen fit to get them close to shore. With the very last ounce of effort and will she possessed, Isobel turned on her stomach. She looped Loraine's arms around her neck. "You must hold on now, cher. Your life depends on it."

Her sister's hands closed together. Spurred on by hope, Isobel pulled and paddled her way to the shore. Then she crawled up to the sand, dragging her sister with her until they were out of the water.

"Forgive me," Loraine whispered just as darkness descended and Isobel knew no more.

****

Elena had never been asked to repeat the story of their beginning before. "The Lady Loraine became the matriarch of my people. The Lady Isobel became our first healer. She showed us how to use our gifts. As with your people, some of mine are stronger in power than others. I'm a throwback to the Lady Isobel. I'm one of the strongest empaths to be born in generations. The pain, the illness, the suffering, the destruction of the human race is too much for most of my people to bear."

"You're a very brave woman," Ariel acknowledged.

"No, Ariel. I'm a very frightened woman. As with the Lady Isobel, fear is a great motivator."

"Yes, it is," Ariel replied. "Yet, there's wisdom to be gained from your story. I, for one, believe that your blue rocks were pieces of the same meteor that created the Nobility. Stefano?"

"It's possible."

"Fascinating," Alexi added.

"Elena," Ariel continued. "What became of the rocks that were gathered? Did anyone save them?"

"I don't know." Elena thought hard for a

moment. "None of the stories, none of the legends say."

"Would anyone know?"

Elena shook her head. "No. I'm the last keeper of the Book."

"The Book?" Alexi asked, his tone intrigued.

"A record of our people, our history, the stories that tell us who we were so we will always know."

"Do you think there are any more rocks in the lake?"

"My people hunted for them, especially once we knew the power they possessed. Then we stopped."

"Why?" Alexi asked.

"For the same reason you have. No one has come back from the quest alive."

The ensuing silence seemed to weigh on them all. "It's why I seek what I seek now."

"Forgive me, but what is that?" Ariel asked, a bit perplexed.

Elena watched both men look anywhere but at her. "I took it upon myself to create a new race. I'm willing to mate with one of your kind."

"We had a deal, nym-...uh, sorry. Elena," Charles sputtered.

"I thought our bargain came before his," Alexi countered.

Ariel laughed, the sound echoing around the hall. "You seem to have created a dilemma for yourself, my dear."

She inclined her head. "Perhaps, perhaps not. I care not whose baby I carry at this point."

"Indeed," Ariel replied. Then she turned and Elena caught a mischievous twinkle in her gaze. "Stefano? I would imagine you would be more than happy to perpetuate yourself, no?"

Stefano coughed and choked, turning rather red in the face as Alexi guffawed out loud. "One for you, Ariel," he said.

Elena watched Ariel try to maintain her composure. She wasn't sure how to react. Yet she felt close to this woman as if they were destined at some point to be friends. "Sometimes levity in a time of great stress is necessary. We're in a grave situation at this moment," Ariel said.

"For you," Elena replied, not wanting to sound hard but resolved to her own duty first. "I have not come here to become embroiled in your problems."

"Forgive me, my dear, but your salvation and ours seem to follow the same path. Believe me, I wouldn't have brought you all here if I didn't need your help. And you need ours. Although now, I think there may be more to our plans than I first realized."

"What is it, Ariel? What's happened?" Alexi asked, his tone full of concern.

"Han-Sing is missing."

"And that's a problem because?" Charles continued, his tone as snide as ever.

"Han-Sing is the only being on earth who knows the exact whereabouts of the Water of Change."

This is not good, Alexi thought to himself. Very not good. "What do you mean missing?" he asked, dread in his tone.

"Han-Sing checks in with one of us every 48 hours. He's nearly eight hours overdue."

"Forgive me, lady, but I'm confused. I don't understand. What is the Water of Change?" Elena asked.

"I beg your pardon, Elena," Ariel replied with a bow. "I forgot that you don't know our full story. It would seem that the same meteor that created you seems to have created us as well. A piece fell into a rock pool during man's beginning. A woman bearing twins touched the meteor. When she did there was a split between good and evil."

"I have known of the Ancient one all my life."

"The good twin became the father of our race.

The Ancient one is the evil twin. Thus we always bear twin boys as our first children. As it was then so it is now."

"True Blood to True Blood," Alexi murmured.

Ariel continued. "The Water, I suppose, stayed in the pool and was re-filled constantly to make more of our race."

"Then why isn't everyone on earth a Noble?" Elena asked.

"My first guess is evolution and natural migration," Ariel replied. "The clan couldn't survive and stay by the pool forever. Sooner or later there wouldn't be enough natural resources to support that many people. So my second guess is that they took the rock and the water with them."

Alexi's mind went into overdrive. "Wait a minute. That's really starting to make a lot of sense. Tara was made by the power of the Chalice, which is probably why she didn't die. The casket that held the Chalice couldn't possibly be as strong as the Chalice itself. Or the Water."

"And from what your brother told us," Ariel continued. "The water Tara used to save them only rested in the Chalice, again not nearly as potent as the real thing."

"Excuse me," Elena began. "But if that's the case, isn't it possible that the real Water can destroy the evil one? And that's why he seeks it?"

"He wants us to die slowly," Charles explained. "One generation at a time. He'll use his evil to change it, taint it, make it totally unusable."

Alexi watched Elena frown. "Again, I don't understand. The Water kills you anyway."

"Full strength. But now we're finding out that diluting the Water somehow or diluting the power of the Water doesn't kill us," Alexi replied.

"Indeed," Ariel agreed. "Which brings me to my next thought. If the same meteor created both our races, why the difference between us? Why don't you have the same powers that we have? Why don't you need the power of the Sun as fuel the way we do? Why are you so attuned to humans where we aren't?"

An interesting set of questions, Alexi thought to himself.

"You're making an assumption the meteor is the same."

"True," Ariel replied with a nod. "But think of the stories for a moment. Over all this time. Shiny blue rocks. Pulsating with power. Coincidence? I think not."

She had a point, Alexi thought to himself. But many more questions arose in his mind. What was this connection, then, between the two of them that enabled him to heal Elena where no one else could? Why didn't the Ancient one fear the Water? Was his security natural arrogance or did the evil one know something about the Water that they didn't?

"I believe you're right, my lady," Elena continued. "And I believe I know why."

"Really? Would you care to explain?"

"Yes, of course," Elena continued. "Our lake is made of salt water, not fresh,"

Chapter Ten

Ariel Gold wondered if she was getting old. Then she wondered if she would be allowed to grow older. Never before, in the history of their race, had the Nobility faced the crisis they faced now.

Could this brave young woman be their savior? Did the fate of their race rest in the hands of a magician? How many decisions had they made that should have been made differently?

Doubt yourself and you lose.

Nicholai? Did she hear him or did she wish so hard that she heard his voice?

Ariel missed him. She missed his forthright honesty and his unshakable belief that they would win. "Fascinating," she murmured. "And yet the difference makes sense."

Ariel took a deep breath then let the air out in measured amounts as she had been taught to do as a child. "Elena. Do you possess any other powers? Any other abilities?"

"No, lady. Not really. We are healers, a simple people; we stay by ourselves so we can survive. We own little; we live off the land. You won't find a cell phone in my village."

"I see." In fact, she did. Ariel longed for that type of quiet life. But hers was the path of leadership and with that path came the responsibility she now carried. None of them knew that Stefano was not the leader of the Council. She was. The Houses wouldn't stand for a female leader. They were too set in their ways. "I have the greatest sense of the Ancient one of all of us. He is near but quiet, as if he awaits our next move. I don't know if Han-Sing is missing of his own accord or if the Ancient one has found our secret."

Turning, she looked straight at Charles. "We need your help again, it would seem."

"I'm still banished."

"True. But for your bravery in saving Tara Valentin and your agreement to aid our cause now, the High Council will waive your banishment."

"My House?"

"Will continue as long as you do not lead. Take the reins and I shall personally see it dismembered. You have shown that you aren't capable of making the right decisions."

"And three people are?" Charles countered.

Hadn't she just wondered the same thing? "Even though you aspire to that which you will never have, what you will never understand is what true leadership is."

"Forgiveness of faults," Elena answered. "Belief in the people that follow you. Inspiration comes from honor, honesty, and integrity."

Ariel smiled. Yes, there was hope after all. If one brave young woman could understand that, they certainly had a shot. "Well put, Elena. And more as you know. What say you, Charles Rhys-Jones? Will you help your people once again?"

"Very well."

"Good, then we need you to seek the Ancient one as you did before. He is near. We need you to lead him down a false path. He will believe you because your motive is revenge. Tip our hand. Turn traitor on us. Tell him you know where Han-Sing is and that you will bring the Water to him. I don't believe he has the Water yet, nor do I believe Han-Sing is dead. I may not be able to find his essence, but I would know if it was gone."

"Wouldn't that play right into his hands, Ariel?"

Alexi asked. "Wouldn't our enemy expect that type of treachery?"

"It's the way *he* would think. And I'm hoping that his greed and his lust for revenge will overcome his common sense."

"Another dead-end," Elena nodded in understanding.

Ariel stared at Elena with frank admiration. "There will be nothing to find. We can't hide something we don't have. But what we gain is immeasurable. We need time. Time to find Han-Sing. Time to create a new plan for the safekeeping of the Water."

"Excuse me, but isn't what you're asking me to do rather dangerous? He's going to be flippin' upset when he finds out we've been playing with him."

"By all rights, Charles, you should already be dead. You have wished for death rather than suffer your sentence. I'm giving you a chance at redemption."

"How the hell am I supposed to do that?"

Ariel smiled. "I have faith in you, Charles. You'll find a way. And I won't send you into battle alone. Dmitri has offered his services."

"That's just ducky."

Alexi smiled with glee and Elena, although she understood the consequences, looked rather horrified. There was a difference between courage and cowardice and that difference was not fear.

"Forgive me, Ariel, but you said you had need of all of us," Elena continued.

"I'm not certain how to destroy the Ancient one. I'm not certain we won't end up destroying a part of ourselves if we do. But I do believe that your idea is the path to salvation. A combination of both our powers might just save us all. You said that your people have never been able to come back alive from their quest for the rocks. But we're stronger than you, better able to find them if they exist. Maybe even contain their power, as the changes to the meteor from your lake will not affect us as they affect you. What is Kryptonite to you may not be poisonous to us. And vice versa. Take Alexi to your home. Search out the meteor pieces. If you can find one, bring it back here. Quickly. We will only have the time that Charles and Dmitri buy us."

"If there's anything to be found, I'll find it, Ariel," Alexi told her.

"I'll help in any way I can," Elena added.

"Good. My jet is ready and waiting at Teterboro Airport."

She turned to Dmitri who simply nodded. He would take care of Charles, but made sure he also knew Charles was expendable. The goal of their mission was of the utmost importance and could not be compromised.

Only Charles looked unhappy. In a small way, Ariel felt sorry for him. But he had no one else to blame but himself. "Just for the record," he told everyone, "this sucks."

Yes, it did. But trying times meant desperate measures. Out loud she replied, "Perhaps. But we have no choice. I love it when a plan comes together."

****

Alexi might as well just start babbling. Babbling had to be better than opening his mouth and not having a word come out for about the thousandth time. "You look tired."

"I am."

"Would it help if you leaned into me? I'd be more than happy to give you some of my energy."

She seemed to fight with herself, but the grateful look in her gaze gave her away. "Yes, please."

"I was afraid you'd say no." He waited while his

energy flowed into to her. "I keep wondering at this ability I seem to have. Do you feel better now?"

"I can't explain this—I don't know what to call your power—but, yes, I feel better."

"I don't suppose you'd care to bank some of that feeling for later, would you?"

She seemed puzzled. "For what purpose?"

Man, talk about unforgiving. "To get you to change your mind."

"I assume you're speaking of Charles Rhys-Jones?"

"No, I'm talking about-," he caught himself just in time. "Yes."

"At least his motives are honest. He makes no claim to be other than what he is."

"Two wrongs don't make a right."

"I'm sorry, but I don't follow," she replied, her body stiffening against him.

"You. Going to him. Asking him."

That she didn't pull away told him how exhausted she really was. "Yours is an opinion of one."

"Okay. Since this is a free country with free speech—." Alexi sighed, disgusted with himself. Snide was not what he was reaching for. "Why is it that every time I try to tell you I was wrong, I end up making things worse?"

"Inherent trait?"

"Thanks a bunch." He laughed. "You could give me another chance, you know."

"I could. But you have other obligations."

He shook his head. "We both have an obligation that is much more important than either one of us right now. We need to be able to work together."

"True and true."

"I'm trying to apologize here. Any help from the audience? I mean, I've worked tough crowds before, but..."

She shifted in her seat but remained silent. Meaning? Loud and clear. Chateau bow-wow all the way. "Listen, I'll make you a promise. Honesty. The truth and nothing but the truth so help me God."

The disdain in her tone was hard to miss. "You've done that before."

All right, he deserved that. "Yeah. And I let my own selfishness get in the way."

She turned in her seat this time so she could look at him. "What do you want, Alexi? Truly. Without obligations, without duty, without honor, without the terror we face. What does Alexi Valentin want?"

He looked straight at her. "I don't know. That's been a problem for me for a long time."

"You'll need to decide soon."

"I know. I also know when you left, life was pretty lonely without you. Everything seemed wrong, somehow. Out of synch." He took a deep breath and confessed, "I need you."

"No," she replied, her disappointment evident. "What you need is Sergei. He'll help you to do what needs to be done."

He gave her a self-deprecating smile. "Sweetheart, what I need, Sergei can't give me."

Her eyes widened then she blushed. He liked that about her. That innocence. She didn't hide her feelings, which ended up being painful sometimes. "Then I truly don't understand. When I kissed you, you pushed me away."

"I'm sorry. I'm a self-centered putz. What can I tell you?"

"That you care."

He drew in a deep breath and let the air out slowly. "What do you think I've been trying to tell you?"

She shook her head. "I don't know. Perhaps that's part of the problem. We're so different, Alexi."

"So?"

"You have your people. Your House. Your act."

"They might not exist if things go wrong."

"I know."

"So you also know, now, why we need to understand one another."

"Now I'm confused. You just said you don't know what you want."

"True. But driving you away hasn't worked. I guess when you live your life not facing up to things, responsibility can roll over you. I didn't know how to handle both your needs, my needs, and the needs of my people."

"Hmm. Honesty. I could get used to that after all."

He turned her back into his shoulder and pulled her close. "Why don't you try to sleep?" He yawned and she started to pull away. "Oh no, you don't. I'm tired. That's all. I haven't slept since you left. And I don't expect to get much sleep after we land."

"Are you certain? I'm feeling much better now."

"I'm sure. And sweetheart?"

"Yes?"

"Don't you think it would be a good idea to let the pilot know where we're going?"

Home.

After wishing for so long to leave, to see the world outside her self-imposed prison, Elena couldn't believe how glad she was to be back. Alexi had talked about the things that were wrong when his world wasn't right. She knew those feelings well. She'd been living outside her skin since she'd started her mission.

Of course, she didn't mind the perks he brought with him. As in the Lincoln Navigator that was waiting for them as soon as they landed in Edmonton.

"Any chance you might want to explain where

we're going and more importantly, how we're going to get there? Time is of the essence here," he told her.

"There's only one plane service that will land on the lake where I live. To get there, we need to leave from Lesser Slave Lake. The easiest way to get there is to drive. Besides, when it comes to traveling, driving is safer."

He seemed taken aback. "Really?"

"Yes. You'd better prepare yourself. The gentleman who owns the plane indulges in his favorite past-time a bit too often."

"I see."

Sight, at the moment, was a matter of opinion. As soon as they left the city and traveled further north and east, the thicker the forest lining the road became. "You seem uncomfortable. Are you all right?" she asked.

"Out of my element, I suppose."

She knew the feeling well. Yet Elena was questioning most of the occurrences in her life. Why had she not known that Nobles lived in Canada? Why did she know so much about the Valentins and no other family? Why was she connected to Alexi in this way? "When I visited Tara, she told me she named the baby."

He smiled. "After my mother."

"Will you, will you reject her as your laws dictate?"

"Not me, never," he replied, his tone emphatic. "Sylvana has the right to live as everyone else in our House. They know what they're up against now and I believe that will set their priorities straight."

Her concern grew as she watched his face tighten. "You say this as if something has happened."

"Noble Pride is dead."

"Oh no!" she cried, horror and sadness filling

her.

"A farewell card from our nemesis."

"I'm so sorry, Alexi. I know how important he was to your family."

"Look, Elena, I'm beginning to learn a lot from you. One of the things you've shown me is how to have hope. Andre told me he believes Noble Pride left behind one, if not two, foals. Something about that tea..."

Elena smiled. The tea always worked in its own way. "I'm glad."

He grew serious. "What we're up against, well, I don't know. But I do know that if I don't bring you back safe... my people...hell Tara, will kill me."

"She's my friend. My sister. I have never had a sister before."

"Am I, Elena? Am I your friend?"

He asked the question with such heart wrenching sincerity that for a moment, Elena didn't know how to answer. "Yes, Alexi, you are."

"Whew. For a moment you had me worried. I just don't want, if you and I have our differences, for it to ruin anything you might have with Tara and Nico. Okay?"

Nicholai.

Elena gasped. She cleared her thoughts and reached deep inside herself. Nicholai. Home. Nicholai.

The car screeched to a halt. "Oh my God, Elena. Are you all right? Speak to me. Please. Is it Tara? The baby? What?"

"Patience, Alexi. I'm all right. So is everyone else. Just drive."

"But—."

"I'm thinking."

He put the car in gear again. "You're freaking me out is what you're doing."

"Alexi, please," she pleaded in exasperation.

"But everyone is okay, right?"

"Yes, nothing has changed."

"Then you'd better start explaining, woman. Because I don't like being scared half to death like that."

Even as she tried to get the words out, her mind kept leaping ahead. "I was just thinking about how glad I was to be home. This is my favorite time of year. New leaves, new growth, spring."

"And you scared the pants off me for that?" Now he was angry.

She threw him a look. "Ariel believes we are made from the same source. What if we are?"

"I don't follow."

"Well, I was just thinking about the tea as well. It works as it is meant to work and not always in the same way."

"I'm not following. And your point is?"

"We are the same yet different."

"Right. I get it. Salt water vs. fresh water."

"Yes. Yes," she replied, her excitement growing. "But what if we combine the two?"

"Combine the two?" he echoed. "How?"

"Your water. My tea. The leaves of the Lady Lorraine and this Water of yours. The Water of Change."

"And do what?"

"If I'm right, save your brother's life."

Chapter Eleven

Could she do that? A sweet surge of hope ran through Alexi. He took a deep breath and let the air out carefully. "Before I put this damned car into a tree, explain. Nice and slow."

"To do that, I need to tell you where the leaves come from."

She was right. "I'm all ears."

"I must ask a promise of you first."

"Okay."

"You must promise not to reveal the truth unless it is absolutely necessary. My people guard the leaves with their lives."

Alexi was a lot of things, but he never broke his word. Ever. "You have my word."

"I stopped the story with the Lady Isobel saving her sister."

"I remember."

"The story continues for Lorraine survived their ordeal. She wallowed in an almost vegetative state for many days..."

Isobel wondered if her mother would ever smile again. "Maman. Please. She will wake up. I know she will."

"If only there was something I could do."

"It is as if she sleeps. Nothing more. Her heart beats strong and true."

Isobel was frightened. She hadn't told anyone about the rocks for fear of being in even more trouble. And she'd taken the brunt of her mother's anger without complaint. As far as everyone was concerned, Lorraine swam too far from shore. They were both lucky to be alive. "You should have stopped her," her mother said for about the hundredth time.

"I tried, Maman," Isobel replied fervently. "I tried."

Isobel sat by her sister's side day and night. The longer she did, the more she worried. Something was not right. And as the days went on, Isobel pondered. Perhaps the key was in the rocks. Perhaps, if she went back to the lake. Searched for them. She would forever remember how they looked. And maybe. Just maybe. If Lorraine touched one again, she would awaken from this unnatural sleep.

Several days later, Isobel found her chance. She'd finished her chores early and received permission to go to the lake for a walk. Even her mother knew she needed a respite from her constant vigil. Her mother also knew, deep down inside, how her sister's illness was tearing her up.

Once she reached the lake, Isobel scoured the rocks and sand along all of the shore where they might have ended up. She found nothing. Then she widened her search to the entire stretch of shore. Still nothing. Despair seared her soul. She would never find a cure. She had failed again.

As she walked along the well-worn path back to her home, Isobel felt a tingling. She stopped. The sensation stopped. She took a few steps. The tingling returned. Yet now it was stronger. More like a vibration running through her body. Like the buzz of a bee by her ear.

Looking around, Isobel could find no cause. She continued walking and the buzz decreased. She retraced her steps and the buzz increased. What was this? What was happening to her?

She would never know what hand of fate caused her to look down at the ground at that moment, but she did. There, in the dirt, tiny blue flecks. She knew the color well.

Hope surged through her body. She began to look around, careful not to disturb the flecks she'd found. Lo and behold, she found more. Then she noticed the strangest thing. The leaves of a plant glowed with the same blue coloring as the rock around their edges.

What is this, she wondered? She thought hard and long. Somehow, she concluded, the rock had changed this plant.

Isobel knew what she had to do. She wasn't quite sure how she knew, but she knew. She reached down to take some of the leaves from one of the plants closest to the blue flecks and put them in her pocket. As she did, she got a nasty shock. All the more reason, she thought to herself, to try to use them to cure her sister.

In spite of the jolt, she picked several. But how to get them into Lorraine? Her sister refused to move. A tea. She would brew the leaves into a tea when her mother left to gather water. She would feed it to Lorraine as she would a child...

"Of course, the tea worked and the secret of our people was born."

"Did they ever find the any more of the rock?"

"No one ever has. But we really don't know if it was one large rock or many small rocks that Lorraine picked up. We will never know. What we do know is that there are patches where the plant grows the strongest. And that there is always one among us that is born with the power to find the strongest leaves."

He made the connection. "Such as you."

"Yes."

"You mentioned a jolt when you told the story. Do you think that's what Nico needs?"

"Perhaps. I don't know how the brew will work."

Alexi's mind kept racing. If there was a chance, even a slim chance his brother would be returned to them. Hope surged through his insides. There had to be one. There had to. "If the leaves don't work, maybe a piece of the meteorite will."

She seemed to ponder his idea for a long time. Or maybe the time seemed long because now he had hope. "Again, I don't know. But I believe in the healing power of the leaves. My people have used them since the very beginning."

All of a sudden, Alexi didn't want to be driving in the middle of nowhere with no end in sight. He wanted to be by his brother's side. "You can't be in two places at once," she reminded him.

Not that he was surprised that she knew what he was thinking, but he was surprised that she understood. "How did you know?"

She gave him a small smile that he caught as he looked over. "Your thoughts are easy enough to read. But even if I could not read them, I would still know. I have a brother too. Remember?"

"Yes."

Alexi thought of Nicholai as he'd last seen his brother, not really cold, but still as stone, barely breathing. Then he thought of his people, the rest of the Nobility, the ones barely beginning like his niece. "When we first met, you asked me if I could make a choice. What you were asking was if I could choose between what I wanted to do and what I knew needed to be done."

"That is correct."

"I'm not sure why, but I keep getting the feeling I'm going to have to make that choice again."

She sighed. "I was unfair to you that day."

"Why do you say that? You didn't know me. You didn't know how I'd react to you or your request."

"True. But I wanted to test you. I wanted you to have to make that kind of choice."

"Umm, I'm lost here. Why?"

"To find out if you were worthy."

Alexi was so stunned at first, he couldn't speak. Worthy? "Me? Worthy? Of you?" he cried.

"Yes," she replied, flinching a little next to him.

"Wow. I'm amazed. No, more than amazed. I never expected this from the woman who was ready to sleep with the biggest sleazeball of the century." A frisson of anger ran through him. "Sweetheart, you have some pair on you, you know that?"

She knew she'd been unfair. She had to know. He heard it in her voice when she cried out, "Alexi. Stop behaving like a child. This instant. Try to listen."

A child? Well, maybe. Sort of. But she was just as bad. Wasn't she? "All...right."

"Can you understand that I faced the same choice?"

She did? "How?"

"The needs of my people outweigh any personal feelings I may have."

Now that was interesting. He'd never considered that she might not want to... "You're not a brood mare, you know."

"Yes, I am." She reached out to touch his arm. "Do you not see? This is the choice I had to make. The choice I have to make."

Was she that willing to sacrifice herself? He shook his head. "Sorry, I'm not cut out to be a martyr."

"'The needs of the many outweigh the needs of the few.' Or the one."

Wasn't that the kicker of kickers? She could quote *Star Trek*. "Kirk didn't buy that and neither do I. He spent the entire next movie trying to save his friend. He also got into a heap of trouble doing it, but that's another story."

He took a second to look at her and caught another fleeting smile cross her lips. "I know the movies. My-."

"Brother," he finished for her.

"I have hope, Alexi. For you and your people. I hope that you will not face this choice alone. I hope that when the choice comes, there will be another avenue to travel. However, for me, my path is set. I cannot, no, I will not, change course now."

Funny, but she really did have a big pair. Just not the kind that could be seen. Five foot nothing, twisted by the pain of the world, and ready to become the matriarch of a new race. She really was something else.

Alexi would never know where the words came from but as soon as they were out, he knew they were right. "Then at least let me be your stud."

"Can you do that with your whole heart and know that you've made the right choice?"

Elena hated to have to have to be sure he knew the consequences of his actions. Once he said yes, there would be no going back. No half measures this time.

"You said you hoped that there would be other avenues to travel," he told her. "Well, this is one road we're going to have to go along together. Just like we are now."

"That's not good enough, Alexi. There may come a moment when you will be faced with choosing between the child you create and the brother you love."

"Then I'll know in my heart what is right when that time comes. But I won't live my life on what ifs. The only certainty we have is uncertainty. Next issue."

"You ran away once."

"More than once, if you're counting. But you don't see me running right now, do you?"

"You may decide to run again."

"That's a chance you'll have to take, isn't it?"

"And the bond?"

"The least of our worries for the moment, don't you think? I'd like to believe we'll live long enough to have that problem, don't you?"

Her heart sank. But her heart had been doing a lot of that lately. "Yes, yes, I do."

To keep the weight of their task from overwhelming her, Elena decided to probe. "What do you feel?" she asked. "I want to know more about you."

"I beg your pardon? I'm talking about reality and you want to know—." He paused, his confusion evident. "What exactly is it that you want to know?"

"What do you feel? Tell me what the Sun does to you. Can you run as fast as a deer? Are you strong enough to lift a car? Why do you have to have the Sun? Can you survive without it?"

He started to chuckle. "I get it. Subject change. No problem. Just give me a minute to answer the questions."

"Not exactly a subject change. Not if we are, well, if we're going to become intimate."

"Hmm. I'm beginning to like the sound of that."

Elena could feel the heat building in her cheeks. Would she disappoint him? She knew her face was beautiful, but would he like the rest? And what would she do once she got there? All of a sudden the knowledge she'd gleaned from her books seemed way too inadequate. "The Sun, Alexi," she reminded him.

He laughed. As he sobered he began, "Let me see now. The Sun." He paused a moment to gather his thoughts. "Think of a bright summer's day. Not a cloud in the sky. What are you doing?"

"I don't know. I'm...let me think. Yes. I'm hanging the wash."

"Good. Now close your eyes. The Sun feels warm on your skin, right?"

"Yes. I can feel it."

Elena closed her eyes. "Now pretend you're

sinking into the warmth," he continued. "Your body is relaxing, like falling into a heated pool of water. The water surrounds you like a glove. A satin glove."

"I like this."

"I'm turning up the temperature. But instead of burning, you embrace the heat, let it flow inside of you. Your muscles relax. But your skin becomes super sensitive. The slightest touch makes you yearn for more."

"You are making me want more."

"Yeah, I know. But hush, this is my game. Now, where was I? All right. There's a place deep inside. Like a vault. The Sun is the key. The rays unlock the wanting deep inside the vault. Tell me," he whispered. "What do you feel?"

She let his words sink in. She closed her mind to their problems and sank inside the image he was building. How did she feel? Funny inside. Open. Ready. Moist. "I'm not sure. I have never felt this way before."

"Oh sweetheart, if you could only see your face right now. Your lips are parted and just aching for mine."

"We can't. We must focus on our mission."

"You just keep on telling yourself that, Elena. But I, for one, am damned sorry I'm behind the wheel of a car right now."

She shivered. "I don't think we're talking about the Sun anymore."

"No, that's where you're wrong. You asked me what the Sun does to me. Just as you feel a connection to me, I'm connected to the Sun. My body responds, sort of like taking a stiff brush and rubbing the bristles against my skin. But not hard. Just enough to make every hair stand on edge, every cell reach out for more."

"That must be uncomfortable."

"No, not uncomfortable at all. For you, think of

someone taking a soft cloth and rubbing all over the surface of your body. Think of that satin glove. After a while, your body responds in other ways."

She tried to imagine what that would be like. "You become aroused?"

"If you go with the flow. By the way, you might want to file away that information for later."

What was it like to 'go with the flow,' she wondered? What would it be like to file that information away only to be pulled out every morning? She had this strange emptiness in the pit of her stomach. As if all the blood had left there and rushed to the place between her legs. "Is this what it feels like to want, Alexi? I mean, truly want?"

"Yes," he strangled out.

"Do you want me?"

"Oh, sweetheart," he groaned. "I don't want to be crude but..." He took her hand and put it on top of his erection.

She snatched her hand back as if she'd been burned. But that place inside, that place that never lied, was pleased. "We can't. Not now."

He turned to her then, almost scaring her with the length of time he gazed at her. His gaze was fire, the Sun, the heat inside her core. So intense, she nearly sizzled. "Don't worry. I'm not normally a patient man. But for you? I can wait."

Chapter Twelve

Alexi wasn't sure what to do, kiss the ground he walked on or get sick all over it. The next time Elena told him something, he was going to listen with both of his ears. She hadn't given him a half-truth or an exaggeration yet. And the pilot read his message loud and clear. Hightail it out of there as fast as his sorry ass could go or pay the consequences.

To take his mind off his stomach, Alexi stared at his surroundings. Man, when she'd said village, she wasn't kidding.

As far as Alexi was concerned, the word remote was one half of the phrase remote control. Not this. As they walked inland from the dock he felt the sensation of the tress engulfing them. Once they reached the village, space seemed to be carved from the woods. Literally. The buildings too were made from their surroundings, from the huge trees, the massive logs carefully measured. They looked to be perfectly aligned. The fronts of the homes were made of stones blasted by time and weather to look better than any molded concrete brick-face he'd ever seen. You'd never find plastic siding here. These homes were as solid as the ground they sat upon.

As they walked, people would stop to greet Elena. They looked at him with open curiosity as he was introduced. Funny, but he didn't think he'd ever get used to them giving him that polite little bow. "Elena?" he asked, touching her on the arm to break into her conversation.

"Yes?"

"I'm not a great flyer. And you weren't kidding

about that pilot. Do you think I could have something to drink? My stomach isn't doing too well right now."

"Oh my goodness, Alexi. You must forgive me. Please. Your color. I should have seen immediately. I'm sorry I did not. Yes, yes. Come."

She led him to a smaller version of the homes he'd seen, somewhat off the beaten path. Not that there was a path really.

She opened the door and he noticed her straighten her shoulders as much as she could and lift her chin, as if she were bracing for something. "Welcome to my home," she told him as she shut the door behind them. Pride was evident in her tone.

He looked around and found the interior rather sparse but certainly not uncomfortable. And silent. That was when he realized that the logs of the home also made up the interior walls. But they were so huge and so heavy; they acted better than the best insulation.

There was a table with chairs in what he assumed was a kitchen. There weren't too many walls, so it was kind of hard to tell. There was a couch and a rug and a huge fireplace. For a moment the horror of the thought that she cooked over a fire must have shown on his face for she answered, "Yes, I use a stove to cook. We have propane tanks that are filled and brought in and we have a generator that runs off propane for the refrigerator. But for heat, we try to use the fireplace and there is a wood burning stove."

A far cry from Vegas. Then he did something he didn't normally do. He put himself in her shoes for a moment. How out of place she must have felt when she came to see him? He remembered her face as her hand ran over the leather of his car seat. "Forgive me. I didn't mean—."

"By all means, forgive the man, Elena."

"Jacques?" A gentleman came shuffling into the room. Her brother? By his looks, Alexi would say yes. Tiny like her. And twisted as she was with much the same limp. "You shouldn't be here."

Perplexed, Alexi wondered why. She looked sad as if she were carrying a private pain inside.

"Your bed is softer than mine. I thought I would borrow it until you returned."

"Alexi? This is my brother Jacques."

Alexi held out his hand. "I'm honored."

Jacques reached out yet did not touch him and Alexi wondered why. Was the man frightened of him? He looked up to see the strain grow around the man's eyes and lips. The look of distrust he expected. The look of disgust, he did not.

Confused, Alexi wasn't sure what to do. Should he just shake and be done with it? Not shake hands? Then he looked over at Elena. For the first time since he'd met her, she was standing straight and tall. And then he looked back at her brother and he understood. Elena drew strength from her brother just as she did from him. More even, judging by the pain in the man's face. He reached out with both hands and captured Jacques' hand in his. He held on for a lot longer than was required by polite etiquette.

He watched Jacques' face go from surprise to disbelief. The man tried to withdraw, but Alexi held on tight. "Elena tells me I'm handy to have around. How do you feel?"

"You already seem to know."

Taken aback, Alexi let go. The strain reappeared in an instant. He wondered why the man was being so ungracious. He caught Jacques' gaze with his and held it, refusing to back down. Elena was his primary concern when it came to pleasing anyone. As far as he was concerned, they could do this friendly or not. It made no difference to him. Eventually, Jacques seemed to gather the answers he sought for he turned away with a shrug and shuffled out of the room.

"That was uncalled for. Alexi is our guest," Elena told his retreating back.

"Is that what you call them these days?"

"Jacques. How dare you!"

A door slammed, ending the conversation for the moment. Alexi watched in helplessness as tears flooded Elena's eyes.

"I'm sorry, Alexi. He doesn't understand."

He made a move to follow Jacques and give him a piece of his mind. No one should be treated like that. "How about if I make him understand?"

She grabbed his arm. "No." He watched her shake her head with sad resignation. "Don't."

He looked down at her and reached out to rub his thumb along her cheek. "Stubborn-assed mule, huh?"

"So I have told him many times."

"I have the power to heal him too."

"I know. Thank you for trying."

"Yeah, well, I don't like seeing you hurt like that. And if he does it again, I'm going to treat him to a little discipline."

She seemed pleased that he wanted to protect her, but he could hear the worry in her tone as she said, "You must promise you will not harm him."

Harm, he thought to himself. There were all kinds of degrees to that definition. Out loud, he said, "Scouts honor." Then he gave her his best innocent look and swiped the letter x across his heart. "What's his beef, anyway?"

"He sees my quest as an excuse."

"For what?"

"Lascivious behavior."

Alexi snorted to cover the bark of involuntary laughter coming from his throat. How Neanderthal was that? And yet, the real world hadn't touched this place much at all. "Time for him to grow up," Alexi replied, raising his voice so Jacques would hear. "Time to join the twenty-first century. Time to realize that the reason we're here isn't fun and games."

"He will, Alexi," Elena reassured him. "He will." She paused for a second. "Eventually."

His fingers slid along the ridge of her jaw to cup her chin and lift her face to his. "I don't like seeing anyone make you sad. Anyone," he repeated. "And if he feels that way," he added as his tongue traced the outer edge of her lips. Oh, man, that tasted nice. Too nice to let her brother spoil the fun. Of course, that little devil driving him couldn't resist a final stab. "Then I hope he chokes on this."

Alexi engulfed her mouth with his. He was sure more than anything that surprise caused her to open her mouth to him. Exactly as he wanted. His tongue explored every inch then returned to every inch in between. At first she remained passive, unsure he guessed, as to what he wanted. Then she became a model student. Until their tongues were dancing and each of them was finding it very hard to breathe.

Whatever he may or may not have known about her became clear as a bell. If not for her brother and the knowledge that she deserved better, he'd have had her dress up to her waist by now and she'd have found herself deposited on the first solid object that fit his height... like the kitchen table.

Uh-oh. That was going to be trouble. Big trouble. How in hell was he going to behave like a gentleman when all he wanted to do was take her here and now? Then do it some more. Of course the table idea had merit. But he could always save that for later.

"Oh, sweetheart," he gasped, finally coming up for air. "I don't know about how you feel, but that was some kiss."

She leaned into him and he realized that even at her full height, she was tiny compared to him. But not her heart. Or her courage. Or her smarts. Or about a hundred other things he'd discovered about her.

"Yes, it was," she replied after taking a deep breath and letting the air out nice and slow. "May I have another?"

He chuckled. He didn't have that kind of will power. "As much as I'd love to float your brother's boat some more, that wouldn't be a real good idea." Oh that ugly word...temptation. Alexi released her before it got the better of him. "I can only handle so much. Besides, we have work to do."

She'd forgotten.

Of course she'd forgotten.

So had he.

But a kiss like that couldn't be bad.

Ever.

And she was beginning to trust him. He so did not want to disappoint her. "There's always later," he promised.

She smiled. "Yes, there is."

"So," he continued. "What do we do now?"

This time she really laughed. "We?" She shook her head. "No, *you* go and get firewood from the stack out behind the house. Otherwise we'll freeze to death tonight. This isn't Caesar's Palace and you won't find a maid, butler, or turn down service around here."

"Gotcha. No problem. I can be helpful when necessary."

"Good. And since Jacques has been known to sulk for days," she told him, raising her voice to make sure it was overheard. "He won't get any of my venison stew. Or my biscuits." She winked at Alexi. "That should get him thinking. He loves my stew."

"Sounds great," Alexi agreed. "But do you think

I could have a tiny little favor?"

She stiffened as if not knowing what he was going to ask. It seemed they were going to have to learn how to trust each other all the way.

"Certainly. What do you need?"

"That drink of water I asked you for."

****

"You can come out now," Elena yelled to her brother. "He's out gathering wood."

"There is plenty of wood by the fireplace. I stacked it there yesterday."

"Exactly." She rounded on him with a vengeance. "What do you mean calling him a man of loose character? How dare you! He is here to save our people."

"By bedding you?"

"Oh, Jacques. We have more problems than just ourselves. When in God's name are you going to understand that?"

"Probably never."

She asked him a question she'd dared not ask all the time they'd existed. "Are you jealous?"

His expression gave her his answer whether his words told her anything or not. "That you can have sex and I can't? Of course I am."

"I bear the same pain you do."

"Like now? You have no idea."

Elena gave her brother a picture of the amphitheater where she watched Alexi's show. "No?"

Comprehension dawned yet she saw nothing but bitterness in his gaze. "Is that supposed to make me feel sorry for you?"

"If that is what you believe, you might as well leave right now."

"I'll leave when I'm good and ready."

"You'll leave like the lady said. Or I'll help you leave."

Elena turned to find Alexi standing in the

doorway. "I couldn't help but overhear." He gave her a little grin then looked straight at her brother, pinning him with his gaze.

She did not want them to fight. Men. They were so...male. "You are not two stags fighting in the woods."

"Tell that to him," Alexi countered.

"I think I need to talk to this man alone, sister," Jacques replied in a quiet tone.

"You want me to leave the two of you together so you can kill each other or something incredibly stupid like that?"

"I promise, sweetheart. No bloodshed. No physical violence."

Did she really believe they could behave?

"Just go, Elena."

All right. She would go see if there were leaves ready to be picked from the Lorraine plants. "I'll attend to part of our mission while you two beat each other senseless."

They both watched her march out the door. "She's not happy with us."

Jacques felt an ease of the pain immediately. "I'm not happy with any of this."

Funny, but the man refused to look guilty. "Are you as gifted as your sister?"

"Yes."

"Then it'll be easier just to show you what's going on. Open your mind."

Pictures flooded his brain of a childbirth and terror, of Elena trying to save the baby, then of a man just like the one standing before him, lying like a stone on a bed. "Just for the record. That's my brother lying there."

More pictures followed of an animal so magnificent; it took Jacques' breath away. Then the sight of the poor creature lying dead on the ground. Then he saw the Council chambers and he listened to all that was said. "You can't be alone anymore, Jacques. You can't think alone any more. We're all in this together whether we want to be or not."

"Can you...do you have the power to heal all of us?"

"No, Jacques. For some strange reason I'm connected to only you and your sister. At first I thought it was only her. You're an added bonus I didn't expect." He watched as Alexi shrugged out of his jacket and put the garment over the back of the chair. "She makes you sick, doesn't she?"

"She's my sister and I can't even touch her." The words sounded sour even to his own ears.

"Life sucks. But I'm not about to die yet. *Je comprends*?"

Jacques nearly smiled. "So does your French."

"Yeah, I guess it does." He watched Alexi twist the chair around and sit in it with his arms braced on the back. "Your race is dying. There's hardly, what, fifty or sixty people left?"

"About that." The pain of that thought was almost as much as the pain he bore from his sister. "And I can't help them procreate."

Alexi shook his head. "That's where you could be wrong. Elena had no trouble living with the people of my House. In fact, she was nearly pain free. You might find you're the same."

If only that could be true. "Do you at least care for her?"

Alexi gave him a disgusted look. "Would I be sitting here if I didn't? Grow up, man. Your sister is willing to become the matriarch of a new race of beings. That's a pretty scary thought when you examine it."

Jacques snorted. "With you as the patriarch?"

He watched Alexi grimace. "Point taken. But for whatever reason, the Fates have decided I'm the guy. So instead of thinking that your sister is a whore, why don't you think of me as part of the family or something?"

Jacques nearly clapped his hands together with glee. "Does that mean you're willing to marry her?"

Chapter Thirteen

Ruh-ro.

Where was Scooby-Do when he needed him? He could use some help with this predicament. "It hasn't come up in conversation."

From what he could tell, that was not a good answer. "We are having the conversation now, are we not?"

"Yeah." Funny, wasn't it? He was willing to become the father of a race without a qualm. Well, almost. He was certainly willing to accept the bond without complaint. Hmm, perhaps he needed to examine that a bit more closely. But marriage? "That's not up to me, Jacques."

"It's not?"

Alexi would have thought that was obvious. "Nope. Not totally. I think Elena would have something to say about it, don't you?"

He watched Jacques scowl. "I'm not talking to my sister. I'm talking to you."

"And I just showed you some really good reasons why neither one of us can deal with personal issues right now." Alexi shook his head in disbelief. "Besides. We are putting the cart before the horse here."

Jacques didn't seem to be happy with that answer. "So you say."

All right. He knew how things looked. There was a time and a place where he could at least be listened to. But it sounded like he wasn't even going to get the chance. "Elena is here to find some of your leaves, so she can help save my brother. I'm here to find the rocks that may have created you so I can try to save all of us."

"You will die," Jacques replied with an evil grin.

And that would make your day, wouldn't it? Out loud, he said, "You will too if I don't. The Ancient one isn't going to distinguish between us. Trust me."

Well, that was the crux of the matter, wasn't it? "Why would anyone care about us, human or not? We're already doomed."

Alexi knew that ignoring a problem didn't make it go away. He'd learned that one the hard way. But he also knew how to be as pig-headed as the best. "I don't think you're reading me, Jack." There, let him chew on some of his own stuff for a minute. "Your sister believes she can save you by saving all of us. Are you just going to let her go off into battle by herself? What the hell kind of brother are you?"

"That's her choice." *Ouch*. Was this guy really this hard and bitter? But as he watched the man give his own body a scathing look, he had a moment of understanding. "What possible help could I be?"

"Oh, I don't know. Maybe be her brother. Love her instead of making her miserable. Something like that?"

"And you believe I don't?" Jacques' tone scorched Alexi with its bitterness. "You know nothing about us. You have a great deal of nerve coming in here and lecturing me about my behavior when yours is no better."

Alexi was willing to concede the point. "I'm talking about family now. I learned what it's like when it's gone the hard way. Just trying to save you some heartache, that's all."

"I don't understand. How would I lose her?"

"No matter what happens, her mind is made up. If you reject me, you reject her. You'll lose. I don't want that to happen. So what I'm trying to tell you is you need to focus on the important first and worry about the rest later."

"So you expect me to simply sit back and allow you to screw around with my sister? Both literally and figuratively?"

Alexi couldn't believe his ears. "You haven't heard a word I've said, have you?"

The man stiffened in his seat. "Elena approaches." He rose with incredible effort. Alexi didn't want to feel sorry for him, but he did. "I don't want your pity. My fate is my own." He shuffled towards the doorway. "You call yourself the Nobility. I expect you to conduct yourself as such. Hurt her in any way and you will think the Ancient one as tame as those cartoon characters that roll about in your head."

****

Elena could feel the tension in the air. "Where is Jacques?"

"He left."

That surprised her. But perhaps it didn't. "I'm sorry, Alexi. He's so wrapped up in his own world. He can't get past his own inadequacies."

Alexi gave her a sad smile. He did understand. "How did you make out?"

"Not as good as I had hoped, better than I expected."

"That will give me tomorrow to find what I am looking for."

"I would take you back to the lake, but it's too late and too dark. Are you hungry?"

"Starving."

He said that with more than one meaning, or did he? Perhaps she was simply reading the feeling into his words. To cover her confusion she began doing what came naturally to her. Cooking. "Then I'll create some of my famous stew."

"Can I help?"

That was new to her. She hadn't thought he

would know his way around a kitchen. "Certainly."

They spent the rest of the late afternoon working together. Every time their hands touched, the thrill would reach deep inside. Those insidious fears returned ten-fold. Would he be pleased with her? How could she measure up to the women he had known?

"The meal was delicious," he said, pushing back from the table after they'd eaten. Well, he'd eaten. She'd hardly touched her plate. Something about not having room between the butterflies in her stomach.

She smiled. "You were right. You were hungry."

He rose. "Do you still need some of that wood? I need to move, otherwise I'll sink."

"That would be welcome. I'll clear the table."

A look crossed his face that she did not fully understand. How inadequate she felt. She knew how to take care of a home, she knew the meaning of work, the pride of performing a job to the best of her abilities, and the pleasure her efforts gave. But not how to receive pleasure.

He came in with an armful of logs that he carried effortlessly. She'd forgotten his physical strength. All of a sudden she wondered if he could hurt her. As he placed the logs in the stack by the fireplace he answered the question in her mind. "Do you really think I could?"

"I'm not sure if I like you reading my thoughts," she replied, nonplused by this connection growing between them.

"I didn't. You're oozing scared right now."

He rose and dusted off his hands. He walked towards her and her heart started beating too rapidly. "This is about making love. Not having sex. I've had plenty of sex and I'm beginning to realize that I probably shouldn't have."

"I don't understand."

"You will." He reached out to cup her cheeks

with his palms. The rough surface of his skin set off little pinpoints of sensation in hers. "I'll only go as far as you want me to, Elena. I promise. Although I may ask for a favor in return."

"Favor?" she strangled out.

"You'll see."

His tongue reached out to trace the outline of her lips. She shivered. Her fists grabbed hold of the front of his shirt. How could one touch ignite her so? "Oh my," she whispered.

"No more talking."

His lips slanted across hers tasting, testing. There was that strange emptiness in the pit of her stomach again. She could taste hints of the stew and wine they'd had for dinner, but the heat of his desire overshadowed them. Raw passion and held in check only by a determined will.

She had no idea how but her hands let go and wound around his neck. Was that her voice? Were those little moans hers?

Still, she was frightened.

His tongue fenced with hers and explored every crevice inside her mouth. The more he explored, the more she felt the fluttery feeling in her stomach grow. Trembling, Elena wanted to know more. She reached around and opened the top button of his shirt. "Yes, sweetheart, that's it. Now the next one," he encouraged.

She undid three or four then touched the skin at his throat. That very first night they met she'd marveled at his physical beauty when he'd changed his shirt. But she had no idea touch could produce such sensation.

First he took off the sweater she was wearing. Then he removed his shirt altogether. He still had on his t-shirt but that followed rather rapidly into the growing pile at their feet.

"Time for you to learn lesson number one."

He took her hands and placed them on the bare skin of his chest. He rolled them over his skin making sure she grazed the nipples over and over again. They hardened into the same small peaks as hers. Then he let go expecting her to continue. Did she dare?

"Don't question. Just feel."

Her fingertips drew lazy circles over his skin. He closed his eyes and she watched his face tighten as he responded. She was almost afraid to look down, afraid to see the result of her handiwork. But she did. There was a hard ridge lining the zipper of his jeans.

"Now it's my turn."

He undid the buttons on her shirt with a shaking hand. She couldn't believe she affected him that much. Once her shirt was open, he leaned back to look at her. Her face flamed with embarrassment. "You are so beautiful."

He slid the shirt off her shoulders and reached around behind to unclasp her bra. She stiffened, unsure of this next move. He let go and trailed feather light kisses down her neck. As he did, his hand slid underneath the material of her bra. She gasped with sensation and his hand closed over her breast. A moment later she cried out as his fingers rolled her nipple into an aching pebble. With his other hand, he reached around, and this time she didn't even notice the material falling to the floor.

She couldn't believe it but the pain, her constant companion, had fled in the wake of sensation.

"Sweetheart, this is where I might need that favor I was talking about."

She looked up to see hot lasers of desire in his gaze. "I don't understand."

"I want to go slow with you. But right now I'm on the edge of what I can take. I don't want to lose control. If you help me release some of the tension,

I'll be able to go at your pace."

"How would I do that?"

He grinned. Of all that she had known of him before, she had never seen anything as sexy as that grin. "Undo my belt."

Could she? She swallowed hard. Her fingers worked at the leather and each time her knuckles touched his bare skin, he sucked in his stomach.

She understood the next step without having to be told. She undid the button and slid the zipper down. A look of relief came over his face. Obviously he was relieved at being set free. Which left her with a dilemma. What to do with him now.

****

Alexi wasn't much into prayer, but he was praying now. He was certain he would come the instant she touched him. He took her hand in his and slid her fingers inside his boxers. He placed them around his shaft and prayed she'd get the hint.

Ah, that felt so good.

At first, she wasn't quite sure how to hold him but he shifted and moved until she picked up the rhythm. Once she had the hang of it, he began to move his hips. Slowly, although slow was killing him right now. Then faster.

Having nowhere else to put his hands, he reached out to take her breast in one and placed the other on her shoulder. As the pressure built inside him, he gave way to sensation and stopped playing with her. But the contact ignited something primitive inside him, something he'd never felt before. And he was glad he was doing this so as not to hurt her.

Although he understood she was a novice at lovemaking, she certainly tried to learn quickly. Her fingers moved down to cup his balls and stoke his fire to a raging inferno. She clasped him again and this time he pumped his hips for all he was worth.

He reached out and grabbed both her shoulders and held on. Like lightning on a stormy day, sparks sizzled and flew and he shouted out his release, convulsing in her hand until he was spent. Yet as he had told her, he spilled no seed.

Alexi found himself nearly collapsed and hanging onto her for dear life. "Thank you."

He could tell she had no idea how to answer. "Now I can take care of you without making you uncomfortable. We have all the time in the world to make babies."

Her gaze told him they did not, but he didn't want a philosophical discussion. Lifting her in his arms, he brought her over to the couch. He wasn't going anywhere near her bedroom until all remnants of Jacques were gone.

He set her down in front of him and undid her skirt. Watching the cloth fall to the floor became one of the most erotic scenes of his life. The skirt seemed to whisper down the skin of her thigh and slip gracefully down the curve of her leg. What remained took his breath away. For as flawless as her face was, her body when unbent was even more beautiful.

Her breasts were large but not overly so, with her nipples sharp and erect. Some might call them pert. He called them perfect. Her waist was hardly big enough for both his hands to span, yet her hips flared out gracefully. For which he was glad. He had plans for those hips.

With a gentle nudge, he pushed her down on the couch. He lifted one leg and took off her shoe. Then he rolled her stocking down, all the while following the material with light kisses. When he was through with one leg, he proceeded to the other. By the time he was finished, she'd fallen back against the couch and her head rolling from side to side in dazed ecstasy. Good.

Falling to his knees, he pushed her legs apart,

wrapped his arms around her, and seared her with a kiss. She moaned and tried to rub herself against him, her body seeking what she had yet to discover. But Alexi wanted her to know all there was to know before they were totally intimate. So he let go and bent down to suckle first one breast, then the other.

Her fingers tangled in his hair. He almost smiled. She had a long way to go yet. His hands traveled the length of her waist, sliding over every inch of her skin. Then with the ease of an expert, he reached inside the waistband of her underwear. Her legs tightened around his waist as she tried to clamp them together. Which was all right. This was uncharted territory for both of them and he'd placed himself right where he was to make sure she couldn't close up, inside or out.

"Easy sweetheart," he whispered, pressing light kisses against her neck. She arched against him and he took full advantage of the moment. His fingers parted her folds and he pushed one deep inside her core. She cried out, but he knew she hadn't climaxed. But she was ready. Oh man, was she ready.

Of course, his own body responded and he once again became stiff as iron. However, her first pleasure was going to be just that. Pleasure. Without pain. So he bent down and started to roll his tongue down to her navel.

She grabbed at his head, tried to close her legs, and Alexi simply smiled. Of course she never saw the smile because his face was buried inside her core. Once his tongue lapped at her a couple of times, she melted and he knew she was ripe for the taking.

Damn, it was hard being noble. But he was going to be noble even if it killed him.

He yanked off her panties, lifted her knees over his shoulders, and started loving her for all he was worth. One arm wrapped around her waist to lift her and get better access; the other, well, there was no reason why he shouldn't enjoy the ride also.

As her climax built, so did his. Her legs shook and trembled. She cried out his name. Her head thrashed from side to side. He focused all of his energy into pleasing her. Plunging his tongue in and out as he would the rest of him. Harder and harder until finally she screamed. He called out her name, his hand working furiously at release. She came all over him as he reached the pinnacle and fell with her. And when the aftershocks finally stopped, he fell against her stomach and her arms wrapped around his head. He'd never known a more intimate gesture in his life.

Chapter Fourteen

The lake sat nestled in the palm of the forest. Tall trees lined the banks on one side. The other was a wall of sheer rock face. In the distance, jagged peaks reached upwards towards the sky. The lake was a natural basin, probably a puddle left behind by a glacier long ago. It wasn't hard to figure that this place was mostly forgotten by the outside world.

Standing on the dock, Alexi scanned the landscape. The rock face was too straight, too smooth to climb and he wasn't a rock climber. There was a way, he was sure, to get to the top. As long as he knew the lake had enough depth, he could risk jumping from that height. And it would save on swimming one length of the lake. "Elena, is the lake deep enough for me to jump from the rock up there?"

One look at her face told him what she thought of the idea although she answered as she always did, considering his words with thoughtfulness. "Yes, I think so. But I know nothing of what is underneath. I don't like this idea at all, Alexi. You could be seriously injured."

"You'd be there to heal me, wouldn't you?"

He reached out to hug her and she slipped away, presenting him with her back. "You shouldn't jest about such things."

"Hey, look, I'm only kidding. I'm not stupid." Her muttered reply told him otherwise. His heart swelled. She really did care about him. "What we could use right now is a boat. I wish I'd have thought about it at that station. You remember, the one before we got on the plane."

"Yes, I remember."

Alexi tried not to think about the plane ride. Then he realized the plane was the only way to get home. "Jacques has a canoe," she continued. "He uses it to follow some of the smaller streams for fishing."

Yeah, and the thought of getting on a plane again was as thrilling as asking old Jacques for help. But they had no choice. "All right," he told her making up his mind. "We ask your brother for help."

Just as Alexi turned to go back to the village, he watched several people carry the object of their discussion down the hill towards the dock. Jacques followed and stood at the edge of the trees. He nodded once then turned back and disappeared into the woods. "You know something, Elena? I might revise my opinion of him yet."

She hugged him hard. "I would like that."

Well, he could try. He watched Elena thank everyone and added his gratitude, but he didn't want an audience for this. Neither did Elena, she ushered everyone back home with a natural diplomacy. "Can you handle a canoe?"

"I can handle anything."

She sighed. "Alexi, we do not have time for you to act macho. We also do not have time for me to prove to you how wrong you are."

"All right, I was just wondering how hard it could be. I mean, you were asking a city boy who lives in the desert, you know."

She laughed. But she also took the time to show him how to step into the middle of the canoe and grab the sides to get in, how to kneel and brace his knees against the insides of the canoe, and how to paddle by making the letter "J" out of his stroke so the canoe would go forward in a straight line.

She made him get in and out of the canoe several times before she was satisfied. "Normally I would paddle from the back but with your strength, it will be best if I sit in the bow. You will need to balance your strokes with mine."

He was going to have a great deal of fun teaching her how to balance strokes between them. But first, they had business to attend to.

"I don't like feeling useless," she complained after they'd reached the middle of the lake.

"You won't be. I need you to be here when I come back up for air. I'm going to try to explore a little first."

Alexi flexed his muscles. He'd fed and then fed some more this morning. Now he needed to move. "You will be careful, won't you?" she asked, her tone worried.

"Of course. I can see underwater unless it's pitch black. And I have trained to hold my breath for a long time."

"I remember."

He did too. Every moment of their first meeting. He shucked his clothes and shivered in the cool air. Then she threw her arms around his neck and planted a huge one right on his lips. Of course, the canoe made a response difficult but when she released him, he knew they were destined for more. "You will contact me, 'speak' to me, often?"

"Yes. Of course."

He was just about to dive in when she cried out, "Wait." Then she removed a chain from around her neck. It was a small gold crucifix. "For me, Alexi. Please."

He nodded. If it would make her happy, he had no problem with it. But it wasn't something he really believed in.

This time he kissed her. Hard and to the point. Then he rose, set her from him, and jumped into the icy water.

Go with God, Alexi.

Elena hated helplessness. She hated inaction more. The combination was going to drive her mad. Funny how the heart could accept what the mind could not.

Alexi kept diving for longer and longer periods of time, teaching his lungs to hold more and more air. When he surfaced, she would pull the canoe close so he could hold onto the side and catch his breath. Each time he went back down her heart lodged in her throat and refused to budge. Each time he surfaced, it would leap out of her chest.

He spoke to her using the connection, telling her time and again that he found nothing unusual. As far as he could tell the rock wall ended in the lakebed. *You mentioned a grotto in your story. I'm not finding one.*

What about a surge of energy? Use your senses. Do you feel anything?

Not yet. But there's a whole lot more area to cover.

She easily sensed his dismay. *Are you all right, Alexi?*

The cold may be a problem later, but for now, so far so good.

Several minutes later he came up for air again. This time he held onto the side of the canoe longer to catch his breath. "Good thing," he told her in between gasps. "I didn't jump. It's not all that deep in places."

"You look exhausted. Tomorrow is another day. You can—."

"No!" he cried, cutting her off. Determination tightened his features. "I'm not tired."

"Yes, you are. Oh Alexi, please be careful."

He caught her gaze with his. Then he grinned. "Plant one on me."

"What?"

"I said plant on one me. Kiss me. A kiss will

make me right as rain."

"Alexi, you are being foolish."

He simply waited. With a sigh, Elena moved to the center of the canoe and he sidled up to her. She'd expected his lips to be cold like the water, but they were warm like the Sun. They were slightly salty and full of promise. Her heart sped up and her insides cried out for more. And all she could do was wonder how lips touching lips could be so erotic.

"Umm. That was fun. Tasty but definitely only an appetizer."

Would he ever be serious? Would she ever want him to be?

As she caught his gaze, she noticed he seemed stronger. Perhaps a kiss was exactly what he needed after all. He lifted up, nearly capsizing the canoe, winked, sucked in a huge breath, then went below the surface of the water again. Another piece of her heart went with him.

Was it possible? He was so...so impossible. Maybe that was why they were able to mesh together. Supposedly opposites attracted. He certainly enjoyed teasing her. She found she enjoyed his teasing.

All of a sudden, Elena realized he'd been down longer than all the other times. She didn't wear a watch, now she wished she did. *Alexi. Speak to me.*

He didn't focus on her thoughts, but she sensed him and his feelings. *Curiosity.* Something had piqued his interest. *Alexi. Listen to me. Mark the spot and come back up. Rest a while then go back down again.*

He shut her off. He refused to respond. Terrified, Elena began paddling towards the place where she sensed he was. His head broke the surface moments later. "What happened?" she cried.

"You...gotta...stop...doing that."

"Doing what? I was sick with worry."

He swallowed, refusing, she realized, to answer her statement. "I thought I sensed something. Once you tried to connect, I lost it."

"Oh." Contrite, she reached out to smooth back a lock of his hair. When she pulled away, he reached out and grabbed her hand, placing a kiss in the palm.

"Thank you." He looked up at her and she knew what he was going to say before he said the words. "You're going to have to tough it out, Elena. I'm a big boy. I can take care of myself."

"I know. But I feel so useless."

He grimaced. "I'll explain all about how dumb that remark is later. But right now, let me do what needs to be done."

Never had words been so hard to speak. "Very well, Alexi. Go."

She closed her eyes and when she opened them, he was gone.

****

At any other time, at any other moment in time, Alexi knew he'd be on top of the world. He'd allow his heart to soar. Hell, he might even shout out his joy to the world. But he had other things on his mind.

Pulling down through the weeds, he found the opening in the rock face wall again. Small but definitely there. He had to clear a space, pulling handfuls of silt and debris from the crevice.

He was only able to get a small area cleared, not large enough for his body but certainly his arm. He backed away and swam a short distance as a test. Yes, the buzz decreased. As he swam back towards the opening, the buzz increased.

Alexi knew every Carney trick there was. He'd learned them while perfecting his magic act. He knew what was behind every door, number one, two, and three, inclusive. But he had no idea what might be on the other side of that rock wall.

Time was running short. He could feel his lungs starting to burn with the strain. With a slight shake of his head, he swam back to the opening and pulled at the few last remaining weeds.

He checked the angle of the opening and found his only entry was going to be left-handed. He grabbed onto the outside shelf of the rock, twisted so that his face pressed against the hard surface, and thrust his arm inside.

At first all he noticed was a tingling sensation. He moved his hand around the surface of the lakebed and still all he felt was the tingling again. Could the rocks have shifted over time? Closed the opening to this small slit so that he might never find the prize?

Alexi had a choice. Continue to try the search or go back up for air one last time. And if he did go up for air, what would he use to dig in the rock with? He had no pick, no hammer, nothing to chip away with.

In frustration, he pulled his arm out and hit the wall with all his might. His hand hurt like the dickens, but his psyche felt a whole lot better.

And the buzz grew stronger.

Now that was interesting. Really interesting. He swam away from the rock searching for a piece of something to use as a battering ram. He found a solid piece of rock a short ways away.

It worked. After he chipped away, he would try thrusting his arm inside again. The tingling grew. He was getting closer. Time was really not on his side any longer. His lungs could only do so much. And they were stressed to the max. He began hammering away at the outcropping to break pieces away and gain greater access into the opening. As he did, he noticed shiny flecks in the rock.

Fascinating. Could pieces of the meteorite have

melded with the rock over time? If so, was the entire rock wall what he searched for?

No, that didn't make sense. Then anyone of Elena's people standing on the top of the rocks would feel the power. But the rock wall could be an insulator of sorts, hiding the meteorite from them.

Alexi neared the breaking point. He had only a few more seconds and he would have to leave and head for the surface. With one last swing, he smashed the rock against the wall. It blasted into pieces and a large chunk came loose.

Pulling the debris away once more, Alexi reached inside. Yeah, there was definitely something in here. The tingling sensation now became like an electric shock. Not quite the jolt Elena spoke of but strong enough to make him want to instinctively withdraw his hand. He fought the feeling and continued searching.

He dug into the lakebed, sweeping his hand through the silt and searching. Pushing his body even closer to the wall, he reached with one last thrust into the darkest depth of the lake. To find the treasure. The hidden treasure.

His lungs were beyond repair. His body, numb from the cold and ready to collapse, simply hung suspended in the water. With his last ounce of will he made a desperate grab at the lakebed.

Alexi had known the power of the Sun all his life. He knew what it was like to hold the energy in, to have ants crawl under his skin, to want to bust loose and send shooting stars out of his pores. But he had never felt power such as this.

Instead of the world going dark, the world went white with light. *Elena*, his mind cried out. Then he knew no more.

Chapter Fifteen

Elena!

She heard his cry from a great distance. She was not strong, nor was she a better swimmer than her ancestor Isobel. But terror gave her a strength she never knew she had.

Diving into the murky depths, she simply closed her eyes. She followed her senses and found him lying on the floor of the lakebed. Pressure pushed at her eardrums telling her she was deep but she realized not as deep as she would have thought. That gave her hope.

Elena lifted his body and latched onto his wrist. She started swimming and her grip kept slipping. Not knowing how else to grab onto him, she twisted him around and wrapped an arm about his chest. But she never stopped, never lost stride.

As she broke the surface of the lake, she pulled Alexi's body up with her and tilted his face to the air. He wasn't breathing.

Treading water, she spied the canoe not too far away. She dragged Alexi to the craft but now faced a dilemma. How to get him inside. She took his arms and laid each one over the side, then she slid below the surface and pushed from underneath until his armpits caught hold of the gunwale of the canoe. Then she did as she'd been taught so long ago. She tilted the canoe and grabbed onto the opposite side, sliding her body along the surface and falling into the bottom with a thud.

Ignoring her own pain, she scrambled to hold onto Alexi and try to do the same. Kneeling on the bottom of the canoe, she braced her back against the opposite gunwale and pulled. She could only get him to bend in half, but it was enough of his body to help expel the water in his lungs.

He began coughing and choking and Elena started crying. She sent up a silent thank you and began pounding on Alexi's back. He was breathing but barely conscious.

"Alexi!" she cried. "You must listen to me. You must hold on if you feel yourself slipping. I can't hold onto you and paddle at the same time."

Fear is the great motivator. Fear spurred her now. She stroked because his life depended upon it, ignoring the strain in her muscles, the burning of her lungs, the exhaustion in her bones. She paddled until she reached the dock, her breath coming in great gasps. Then she pulled the canoe along the dock until it wedged into the sand at the lake's edge. She threw the paddle onto the ground and jumped out. She took hold of both his arms and rolled him off the canoe and into the water then dragged his body up the shore. Putting him on his back, she rubbed at his skin. So cold. Where was the fire?

Looking at the sky, she cursed the clouds. Why could it not have been a bright sunny day? Why was the Sun playing hide and seek with her when she needed its energy so much?

She tilted his head and put her cheek near his nose. A light puff of air touched her face. She put her hand against the side of his neck and felt his heartbeat, though to her, the pulse felt weak and barely there.

Elena knew how to heal humans. That came naturally to her. She had no idea how to heal a Noble. She ran her hands over his body, rubbing his skin, trying to work some warmth into him. She called to him with her mind. He didn't answer.

Reaching inside herself, Elena put her fingers to

his temples and made a connection with him. She begged him to fight the lethargy and follow her back to consciousness.

And then she realized.

Elena pulled away slowly but she pulled away. Once outside, she looked down at his hand. She hadn't seen, hadn't thought. His hand was tightly closed in a fist. It took only a moment for Elena to realize she needed to remove the source causing Alexi's unconsciousness before he would come to. She ran back to the canoe and pulled out a small leather pouch that she used to carry herbs. Inside were some of the strongest Lorraine leaves she could find. Then she searched the shoreline until she found a small stick wedged in the sand.

She ran back with the pouch and opened his fingers. There, resting in his palm, he held onto tiny bits of blue, so blue they hurt her eyes. She scraped the sand and the flecks into the pouch, careful not to touch them, then sealed the top. Then she splashed water into his palm to wash away what was left in his hand.

She placed the pouch on the dock and returned to her patient. As she'd thought, he seemed to be breathing easier. And his color seemed better. Or was that simply her mind and wishful thinking?

Torn, she wondered if she should leave him and go get help. Not that her people could heal him. That was her domain. But a fire and shelter would be better than sitting at the water's edge on a chill, cloudy day. She started to rise when she found herself stopped by a hand clutching her wrist. Her cry of fright turned to a shout of joy as she realized she was staring into his stormy gray gaze.

"Alexi." She said his name over and over again in between her tears. Then she realized he wasn't speaking back.

****

He wanted her. Not just wanted. Really wanted. As in he was one step away from losing total control of his body and his mind.

He read the surprise in her gaze. Reaching up, he put his hand behind the back of her neck. He pulled her head down to his. There would be no gentleness, only demand. His lips ground against hers, searing her with his kiss. At first she dove into these uncharted depths with him, her answer as fierce and as wild as his. Then she stopped as if realizing what she was getting herself into. She was confused. But how could he explain?

She reared back. His answer was to pull her down on top of him. She fought his strength with her own. She didn't understand. She would never understand the forces that were driving at him, in him, through him. She would never feel the thousand-watt charge running along every circuit in his body. Or know the charge ended right between his legs.

He won the battle with ease. His mouth ravaged hers, taking, and demanding response. She held back, he could taste her uncertainty. This was not the Alexi she knew. But it was. This piece of him was just as much a part as all the others, a fierceness he'd never shown her before. He would never hurt her, could never hurt her.

He took her hand and pushed it down inside his boxers. Using his hand to guide her, he showed her exactly what he wanted. He wanted hard and fast and he wanted satisfaction.

Would she accept this demanding side of his nature? Would she go with his flow as he was asking her to do? Making love, he realized in that moment, was a game of trust. Did she trust him enough to let go with him? Was she daring enough to take the freedom he was offering and run with it?

Her lips softened against his and his heart

nearly leaped out of his chest. Then she changed tactics on him, kneeling down, pushing his boxers down over his hips, and bending over to take him in her mouth.

He moaned at the warmth of her mouth. She ran her tongue over his erection and sparks flew. Each touch sizzled through him as if she were setting off a string of firecrackers.

And that was when he knew. Whatever fate had divined for them, talking about making love and spilling his seed inside her, and actually doing it were now one and the same. He could feel the heaviness grow in his groin. But he held on. Release now. Only release.

The heavens opened up. He screamed, his cry echoing through the trees. He came with the force of a lightning bolt, hard, quick, fast, and so intense he nearly burned to a cinder. And he kept coming. Spasm on top of spasm, pure pleasure, but a pleasure as near to pain as one could get.

Once he stopped, he lifted his body and latched onto her mouth. He wanted her to understand the need, the insatiable appetite that grew upon itself. The more he fed, the more he wanted. The more he wanted, the more he had to feed. But at least he could speak now. "Forgive me," he whispered against her lips.

****

Deep down inside of her, Elena knew she was about to receive more than any book could ever explain. She was probably the most conservative being on the planet, comfortable within her own skin, not needing anything more than what she already had. Alexi had just told her, in no uncertain terms, to forget any preconceived notion she might have about sex. He was asking her to go on a magic carpet ride with him.

In the space of about two heartbeats, Elena

knew what she really craved, why she melted with him and no other. He was her magician. He was wild, fun-loving, daring, scary, all the things she was not. And she wanted him. She wanted his fire, his passion, his lust for life. She wanted to let go, give herself over to him, let him take her to places she couldn't even dream of.

He was asking her forgiveness when there was nothing to forgive. She wanted him as much as he wanted her. If that meant pain, then so be it. She'd known pain before, lived with pain all of her life.

They were nothing compared to the hole in her heart, the hole he'd carved while swimming around the bottom of the lake. She never wanted to know terror like that again.

So maybe he did need to be forgiven after all.

****

An appetizer was not going to be enough. Alexi burned with need even though he'd just experienced the most intense orgasm of his life. He wanted her so badly, he shook with need. He wanted to go fast yet she wouldn't let him and the more he tried, the more Elena slowed him down. Each time he tried to ravage, she soothed. He kissed her so hard her lips scraped up against her teeth, so she pulled his face back with her hands and nipped at his lips. His chest heaved with excitement so she used her fingertips to soothe the skin at his temples. He brought fire as his mouth engulfed hers and she became as cool as the lake next to them by withdrawing. She wanted him to understand he wouldn't get what he wanted until he let her set the pace. And once they reached a balance, once he was able to find a modicum of control, she responded in a fashion that took his breath away.

Their tongues danced. Not slow. There could never be slow or lazy now. Not while his body sizzled with electricity. But she made him understand that simmer was better than shooting sparks. Flames that burned too hot, too fast, ended up putting themselves out, and he had an objective to reach first.

Her clothes were wet and chilled, yet because of the heat he exuded, he knew she wasn't cold. His fingers shook as they tried to unbutton the buttons of her blouse. Once he accomplished that task, she helped him by trying to shrug out of the garment. While she struggled to get free of the wet cloth, he took full advantage of her predicament.

Unclasping her bra, he let her breasts fall into his waiting hands. Since she was already in a sitting position, he lifted up and began suckling first on one nipple, then the other. "Not fair," she moaned.

He chuckled at her protest, after all it wasn't fair to play with her when she wasn't able to return the attention, and started nipping at her with his teeth. She sucked in her breath and flailed at the blouse until she was free.

Her arms wrapped around him and he felt her stretch her head back as far as it would go. She gave him access to all of her and the knowledge burned as hot as the fire in his groin. He wished, for a moment, he could stand outside himself to see the picture she made. Elena thought of herself as ugly. He knew she wasn't. She was beautiful, made even more so by the throes of their passion.

Of course his physical body had other ideas, and brought him back to earth with a jolt. He let go of her for a moment and shucked his underwear. He was hard as steel, harder even, for his mind knew what he'd yet to experience. She was going to be like a velvet glove, surrounding him with desire.

Alexi fell back to the ground and flipped over so she was lying beneath him. His hand worked at the snap of her jeans then opened the zipper. Each tick of the metal resounded inside him, making him terribly aware of the prize underneath.

How soft and warm her skin was. How frustrating to only be able to slide his hand inside the waistband yet go no further.

Alexi growled with frustration. If a wet shirt posed a problem, wet jeans were near impossible to remove. And lying down wasn't working, even though she was trying to help.

Instead, Alexi lifted Elena until she stood before him. He took a moment, for that was all he could spare, to rake her body with his gaze. She was far from being an ogre now. Her body showed no sign of pain. Indeed, she seemed more like a gypsy, earthy, sensuous, a woman proud of the power her body held.

He couldn't resist kissing the soft skin of her belly while his hands pushed the fabric over her hips and down to her knees. He pulled back to allow her to step out of them then returned to his prize. He nipped at one hip then the other, soothing each bite with a lathe of his tongue. He made sure she didn't notice her underwear taking the same path as her jeans.

She was so beautiful.

Lifting up onto his knees, he took her breast into his mouth and slid a finger along her opening. She cried out and her fingers tangled in his hair. But the pressure of her hands told him the truth of the matter. She wanted him as badly as he wanted her. He reached inside, using her moisture to ready her for his entry. First one finger, then two. Stretching. Opening. And when he was certain he'd crossed the line of no return, he touched her nub with his tongue.

Her knees buckled. He caught her before she fell and lowered her to the ground. She was ready and so hot, he was certain he'd be scorched. Funny how the tables had turned. He was the one out of control, yet her mouth was all over his, her body writhed, seeking fulfillment, she kept begging him for release.

He was more than willing to oblige.

Alexi lay down on top of her and nudged her legs apart with his knees. He lifted up onto his elbows, caught her head with one hand, and drove his tongue deep inside her mouth. He sought her core like a heat seeking missile.

Once he was poised at her opening, he spread her legs until they could go no more. Then he pushed. Once. Twice. The fire in his blood demanded that he pound away at her. No gentleness, no finesse, just raw need. But she was a virgin. And he held onto that last piece of sanity for all he was worth.

Rocking back and forth, Alexi slowly worked his way inside. God she was so tight. So hot. Sweat dripped from his temple with the strain. Then the most amazing thing happened. She caught his head between her hands and forced him to look at her. She told him with her gaze that she understood his need, she could handle the wildness; she wanted to embrace the animal inside him.

He bent his head and kissed her with all his heart. With one thrust he broke the barrier and buried himself to the hilt. She cried out and he absorbed her pain. He'd forgotten he could do that. So had she. She smiled against his mouth and began pushing her hips against his.

Oh, she had to be kidding.

Lifting up onto his elbows, Alexi made sure he rubbed against her nub as he thrust in and out. He felt the heaviness inside build. He'd never let go of his seed before, so he wondered how it would feel.

Her fingernails raked his back. He reveled in the pain. She tried to claw her way inside his body. He countered by thrusting his into hers. He'd wanted hard and fast. She gave him overdrive.

A tight pressure built deep inside. With one last gasp at sanity, Alexi reached between them and started working her nub. He could feel her rising, climbing, reaching for release. The higher she climbed, the higher he climbed with her. Until she shattered.

She clamped around him, her muscles rippling, clenching, squeezing. Between the heat, the sensation, the need, he was a goner. He reached the summit then jumped beyond it, and in the space of his next breath, came as he never had before. And with his climax, he shot his seed into her womb in spurts of never-ending pleasure.

Chapter Sixteen

When he rolled off of her, Elena knew she'd lost a piece of herself. Were there any words? Could she describe how she felt? That she reveled in the slight soreness between her legs. That her heart leaped with joy that she may have created a child. What she craved for so long could now be a reality?

He pulled her close, showing her a side of him she'd never guessed at. Such tenderness. Such care. The kiss he placed on the top of her head reverberated all the way down to her toes.

Snuggling tight against his chest, she listened to his heartbeat. For all her life, she'd associated that sound with dread. A human heartbeat meant pain, the steady pound of blood flowing through arteries and veins became a migraine. Now there was only joy.

Elena had let herself flow with him. In return, she became part of him. What an amazing difference between a man and a woman. He was so...so linear. Even when she sensed his thoughts she'd only known them with a purpose in her mind. Now she understood his purpose as well. Funny, but the discovery wasn't quite what she expected.

As a woman, Elena was an emotional being. She always tried to see the entire picture. Alexi, well, Alexi was straightforward. Point A went to point B. No deviations unless logic showed up. Or needs. Or desires.

Was this the bond? Was there a description she could have used for it? Before she would never have understood, she would never have recognized their differences because she would not have been able to comprehend them. Not in the truest sense of the word. Now she did.

The bond meant she'd become part of him. Not as herself but as him. She knew his senses as he knew them, processed his thoughts as he processed them. The difference between male and female disappeared. What was left fascinated her.

"Are you sorry, Alexi?" she asked, her one fear that he might regret his actions. Saying and doing were two very different things.

He lifted up on his elbow and gave her one of his heart-melting grins. "You didn't need to ask that question, did you?"

"No."

He bent down and gave her a slow, sweet kiss. "I've always understood the bond in my head. But I never quite realized what it meant. Really means. It's amazing."

"I know."

She could feel his wonder matching her own. She could also feel something else nudging up against her hip. All of a sudden thoughts and pictures ran through her head. Vignettes. Of how he saw them together. She blushed.

He laughed. "I'm stunned that you can still do that after what we've shared. What we will always share. At least I hope what we will share."

"What do you mean?"

"You can build walls, Elena. When you want your privacy. The bond is about completion, not invasion. You still have to be able to be…well, you."

"That makes sense." And she was glad for the knowledge. No being should become another so totally that they lost themselves.

"But not too many. Because I kind of like knowing that you get all hot and bothered when I do certain things. Like this." He rimmed the shell of her ear with his tongue. "And this." He spread light kisses all the way down the arch of her neck.

"Alexi," she strangled out. Hot and bothered were mere child's play compared to what she had in mind. "Those pictures?" she continued.

"We have plenty of time."

And she was more than ready. But first she wanted to explore. Elena rolled and swung her leg over his waist to straddle him. Her hands glided over his chest and she marveled at the sensations in her fingertips. Or was that because he was doing the same to her? She tweaked his nipples and he sucked in his breath. He tweaked hers and the sensation started a slow burn in the pit of her belly.

She bent over and bit her way down the side of his cheekbone, and learning from him, let him know the sensation of her tongue around his ear in return.

He gasped and lifted up to take one of her breasts in his mouth, worrying the nipple between his teeth. A live wire burned all the through her and the embers caught fire.

There would be no holding back. She pulled his head away and plunged her tongue deep inside his mouth. Her breath mingled with his breath. Her sensation became his sensation. Soon all they shared was pure pleasure.

She wanted him inside her. She wanted the pictures rolling fast and furious through her mind. She got off of him but stayed on her hands and knees with her back to him. She couldn't see him smile but she knew he did. A long, knowing grin that told her she was going to get exactly what she wanted.

He spread her legs then sat back on his knees. He pulled her hips back until she was forced to sit down. As she did, he impaled her on his erection, pulling her down until she could go no further.

Her muscles clenched and clenched all around him. Her body wanted him to move. "Slow down, greedy one," he whispered against the back of her neck.

She knew what he was doing. He was forcing her to wait. He wanted to be in command. Oh, sweet, sweet torture. To feel every inch of him, to burn with the fever of wanting, but not to assuage the itch.

His hands came around and began playing with her breasts again, rolling the nipples, pulling gently. Each stroke sent fire shooting through her belly. He continued to kiss the back of her neck, her shoulder, whispering words of what he was going to do next.

She started begging. "Please, Alexi. I can stand no more."

"Talk dirty to me. Tell me what you want me to do."

Could she? He continued to play with her breasts and shifted a few times to give her a hint of the reward if she played his game. She gave into his demands with some of her own. As she told him what she wanted, no begged for what she wanted, she started to move up and down on his shaft. This time he let her, using more and more force with his hands on her hips until she didn't know where she ended and he began.

He pushed her forward so that she had to rest her hands in the sand. He held onto her hips and thrust into her harder and harder. She could barely breathe, her entire being centered on the joining of their bodies.

She could feel him tighten inside of her. His hands pulled on her breasts but she wanted more. She got more than she bargained for. He lifted back and held her hip with one hand while he played with her nub with the other. He stroked her in time with his movements until the force of them echoed through the trees.

The connection made them one.

She could feel his body fill with semen. She

knew he could feel the readiness of her womb for the gift he was about to give her. Together, they reached and clawed their way to the peak of sensation. Then leaped beyond.

He thrust once, twice. He cried out in ecstasy, a split second later she screamed and exploded all around him. She could feel the hot jets of his life spurt into her and she couldn't stop coming.

Elena had no idea how much time passed. Alexi had collapsed on her back, drinking in huge droughts of air. "That was incredible," he told her.

He hugged her around the waist, hard, then let go. He rose first, then reached out a hand to help her up. Both of them were full of sand and Elena felt the stickiness of his lovemaking between her legs.

"You do realize how awkward this is going to be," she replied. "The entire village is going to know."

"Jealousy. Pure jealousy. I mean, I would offer my services—."

She swatted at him with her shirt. God help her if he ever stopped teasing her. "You do and you may be missing an appendage."

"A what? Oh," he chuckled. "I get you." He helped her on with her shirt. "I like it when you turn green on me, you know. Your eyes get all narrow and dangerous. As if you're gonna spit fire and stuff."

"And you, Sir Dragon? Is that not fire I see coming from you as well?"

"Yeah, I guess. You know you're going to have a lot of explaining to do to Chuck."

She laughed. "True. I will. But I don't think he'll mind if I hand him some of his money first."

****

The object of their conversation, at that moment, was sitting in a car fuming. Charles didn't like being used. He also didn't appreciate stupidity. But right at the moment, he was getting an overdose of both. "Where the hell are we going?" he asked as they sped southward on the Garden State Parkway.

He watched Dmitri smile. "I would have thought that was obvious."

"Not exactly. But be that way. I know where the car is going. What I don't know is our destination."

"Good," the other man replied. "You can try to figure it out until we get there."

Games? He wanted to play games? The only game the Ancient one knew was death. And, as far as Charles was concerned, that wasn't a game. "How in hell's name would you know where he is?"

"I would say I have a fifty-fifty chance of answering that question correctly. I'm either right or I'm wrong. Not bad odds."

Oh this was just wonderful. Stuck on a joy ride with a flippin' know-it-all, going who knew where, but knowing life was going to get very short once they arrived. "Look, Konin. I don't like you. You don't like me. Fine. No problem. I don't want to be here. You don't want me to be here."

"Am I supposed to feel sorry for you or something?"

"No. You're supposed to let me off at the next rest stop."

"No can do, I'm afraid," Dmitri replied. "The Ancient one won't talk to me."

Charles clenched his jaw in frustration. "You think he's going to talk to me?" Man, they were so stupid. "First of all, he's not even going to talk. He'd just as soon blink as remove me from the planet."

"You'd better hope he doesn't."

"I don't think you're hearing me here, so I'm going to go real slow. He...won't...listen. Can't you get that through your head?"

"Your job is to make sure he does. He needs to know we want to make a deal."

For the love of whatever name anyone could

think of. "He isn't going to make a deal. Don't you get it?"

He watched the man shake his head. "Tsk, tsk. Your stripe is showing."

"Call me anything you like," he retorted, clenching his fists to keep from using them. "But what you're trying to do—"

"What *we're* trying to do," Dmitri corrected as he cut him off.

"Whatever," Charles muttered; cursing the man, the Nobility, and all the bad luck he'd had lately. "Dead is still dead. *Morte. Fini.*"

"If that is the price, so be it."

Man, why did everyone have to go Noble on him at the worst possible moment? "Hey, look. If that's what you want, go for it. Be my guest. But I don't feel like taking a trip to the afterlife just yet."

"I can understand why," Dmitri replied with a smile. Charles didn't like what he saw in that smile. Came a bit too close to home. "You made a deal," the man continued. "I'm here to make sure you don't back out."

"Is that a threat?"

"A promise. If you don't hold up your end of the bargain, you will be dead anyway. Pay me now or pay me later. You have better odds with him than with me."

"Really?" Charles sneered. The next thing he knew, a fist had hold of his shirt and was squeezing the cloth tight.

"Would you care to ask that question again?"

Charles got the message. "You can let go now." When Dmitri did, he made a point of straightening the material of his shirt and brushing away some non-existent lint. "So, I guess I'll go back to my original question. Where are we going?"

Dmitri sighed and Charles could tell the man's patience was wearing thin. "If you ever have children, do not let me know. I will be forced to end their lives before they reach the age of three."

Charles laughed. "That's an optimistic statement. You're assuming we'll live through this."

"We are going to his home." Dmitri didn't sound happy. Good. "You know where that is, of course."

He did. Just outside Atlantic City. "I thought the place went up for sale. Wasn't that why Tara Valentin went there?"

"It was. It was a set-up. The sales listing was rescinded the next day. We have been watching the place since Tara and Nicholai vanquished him."

"Vanquished? Hardly."

"To win a battle is to win a battle, no matter how small or insignificant you may think the victory."

"And the war?"

He watched Dmitri's face tighten. "That remains to be seen. If we do as we are expected and Alexi finds what he is searching for, I just may have to remove your offspring from this planet after all. Say another word and the car will stop. If it does, your chances at procreation will diminish. Greatly."

Oookkaay, so he didn't like the way the other man grinned as he uttered the threat. Charles liked his nether region just the way it was. Time to step back. "Do I at least get a last meal?"

"Certainly. Your choice. Burger King or Taco Bell."

Someday, Charles thought as he sulked. Someday, he was going to be treated with respect.

Chapter Seventeen

Two plane trips. Alexi sighed. He'd come close to kissing the ground as he got off the first plane, but the second? Elena gave his hand a squeeze of encouragement. To thank her, he lifted her hand to kiss her palm. She melted, her face becoming warm and soft and liquid. That he could give her such pleasure amazed him. That he did made him smile.

And right now he had little to smile about. He stared at the cell phone in his hand. The success of their mission had torn him in two. His next call would be to Ariel to advise her of the outcome of their mission. But his heart had no desire to travel up the Hudson River, needing instead to go south to the Jersey shore and to his brother.

Was there no end to the choices in his life? He had to wonder. He certainly had a penchant for putting himself in impossible situations. "Why, Elena? Why does it have to be this way? I keep asking myself if this is some kind of punishment for playing the fool."

"You can't ask yourself that question. It's not fair. You've done nothing wrong. These are trying times. Times of great courage. That's all."

"My head knows I have a duty. I know what I have to do. And yet, my heart lies with Nicholai."

She squeezed his hand again. "I told you once that I believed in you. I believe in you even more now."

"They'll never understand the power, Elena," he continued. "The Houses will fight each other as they have done for centuries, scrabbling and scrambling for what scraps they can get. With the hope that they come out with a piece of the bigger prize."

"I won't lie, Alexi. I do not understand your people. I don't understand the way they think. Our discovery is for everyone, not one House or another."

"I know," he concurred. "And by the time they get their act together, it may be too late."

She nodded. "I believe I also told you that you may be the one to pull them together."

"That's Nicholai," he scoffed. "Not me."

She rounded on him. "No, Alexi. You. Not your brother. You." Why did she believe in him? "Because of who you are, Alexi. You are the magician. If anyone can pull off the miracle of their cooperation, you can."

She didn't understand. She never would. But for her sake, he continued to think out loud. "All right, let's follow this through for a moment. They'll never truly trust each other, but let's just say I can get them all to call a truce. What then?"

"You tell them the truth."

"I tell them the truth," he repeated. "I tell them the Water is missing. I tell them the foundation of all they have known for all of their existence may be gone for good. What do you think they'll do then?"

She nodded. "I see your point. I suppose your first step is to keep them from panicking."

"Agreed. So I tell them about the mission I went on and that it was a success. But now I have to also tell them that I have no idea how the flakes will react. By themselves, they could be useless. Or they could be so powerful they will destroy anyone who comes in contact with them."

"Or they may be able to make more of the Water. But perhaps this time without the threat of death."

"Or the Water won't work at all. So what do you think they'll revert to?"

"Their own personal gain, I'm sorry to say."

"Exactly."

"Then they need to be made to see the truth. They face their own extinction if they do not cooperate."

"To do that, I'm going to have to find Han-Sing first. If I can, if I can at least find the Water, I'll have a chance at making them join together." Alexi threaded his hands through his hair. "God, I hope I'm not too late."

"Where will you start?" Elena asked. "Trying to find one being on a planet of so many. Even with the connection..." Her voice trailed off.

"I'm not sure."

"Use your instincts. They are your best asset. What do they tell you now?"

"To start thinking like my brother," Alexi answered without hesitation. "Han-Sing had to have gotten to the Chalice before Nicholai and Tara and removed the Water. Nicholai told me that the priest in the church said it was simply Holy Water in the Chalice that Tara used to defeat the Ancient one the first time."

"Do you think he hid it somewhere?"

"Probably. And he probably followed that old adage about hiding things in plain sight. But without knowing where, we'd be trying to find a needle in a haystack. I think our first stop is to talk to the priest. He's at the church up in New York State. Ummm, I think it was—yeah, St. Francis something or another. But I know where. Geneva, New York."

All of a sudden, Alexi noticed Elena had grown quiet. "What's wrong? Don't worry. We'll find him."

"I know. I have always believed in the goodness of faith."

"Then what's bothering you?"

He watched her frown. "People follow the path

they are meant to follow, Alexi. I can't go with you."

"What do you mean? I don't understand."

"I'm a healer, Alexi. You must follow the course that has been set for you. So must I. I must go to Tara and try to save Nicholai."

His eyes filled with tears. He couldn't believe she cared so much. He thought of the love that Nicholai and Tara shared and knew this was part of that love. Elena gave him a quizzical look back. Alexi's heart was beginning to tell him things he wasn't sure he could handle, certainly not when he was trying to make a decision about his brother's life.

Elena reached out a hand to grasp his. "You must have faith."

"I do. I was just—."

"I carry no child yet, Alexi, if that is what you fear." He looked at her in horror. Did she really think he'd thought she'd endanger the life of an unborn child? "Forgive me," she continued. "You took my meaning incorrectly. I simply meant you still have a bargain to fulfill."

He grinned. "I was trying to say thank you. But now that you've reminded me of my conjugal duties, perhaps you'd like a lesson on flying?"

She threw him a look. "Perhaps. Someday. But right now you have a phone call to make."

Indeed he did. And he had a feeling Ariel was not going to like his idea one iota.

****

Elena had never been near the ocean before. Listening to the constant roll of the waves soothed her in the same way as the lapping of the water against the shore of the lake soothed her. She marveled at Tara's home; the pieces, the statues, the items that all had special meaning or told a story. She thought of her spartan existence and realized that sometimes having things was better than not.

Walking into the solar, she watched Tara as she brushed the hair off her mate's forehead. So much love. Elena held onto that love. She held onto the hope in Tara's heart. She needed both desperately for she had no idea what she was about to do. Of course, intellectually, they all knew that. But Elena prided herself on being a healer, on being able to make the right decisions to save a life. Not end one.

Sylvana started crying and with a pang of envy she watched Tara pick the baby up. She carried no child in her womb yet. And that was probably a good thing. She had no concept of the power held inside the pouch she carried at her hip. She could feel the power; she could sense the power in Alexi, but the thought of harming an innocent by touching the contents... No, let Fate toy with her as it would.

Which left her right back at square one. Brew a tea or place one of the flakes in some water thereby, perhaps, creating the Water of Change? If she brewed a tea, how long did she let the leaf steep? Normally, the stronger the better. But now?

"Here," Tara said, coming up beside her. "Take Syl for me for a sec, would you?"

The baby smelled like babies do, fresh and clean, and Elena let herself drown in the goodness. When she lifted her head, Tara was standing there with a huge smile on her face. "I don't know what to do, sister."

Tara simply shook her head. The smile turned wry before leaving altogether. "Duh."

Elena watched as Tara reached into the refrigerator and pulled out a bottle. "But what if I—" She couldn't finish the rest of the thought.

"Doubt yourself and we lose," Tara rounded on her. "Hasn't any of Alexi rubbed off on you yet?"

Puzzled, Elena stared at her friend. "What do you mean?"

"Use your instincts. Go with your gut."

Astonished, Elena replied, "At a time like this? You would accept my best guess?"

"Of course." Tara shook her head again and took the baby back. "Because it's your guess. I believe in you. Just as I believe we'll win."

"I have faith."

"I know you do."

"But I'm not God."

"Exactly. That's why I accept that you can fail and that your best guess is worth a hundred, no a thousand, doctor's cures."

"Thank you," Elena breathed.

"No, Elena. Thank you."

Tara turned to leave and Elena could not stop the question. "Why do you feed Sylvana from a bottle?"

"She won't take my breast, Elena. She's human. I'm not."

Elena reached out and squeezed Tara's shoulder to help wipe away the pain. "You're very brave."

"So are you."

"I guess it's hard not to have any family around you."

"That's not true. My brother Morgan lives right here on the Island."

"He does?"

"He's special, you know? He lives with the nuns at the Retreat."

"I'm sorry."

"Don't be. I'm not. Just go for it, kiddo. I need my mate back."

Elena sat at the kitchen table for a long time staring at the pouch. She closed her eyes and tried to reach into her memories. What would Isobel do right now? She'd needed to make the same decision. Had Isobel hesitated? Or had desperation overridden her fears?

She imagined a pair of sturdy arms circling her

waist. She could almost feel the light kiss on the top of her head that ran all the way down to her toes. Then, as suddenly as she knew Alexi was with her, he was gone. But his care and concern lingered.

Use the love.

Was that the key? Isobel's love for her sister. Tara's love for Nicholai? Her love for Alexi?

Love? Was she certain?

Yes, from that devilish grin that melted her bones to her pride in knowing what strength it took for him to become the man he was now. He'd grown into what he thought he would never be, a leader able to make the most difficult of decisions. He'd become strong and true in his heart and his soul. Passionate beyond belief.

Yes, she was in love with him. Heart, soul, and body.

Use the love.

Elena opened the pouch. Her fingers tingled as they neared the leather. Thick and sturdy and weathered over countless years, the pouch had acted as some kind of insulator.

Closing her eyes, she let destiny guide her hand. As soon as she touched one of the objects inside, a jolt ran through her arm and into her brain. White light invaded and she fought to keep a hold of herself. She hung on, battling, fighting the power that tried to overwhelm. And once she knew she had won the battle, she opened her eyes again.

Her fingers were wrapped around a single Lorraine leaf.

The leaf pulsed with power, glowing blue and silver around the edges. This would be enough, more than enough, for her purpose.

From another satchel, Elena removed a bottle of water she'd taken from the lake. She'd always made her brews from the lake water and trusted it as none other. In a small pot, she brought the water to a boil.

Then she placed a leaf inside.

At first, nothing seemed to happen and Elena wondered if anything would. Then some of the color around the edges transferred into the water. Once the leaf stopped pulsing, she pulled it out and laid it on a towel to dry. It still glowed but seemed almost to rest now that its work was done.

She poured the water, now blue and silver, into a mug and let the mug cool before taking it to the solar. As she entered the room, she prayed that the love they carried would be enough.

****

A fire scorched his throat. He walked along a parched desert plain. He could feel his mate near him and he could hear her voice when she spoke to him. But he could not find her. He had no idea where he was.

Nicholai Valentin continued to walk. The scene never changed, the wind never ceased, always dry, and always dead. Nicholai knew an unending thirst. A physical one to be sure. The fire in his throat was real. But also a need to see something different, a piece of color, a hint of moisture, something, anything that would take him from his desolate journey.

All of a sudden the winds kicked up blowing bits of dust like tiny shards of glass. They stung, but he welcomed the pain. To feel pain meant he was still alive, still willing to fight to find his way home.

The ground began to shake. Small rumbles at first then deep tremors. He tried to keep his balance, but the shaking would not allow him to stand. He crawled, keeping his head low to shield his eyes from the flying debris, and tried to find shelter.

Was this, then, the answer to all that he was? Reduced to crawling like a blind man with no direction and no way to find one? Was this the lesson he needed to learn? How the pride must fall in order to be reborn again?

How many times had Stefano told him? Over and over again. Not to let his emotions get the best of him. His only answer was that he did not understand how trying to destroy something as evil as the Ancient one could be so wrong.

Of course it wasn't. But by not using his head, by not waiting, by jumping before finding how deep the hole was—well, that put the entire Nobility in jeopardy.

To err is human. At one point he would have uttered the words with the greatest disdain. Now he could not. He'd made a mistake, a human mistake, and he was stuck in the middle of the consequences.

As the dust swirled and bit at him, he choked on that error, swallowed what was left of his pride, and prayed he could find a way out of the mess he'd created.

All of a sudden, a warm liquid slid down his throat. No longer parched, he gulped and gulped. Just in the nick of time. Tea to go with his humble pie.

Chapter Eighteen

Charles shivered in spite of the warmth of the spring sun. Weeds grew over the high brick walls and nearly covered the metal gate in front of him. Thick grass grew rampant over the grounds making him wonder how anything lived in this environment. He'd never thought he'd live to see the day he'd enter this house. But that was the point, now wasn't it? He was dead already. So was Dmitri.

His skin crawled just standing there, tiny ants with sharp pincers attacking him just beneath the surface. Didn't Dmitri know fear? He had to guess not, for the man just shoved him aside, broke the chain that held the gate together, then swung the pieces apart like he flippin' owned the place.

Charles could only stare. He certainly knew how to appreciate a decent pair of balls even if he really didn't have any of his own. After all, he liked to think of himself as the brains behind the scenes, not the brawn. But Dmitri bordered on, well, he had only two words: stupidity or courage.

Right now he chose stupidity.

"He's not here," Charles told his compatriot in crime.

"How do you know?"

The question was asked with just the right amount of impatience. Just enough to really aggravate an already impossible situation. "Because I'm not the bravest individual in the world. And when he's around, I'm scared shitless. Does that answer your question?"

Did they all do this just to make him suffer? If

anything, he knew he was a realist. He knew what he was. He knew his attributes. He knew his faults. He certainly knew his shortcomings. And he knew when it was smart to fear. And right now, he was at the head of his class.

"You're sure?" Dmitri questioned again.

Talk about a good working relationship. "Look, you can go and search the grounds if you don't believe me."

"Don't mind if I do," Dmitri answered. "And you can come with me. I wouldn't want you to get lonely."

"Gee, thanks."

What had once been a stately home, in the fashion of a Southern mansion, now reeked of decay. Not that stones or wood could feel. But somehow the Ancient one had even been able to suck the life out of those inanimate objects for the house seemed worse than dead to him with no hope of life ever returning to it.

They covered the grounds with a thoroughness that had him clenching his teeth in exasperation. But he had to give Dmitri a little bit of credit. He was trying to plan. The man made note of all the windows and doors and what rooms they were in as they circled the house.

He also gave him a silent pat on the back for stepping back when he reached out to open the door. "I tried to tell you."

Dmitri took a deep breath. "I have never been afraid of anything in my life," he said as he exhaled. Charles watched him take another breath then reach out again. He was impressed. He had to give the man his due. Courage. Definitely, courage. Foolhardy, but courageous. Because Charles certainly didn't want to touch that doorknob.

He knew the feeling. Like stepping into a pit of snakes, slithering and sliding all around, nowhere to step, no way to escape. One false move and who knew which one would end his life.

The door unlocked and opened as soon as Dmitri turned the knob. As they entered, Dmitri checked a wall fixture to see if the lights worked. They didn't. "He is waiting for darkness to fall. I don't want him to have that advantage. Let's see if we can get the lights going."

They spent the next couple of hours doing just that. The blaze of light from the hallway was a welcome sight, even for Charles. "You know, you're pretty sure he's going to be here."

"He knew of our presence the minute I touched the door."

"But that doesn't answer the why."

"At best, a thirst for knowledge. He wants to know what we know. At worst, curiosity. After all, we are playthings to him, are we not?"

"Yeah, but I was hoping—." Charles stopped speaking, frozen by the chill in his bones.

"What?" the Ancient one drawled.

A frisson of fear ran up his spine. He'd been hoping to cut and run. "Oh, I don't know. Invite you to a garden party. Have tea on the verandah. How about this? Let's all have a rousing game of Canasta."

The Ancient one laughed. "Charles, my old friend. How I have missed you. Especially your wit."

Yeah, well I haven't missed you. Out loud he answered, "Sorry. Social schedule from hell. What can I tell you?"

"That you'll be seeing that named place very shortly."

"Does that mean you don't want to make a play date?"

He really hated the guy's smile. Gave him the utter creeps. "And you, Dmitri? Are you ready to join your friend there?"

"Not what I had in mind."

How did that man keep his tone so even, so unaffected? "I came here to make a deal, not spew social drivel. So let's get on with it, shall we?"

"A deal? How interesting? Is this true, Dmitri Konin?"

Dmitri nodded. "You want the Water. We know where Han-Sing is."

"And you expect me to believe you are willing to sell out the Nobility? I mean, Charles I can understand. He'd sell his own mother for the right price. But you?"

Charles breathed an inner sigh of relief as the Ancient one turned his attention to Dmitri. He could only hold the evil one at bay for so long. He was insidious, trying to search the maze Charles had erected in his mind. But he'd seen the tic. The little tic in his cheek that let Charles know all was not paradise in the Garden of Evil.

"You know why I'm here," Dmitri answered.

"Any why you'll never procreate."

Charles' jaw dropped. Dmitri gay? Impossible. Or was it?

"Do we have a deal?" Dmitri asked in a clipped tone.

"How much, Charles?" the Ancient one turned to ask him.

He let the man see a picture of his current digs then smiled. "Enough is not enough."

Man, that laughter of his really went through a spine. "Why are you so easy to please, Charles?"

"No particular reason."

"And you Dmitri?"

"You have no idea what I want, so don't even try."

An awed Charles watched Dmitri's expression change. He'd never seen the man soften, ever. So whatever he was promising Dmitri, the Ancient one had Konin's number to be sure.

"Done deal." The Ancient one clapped his hands then rubbed them together. The sound echoed in the same way a nail must have sounded, hammered into the wood of a coffin. "You have twenty-four hours."

"Agreed," Dmitri replied.

Now that was just wonderful. A time limit. They had to be crazy. "Hey boss man? You think we could make that forty-eight? We may have some transportation issues. I sure as heck don't want to lose my life because a flight got delayed or something like that, you know?

The Ancient one considered the request then nodded. "I'll be waiting."

As soon as their nemesis was gone, Charles rounded on Dmitri. "I don't know what he promised you, but—."

"I had to be convincing."

"You didn't have to put a time limit on it, did you?"

"I saw no reason not to."

That was just peachy. "So you thought it would be acceptable to cut our legs off at the knees. Man, I hope you have your affairs in order. You just signed our death warrants."

"Have faith, Charles. We're not dead yet."

Frankly, he didn't have any. Which was why his next thought was how hot it really was in hell.

****

Alexi wondered if they could turn the heat up any more as he sat in the vestibule of the church. He worked at the collar of his shirt.

"Would you like a glass of water?"

"That would be nice."

She handed him a paper cup. "Thank you, umm—."

"Rita."

He nodded and drank the contents in two gulps.

174

As he was throwing the paper in the trash Rita said, "Mr. Valentin? Father Jim will see you now."

"Thanks."

He walked down a narrow hallway and through a set of old, dark stained wood doors into an even older looking office. The room reminded him of a library, cluttered but with its own sense of order. "Good to see you again, Mr. Valentin."

Again? Wait a minute. The man thought he was Nicholai. Did he play it straight or pretend? "I'm sorry, but you have me confused with my brother, Nicholai. My name is Alexi."

"I beg your pardon," the priest stammered. "So now you will have to forgive me. I thought I was meeting your brother to see about joining our parish. Did you wish to join also?"

Alexi frowned. "Look, padre. I don't have time to beat around the bush. You know exactly who and what I am, so let's cut the bull and get to the point."

The elder gentleman leaned back in his chair, clearly unhappy about the situation. "Very well."

"You had an arrangement with a gentleman. He asked you to keep a certain item safe. In return, you received what I am sure were very generous donations to your parish."

The man nodded, his face totally serious. But there was also another fear in his gaze. Did Han-Sing have something else to hold over the man's head? "Continue."

"He contacted you not long before my brother and his wife came here."

"He did."

"Did he say anything different? Do anything out of the ordinary?"

"Not that I recall."

"I need the number you used to contact him."

"I can't give it to you."

"I'll take it if I have to. You know I can."

"My son, you seem under a great deal of duress. Perhaps—."

Alexi never let him finish the sentence. He jumped out of his seat, slammed his hands down on the man's desk, and leaned over so his face was only inches away from Father Jim's. "Don't play with me, padre. One touch and I'll know everything anyway. And I won't be kind with the knowledge. So we either do this the easy way or the easier way."

"All right, all right." Father Jim cringed but backed down. "It's not necessary. Here is the number. It belongs to a cell phone. I have called several times. There has been no answer."

Alexi sat back down and wrote the number on a piece of paper. Then he asked, "Why?"

"Why, what?"

"Why did you call the number?"

"Because a day or two ago I knew something was wrong."

"What do you mean, wrong?"

A wind, like the one that blew up when your brother was here, passed over the church. Scared me half to death."

"Do you know why that wind passed over the church?"

"As a priest, I suppose I have an intuition about evil. That wind was evil."

Alexi processed that statement for a moment. It was also possible that the priest had some Noble blood in him and didn't know it. "Anything else?"

"Only that your friend is a very nervous man. I don't want to know why. Especially with the way things have happened. But I'm very concerned. He usually comes back by now."

"Wait a minute. I don't understand. Comes back?"

"Yes. When he comes, he contacts me. He has over the years. I'm used to a pattern."

"A pattern? How?"

"He would either make a withdrawal or a deposit."

"Like a bank?"

"I suppose you could say that."

Alexi tried to process that statement. A safe house? Did that mean there were others? Could they all be churches? It was possible. "Thank you, Father Jim. And I'm sorry I had to get tough with you. Trying times require dire measures." Alexi held out his hand as he rose.

Father Jim shook it. "Have patience. Han-Sing will show up. He always has."

Not this time, Alexi thought to himself. He smiled at Rita as he walked out and she rose, motioning to him to follow her in silence. "Mr. Valentin?" she asked when they were out of the rectory. "I couldn't help but overhear."

He felt a bit sheepish. "Sorry about that. But I've got some problems that need to be fixed pronto."

"I understand."

"You do?"

"Yes, you see, Father Jim doesn't know it, but I know the man you're looking for."

"You do?"

"Yes. I caught him in the sacristy one day. At first I thought he was a thief. Then he explained that we were holding something very sacred to his family and his people. I didn't want to know what it was. Then he told me I could help. He gave me this and told me if anyone came looking for him, with, well—."

Alexi grinned and his hand strayed to one of his slightly pointed ears. "Yeah, I guess they're a bit unique."

She handed him a piece of paper.

Alexi's heart soared. "Thank you, Rita."

"He really was a nice man. I'll pray that he's all

right."

"Thank you."

She looked at him and gave him a bit of smile. "Go with God, Mr. Valentin."

"You, too."

Funny, he thought as he got into his car. She'd meant it. Then he realized he was still wearing the cross Elena had given him.

He looked at the piece of paper in his hand then tried to steady the trembling. Printed in Han-Sing's handwriting were the words: St. Francis DeSales.

Chapter Nineteen

Elena looked over to see Tara sit down next to Nicholai. The sister she never had but wanted very much was near the breaking point. Elena's heart wrenched at the sight of Tara's slumped shoulders.

Elena wanted to speak. She wanted to explain. But what was there to explain? All the hope, all the promise, all the expectation. Gone. "Tara, I—."

The woman swung around with such agony on her face, Elena couldn't continue. At first, as she searched, she'd felt Nicholai's essence. Elena truly thought she would be able to guide him to light. Then time passed. And more time. And he didn't awaken.

When Tara turned away, Elena's heart broke. She'd failed but didn't know why. The leaves never failed. Ever. The fault had to be hers somehow. Was her faith not strong enough? Her love for Alexi too new to be tested?

Failure.

The word pounded inside her brain. Worse still, the word became a stake in her heart as she watched Tara crawl inside herself from the grief. Elena was so immersed in her own misery she jumped when the telephone rang. As it continued to ring, Elena realized Tara had reached defeat. "Hello?"

"Elena? What are you doing answering the phone? Has something happened? Is Nicholai—?" She heard the catch in Alexi's voice and her misery increase ten-fold. "Is he dead?"

Oh God, she hadn't even considered that a possibility. "No, Alexi. He's not dead."

"Thank Goodness," he breathed.

"He is—."

"What?" Alexi cried, interrupting her.

"Unchanged," she sighed. "I have failed, Alexi."

A long silence ensued, one she never wanted to hear again. "Do you know what went wrong?"

His tone was so cold, so bleak. "No. I wish I did."

"Wishes aren't good enough."

"I tried my best, Alexi. My best wasn't good enough. The power of the leaf wasn't strong enough." *My faith was not strong enough.*

He heard her unsaid words. She was certain he did. Yet he refused to answer them. The fault was hers. "Where's Tara?"

"She sits by Nicholai and doesn't move. Even the baby's cries have little effect."

Another silence she'd rather forget. "I'm on my way. But I need you to do something for me first."

"Anything." Anything to redeem myself.

"Go to the computer in the den." Elena followed his instructions. "Is it on?"

"Yes, it is."

"Good. Get on the Internet. I need you to Google something for me."

"Google?"

"It's a search engine," he explained. "A way of finding information quickly."

"I see." It took a few minutes but she finally got to the website.

"Put in St. Francis DeSales Churches."

Could his tone seem any colder, any more sterile? So businesslike as if they had never shared an intimate moment. "There are so many."

His sigh reverberated through the phone. "I'll call Ariel. We'll have to narrow the search to the New York metropolitan area first. Han-Sing lived in New Jersey but also had an apartment in the city. I'm going to venture a guess and say he hid the

Water nearby so he could gather it quickly and get out of town fast. Where's the one in New Jersey?"

"Vernon." She frowned. "Alexi, I don't understand. What did you find?"

Another silence. Her stomach fell as the thought that he didn't trust her anymore hit home. "We've been thinking that the Water is in one container or only in one source. What if it isn't? I think Han's idea was to minimize the risk so he split the Water up into smaller quantities and hid them individually."

"Then they could be anywhere."

"You would think that. But when I talked to Father Jim he said Han would show up every couple of years and either bring the Water or take it away. Like making deposits and withdrawals at a bank."

"So you believe he continually shifted hiding places."

"Yes."

"But how did you narrow down the search to these churches?"

"He had to have some kind of a network with a common theme. Why he chose these particular churches, we'll never know. The only reason we do is because he left a clue with the secretary at the rectory."

"Why not the priest?"

"Because Father Jim is the first person the Ancient one would question if he ever tracked the Water down."

"He never did the first time."

"Because Tara and Nicholai got there before he could."

"But why not now? As we did?"

"Because the Ancient one is waiting for us to go find the Water for him. He's letting us do his work."

A very bad feeling seeped into her bones. "Then aren't you leading him right to it?"

"I suppose. But hopefully only one small piece. He may never know about the connection between the churches."

"He'll find out eventually. You know he will."

"Do you have a better suggestion?"

"I think I do." Would he trust her? After all that had happened?

"Okay. Talk to me."

"Don't call Ariel. All the Ancient one knows is that you went to this particular church. It would make sense to him."

"Go on."

"Get some of your people to hide Father Jim and his secretary. Then start your search. Quietly."

"What about Dmitri and Charles?"

"Tell them to meet us at Nicholai's home."

Another silence. Yet this one seemed to hold a faint sense of hope. "All right. I'll send for Sergei. He's at our apartment in the city. He'll make the arrangements then it would be easiest for him to start at the church you said was in New York."

"Belle Harbor."

"Got it. I'll go to Vernon."

"I'll meet you there." Oh how his hesitation cut like a knife. Yet she deserved no less. "I know my way around churches better than you. Besides, I'm a woman."

"That explains a lot."

"Women have latent detective tendencies. We have to. We bear children." *Smile, Alexi. Oh God, please smile. Let me know I haven't lost you completely.*

"I'm about two, maybe two and a half hours away." She read him the directions, which repeated several times. "Got 'em."

"I'll see you there."

He clicked off without answering and her heart fell. She rose and the pain in her bones seeped straight into her soul. She put on her cloak, found Tara's car keys, and left the house. Tara never acknowledged her going. Never before had she felt so alone as she did when the door closed behind her. Failure was such a lonely place to be and her chance at redemption was slim at best. Could things get any worse?

****

Alexi pulled into the church parking lot feeling raw. He'd never counted on anyone, always kept himself away from that kind of entanglement. Now he knew why. Counting on people meant hoping they didn't let you down. Invariably, they did.

He watched Elena struggle to get out if the car. His heart clenched then he dismissed the pain. She was still the most beautiful creature he'd ever seen. But for all her beauty, inside and out, she hadn't been able to finish the show, master that last trick.

He shook his head. Bitterness wasn't going to get him anywhere. She'd tried, hadn't she? Nicholai was still alive, wasn't he? Alexi never quite understood the word disappointment before. He did now. "Elena."

Her gaze begged him to forgive her. But there was nothing to forgive. "I took the liberty of going inside while I waited for you to arrive," she said. "No one seems to be about at the moment."

"Let's take a look around."

"They will not think we are trespassing?"

"We have to get caught first." She looked at him as if something were missing then lowered her gaze. Sure, something was missing, but he didn't have much to smile about right now.

The church was small and sort of modern, made mostly of wood and glass. "Looks like something out of the seventies," Alexi commented and they walked around the building.

"Eighties, actually. I took the liberty of looking

up the history of the church before I left. They seem to have joined with another congregation. Our Lady of Lourdes."

"Does that mean anything?"

"I'm not sure. It may." She stopped walking and reached out to stop him. Her hand burned through his sleeve. All of him wanted her with a hunger that left him breathless. In spite of being on the grounds of a church. In spite of feeling so hollow inside, he didn't know if he'd ever find his insides again.

"Look," she breathed.

Alexi didn't understand. They'd followed a path and now stood before a statue set inside a curved rock wall. "I don't get it. A statue. I guess you'd call this a grotto."

"Our Lady of Lourdes. Water. Do you *get it* now?

Bell ringing time. Of course. But where? They were on a stone path with a rock wall made of hundreds of stones. A small container of water could be hidden anywhere. "Yeah, but getting it and finding it are two different things."

"Let me think a moment." He watched her walk up to the statue then kneel down on the hard stones in front. His gut wrenched from pain at the sight. He was being unfair to her but didn't know how to stop. He kept hitting that empty hole in his soul, the one he hated feeling so much that he avoided the possibility of ever being let down.

"The statue won't talk to you."

"Don't be too sure of that. Having faith is better than not having faith."

"Even when that faith fails you?"

She closed her eyes at the sting of his words, but instead of protesting, simply bent her head. As he looked on, her countenance changed, softened, and he marveled that she could find solace in whispered words. He didn't understand that ability, probably never would. "Faith is always there, Alexi. Waiting for us. Sometimes finding that faith is the hardest part. Sometimes holding onto that faith is even harder." She struggled again to rise and this time he reached out to help. He knew she was in constant pain so he let his hand linger to give her some ease. "Thank you," she added, taking a deep breath. "The lady is the key."

"Why do you say that?"

She switched gears on him. "Tell me about Han-Sing. What was he like?"

He had to wonder for a moment if she wasn't losing it. She gave him a wry smile and he shrugged. "Very straightforward. No bullshit kinda guy. Nervous. Smoked like a fiend. He'd be dead right now if he wasn't a True Noble."

"Put yourself in his shoes for a moment," she encouraged. "Would you want this task?"

He shook his head. "No way. So let's try to think like him. Let's see. Smart. Smart enough to split the Water and minimize the risk. Smart enough to change hiding places but have one central theme so one clue would create a domino effect and lead us where we needed to go. Smart enough to make the task look impossible but still keep it simple. Yup. You're right. That would be the statue. Let's take a look."

Because of his height, Alexi started at the top of the statue while Elena checked the base. True to her word, she examined every nook and cranny like a detective straight out of one of those crime shows on television.

All of a sudden, Elena whipped her head around. "Someone is coming."

She flipped up her hood and struggled to her knees again. He stood behind her and laid a hand on her shoulder. To the outside eye, they looked as if they were praying to the statue. Alexi even bent his head and closed his eyes to make their act more realistic. The footsteps stopped and began retreating. Alexi sneaked a quick peak. All he caught was the sight of black pants and a black coat out of the corner of his eye. Probably the pastor or a priest not wishing to intrude.

"He is gone," she told him a moment later.

Alexi helped her to get up. She had a huge smile on her face as he did. "What?"

"Come. Look." Right at her eye level as she kneeled was a basin made out of the statue's cupped hands. A crack ran along the entire circumference of the top of the bowl. Alexi had a small pocketknife on his key chain and began loosening the plaster of the basin. Elena lifted one side, he lifted the other. Underneath rested not a container but a vacuum-sealed bag that surrounded a smaller bag, and a smaller bag.

In his excitement at their discovery, Alexi missed one very important fact. One which hit him like a ton of bricks. He felt nothing. No power, no zing, no life, nothing. He glanced at Elena's face and knew the truth. Decoys. Probably all of them. Han-Sing had led them on a wild goose chase. Another maze within a maze. But now time was running out. And failure just wasn't an option anymore.

Chapter Twenty

Tara was beyond tired. Throughout her life, she'd fought, kicked, scratched, and clawed. Defeat never occurred to her. But there had only been one of her in those days. Now there were three.

At first she'd held onto hope as one would a lifeline. Missing Nicholai was like missing most of her heart and all of her soul. Even the abject joy of her daughter could not bring her to a place where she could simply exist. He was her. She was him. They were bound beyond life.

Which was why she felt like she was dying.

Lifting her head, Tara realized Elena was gone. It didn't matter where. Nothing mattered anymore. Even Sylvana failed to spark any interest. She rose, went through the mechanical motions, fed, changed, and cared for her baby. She would hold her in her arms, rocking her, wishing she could sink inside her child and find some life. A spark. Anything. Even anger. Not this gray, marshmallow funk she was drowning in.

Her funk was the reason she didn't hear the doorbell ringing until Syl started to cry.

Thinking Elena had returned Tara rose to answer the door. Her jaw dropped when she saw who was standing before her. "Morgan?"

His face scrunched and her brother shuffled his weight from side to side. Tara shook her head. He would never change, could never change. His mind was slow, but he was so very special. Opening the door, she ushered him inside the house. "What is it, Morgan? Are you in trouble?"

He carried a messenger bag over his shoulder, which he lifted off and over his head. "Is there something in the bag, Morgan? Something for me?"

He nodded yes, then no. Typical Morgan. Tara thought back to the one time he was lucid and pain knifed her already damaged heart. He kept shifting his weight between his feet, a sure sign that he was excited. "You...need."

True. She needed many things. First and foremost, her mate back in her arms where he belonged. But, she smiled, her first true smile in a long time, she also needed Morgan. He was her brother. Her flesh and blood. In spite of his problems, he loved her. "I need *you*."

Tara hugged him. He never usually hugged back. Never realized he was supposed to, she guessed. But it didn't matter. He smelled of the sea and the convent and both brought back untold memories.

As she let go of him, the hand clutching the bag lifted towards her. "You...need," he insisted.

She sighed. He wouldn't stop until she acknowledged what he wanted her to acknowledge. She wondered for a moment if that was good or bad. Being of single-minded purpose could probably be both, so she took the bag out of his hand. Inside rested a piece she was very familiar with; the casket that held the Chalice that held the Water of Change. "Morgan, you shouldn't have brought this here. You're supposed to keep it hidden, safe, at the Retreat. You must take it back this instant."

He shook his head. "You...need."

Oh, Morgan, she thought. So beautiful in your simplicity. "Sweetheart, no. The Chalice isn't strong enough. The Water from inside the Chalice isn't strong enough."

He shook his head again, his movements becoming more agitated. She sensed his frustration, could feel her own welling inside. Damned delayed relay switch. Communicating with him was the challenge of all challenges sometimes. "Go slow, Morgan. Take your time."

He swallowed. "Inside. Inside."

Tara figured she'd better go along. She took the case and brought it over to her dining room table. She opened the lid, her heart in her throat. There was no telling what Morgan was capable of. However, she breathed a sigh of relief, the Chalice wasn't inside, for which she was extremely grateful. "Now what, Morgan? I don't see anything. I don't know what you want me to see."

She did, however, feel. Since she'd already come in contact with the casket, she knew the power it exuded. But this was different. Stronger. Which made her curious. "Inside," he repeated.

She watched in fascination as his fingers trailed over the outside edges of the wood and inlaid silver and gold. A lover's caress, she thought. His fingers touched the carved out portion that would hold the Chalice and his face softened. Tara likened the expression on his face to that of a drug addict getting that first taste of being high again. Could that be? It was certainly possible. The only time he'd ever been lucid was when he received the power of the Water from the case.

Funny, but the power, although well remembered, seemed much more real to her. The thrum and tingle. Growing until all she felt were the surges running through her body.

She shook her head. She wasn't imagining the power. Thousands of tiny sparks jumped from synapse to synapse all through her. More powerful than the Sun. More powerful than she remembered. "Morgan? What did you do?"

Did she dare to hope? Did she dare to question?

Inside, he'd said. Could there be something

189

hidden inside? Tara searched along the outer edges and felt for a catch of some kind. As she slid her finger along, she pushed, and all of a sudden the portion that held the outline of the Chalice sprang open. "Hidden inside?"

He smiled. Such a beautiful smile.

Tara lifted the piece with trembling hands. Like turning the page of a book, the case opened on a hidden binding. The thrum increased ten-fold and Tara staggered back. Taped to the underside of the wood rested a plain silver flask.

Morgan's gaze cleared as he touched the flask. "The ability to be with you is getting harder, Tara."

"This is the true Water, isn't it?"

He nodded. "Use it as you see fit, sister. I know you will do what is right. For all."

So many questions. So many questions that would go unanswered for as soon as his fingers left the flask, the clarity of his gaze declined. "I love you, Morgan."

"I love you too, Tara. Time grows short. He is fading."

So was her brother. Reaching up, she kissed Morgan on the cheek. "Thank you."

Tara knew now she couldn't do this alone. She sent out a silent call to the only being on this earth that she trusted to heal her mate—Elena.

****

Elena sensed the power even before she got out of the car. She turned off the ignition, opened the door, and got out. The metal of the car was cold, very cold, in contrast to the air around her. The air shimmered with fire and she let the heat of it seep into her bones. The pain of humanity melted in its wake. She stood and straightened, knowing the force she felt exceeded even her wildest imagination.

Alexi pulled his vehicle beside hers. He got out of his car, his face intent with what seemed to be a different purpose. As he staggered, his gaze flew to hers. Inside she read a thousand questions she could not answer. Those rested with Tara and Nicholai.

"A moment. That's all I ask. We need to talk."

Aghast, Elena simply stared at him. "Your brother's cure lies but a few feet away and you wish to talk?"

"Yes," he confessed, raking his hands through his hair. "Two plus hours in a car is a long time to think."

"Think later." She turned and he stepped in front of her.

"Elena, please. You must listen." He took a deep breath and the words all came out in a jumbled rush. "I was wrong."

"Of course you were." And standing there wasn't going to change anything, she thought to herself.

She sidestepped around him and began a gaited walk-run towards the house. He caught up with her after only a few steps and tried to slow her down. "That's it? No I-told-you-so's?"

"Alexi," she cried, exasperated beyond belief. "We don't have time. This isn't about you anymore. It's about your brother." She made a circle around him and tried to continue on her way. "Besides, when I leave you alone to figure things out, you eventually get them right."

He caught up with her again and started helping her up the stairs. "I'm not used to caring."

"I know."

"So I'm not used to people letting me down."

"You will learn. Now will you please let me go? I failed once. I do not wish to do so again."

He stopped her on the landing of the stairs. "Failed? I think you got that backwards. I failed you, not the other way around."

He didn't let her answer. His head bent and the next thing she knew, his mouth covered hers. She couldn't help herself. She melted. He was liquid fire, even more potent than the air around them. As his tongue mated with hers, she sighed. Her body rested right where it needed to be. But this was madness. Time was running out. Nicholai needed, well, he needed both of them.

"Alexi. We are not important right now," she told him, tearing her mouth from his. "Please. I beg of you. We must go inside."

"Only if you forgive me."

"That will take longer. And will not happen at all if you do not release me this instant."

He nodded and stepped back. "All right. But we're not finished yet."

"Not by a very long shot," she agreed.

A moment later she reached Tara's door, Alexi following right behind her. She rang the bell and he pounded on the door.

"Tara. Open up," he called.

"Can you save him?" Tara asked as she let them in.

"He is fading."

Fear racked her gaze. "I know. What do you need me to do?"

Elena reached out and gathered Tara in her arms. "Love him. Believe in the power of goodness."

"You didn't say believe in me," Tara remarked as she let go.

Elena smiled. Learning lessons was hard for all of them. "I'm a vessel, Tara. I can't be more."

Tara nodded and Elena ran-walked into the dining room. She walked over to the table, unable to catch her breath. So this was the Water they spoke of. The beat of all Life pulsed within it.

All of a sudden, she noticed a young man standing next to her. Extremely close, as a matter of fact. Her gaze flew to Tara's. "My brother, Elena. This is Morgan."

The resemblance was easy to see. Elena held out her hand in greeting, confused when he didn't take it in his grasp. She looked at Tara who merely shrugged then back to Morgan who simply stared. Yet, instead of dropping her hand, she reached out to grasp his anyway. As she did, she knew his true nature immediately. Morgan's impairment hid an exceptionally gifted mind.

I don't know what to do, she confessed.

Do what you do best, healer, he answered.

But how, she wondered? The connection between them faded just as quickly as it had come. Elena knew she had to go with her instincts. "Alexi. Get my pouch. Take out one leaf. Tara, I'll need a small pot. One to boil the Water in. And a towel of some kind.

Tara handed her a dishtowel. She used the cloth to open the flask and poured out about half the contents into the pot. Then she let Alexi add the Lorraine leaf. The leaf glowed very brightly then faded, but the colors remained sharper, clearer, richer. She closed the flask and replaced the container inside the casket. Then she closed both the inside portion and the lid. The aura weakened considerably. Obviously the case acted as an insulator of some kind.

Elena took the pot back to the kitchen and brought the contents to a boil.

"Look," Alexi cried. He grabbed her hand, holding her fingers tight.

The leaf began to pulse and glow, like that of a heartbeat. Or perhaps she was simply too nervous to separate her own heartbeat from the leaf.

After a while, however, the Water began to change color. Where once the leaf glowed blue as the daytime sky of summer, it now glowed as green as a field of grass. Once the change was complete, the leaf pulsed no more.

Elena turned off the heat then went to the cabinet for a mug. She poured the water into the mug then put it on the counter to cool. She turned and realized Tara's brother wasn't in the room. "Morgan is gone?

Tara nodded. "He is so locked inside himself."

"He brought the Water, didn't he?" Alexi asked.

"Yes."

"Where did he get it from?" Elena wondered out loud.

Tara shrugged. "I don't know. I'm not sure we'll ever know. It's getting harder and harder to reach him."

"The churches were just decoys," Alexi told Tara.

"That makes sense. More sense than you would think." She walked over to Nicholai who seemed to be resting easier. "Go for it, sister."

Elena shook her head. "Sorry. I think this one is yours."

Tara's hands trembled as they took the mug from her. Her eyes widened at the power between her fingers. "Nico, I love you with every breath my body takes. I need you back where you belong. Please come to me." Alexi lifted his brother's head and Tara began spoon-feeding him the liquid. She went slowly, barely wetting his mouth at first. When Nicholai swallowed, she would give him a little more, then a little more after that.

Elena closed her eyes. She searched for Nicholai's light. She could feel him near. "I'm not the one to guide him, Tara. You are." She looked over at Alexi. "You both are."

She stepped back and away and let them in. The sin of pride was a cold sin and she refused to allow her pride get in the way of what needed to be done. In truth, she was just that. A vessel. She was not the one who had the power to heal. That power channeled through her. And she was thankful for the opportunity to remember it.

"He's not coming around," Alexi said, dismay in his voice.

"I didn't expect him to. Not right away. He, too, has to find himself, find his way back to us. You must have faith, Alexi. When you stand at that cross-road, when you believe all is lost, when you cry out at the injustice of the world or ask why did this have to happen now, happen to me, happen to my family; look inside yourself and you will see the truth. There is right in this life and there is wrong. We fight the wrong because we believe in the right. We continue to fight because we have hope that we will win. Don't give up. Faith is your sword. Hope, your eternal light. Believe, Alexi. Believe."

Chapter Twenty-One

Time passed with the speed of a giant turtle. Each second lumbered into the next until Alexi thought he'd go mad. Energy from the Water raced through his veins. He stood. He sat. He paced. Fear seared his heart. Why didn't Nicholai wake up?

Elena asked him to believe. He wanted to. He tried. In his heart, he knew they'd done all they could. The rest was up to his brother. Still, Alexi wanted to do something more. Anything.

Dammit, Nico, quit f—ing around.

Alexi needed to get out. He walked to the closet, threw on his overcoat, and left the house. He heard Elena follow. Part of him wanted her to follow, part did not. But he was already alone with his thoughts so staying that way wasn't going to help.

After living in the desert for so long, Alexi wasn't used to the dampness of the sea air. He shivered in spite of the fire in his blood. The Sun had already set, the sky striped with pink and gold, while he stood surrounded by the deepening dusk. He knew the exact moment she joined him, he would always know.

She didn't speak, didn't have to. She clasped his hand with hers and squeezed. He held on, needing her just to be there with him.

He wasn't sure why he started walking. He simply headed to the stairs, pulling Elena with him. She hesitated then nodded. A few minutes wouldn't hurt.

Tara's townhouse complex extended out over the bay so Alexi started walking in that direction. To his right, he noticed a large amusement complex. He tried to imagine being on this island in the middle of summer. He guessed there couldn't be a better time to be alive.

Alexi had no idea why he stopped, he had no plan to pull her into his arms, but the action was so right he wondered why he'd waited until now to do it. She opened her mouth in surprise and he took full advantage.

Without realizing, Alexi had headed towards the amusement park. Part of the park rested on planked pylons made of stilts, the same wood he'd seen houses rest upon. The outside pieces were cut like a fence and set next to one another to create a wall.

He pushed her back until she stood against the wood. He took both her hands in his, spreading her arms, and pinning them to the wall. This left Elena spread-eagled and defenseless. Of course, he knew better. But the pose suited his male vanity. He wanted control of something in his world.

Alexi decided he wanted company in his misery. He ravaged her mouth, drawing every spark of response he could out of her. He didn't lift his head until her chest heaved against his, until they were both breathing so hard, the very air swirled around them.

"Alexi," she protested. "We can't do this."

"Says who?"

"A police officer for one," she choked out.

She had a point. But Elena had also asked him to believe. He was sure he wasn't meant to walk around with a raging hard-on for the rest of the night. "Let him try."

He bent his head again, but Elena turned her face away. Oh well, he thought. He could play that game too. He kissed and nipped and sucked his way down the luscious curve of her neck.

"Alexi, please. This is not right."

He lifted his head. "What isn't right, Elena? That we should be making love? That we should be celebrating life when Nico's life hangs in the balance?"

The fire from the Water still burned intensely in his blood.

"Yes," she strangled out.

"That's where you're wrong." Alexi bent lower, still not releasing her hands, and suckled her breast through the cloth of her shirt. "You told me to believe. What better way is there to believe in life than to make love?"

The resistance in her body softened. She kissed his head. He would have smiled, but for the nipple he was worrying between his teeth.

"We can't do this here. We will get caught."

He chuckled. "Have faith, Elena. I'm a magician."

Her body shook with repressed laughter. "You're good. You're not that good."

He took that remark as a direct challenge. "You wanna make a bet?"

"No."

Because she knew she would lose. He couldn't resist her lips as they formed the little 'o' of the word and he kissed her senseless. But of course, now they had a very real problem to conquer. Public displays, even in deserted parking lots, could get them arrested.

He let go of her hands. "Slide your arms inside my coat."

He unbuttoned her coat and drew the material inside to make a tent of sorts.

"Alexi. You can't. Not here."

Rather enjoying her discomfort, Alexi grinned. "The parking lot is deserted, there are no lights. It's dark and getting darker by the minute. My coat is black, the piling is black. Someone would have to be on top of us to see."

His hand reached inside the material of her blouse and lifted her breast out of her bra. He played with her distended peak until he felt her relax once again. "Unbutton me."

"Alexi. You can't be serious."

His gaze, full of the fire burning in his blood, told her he was dead serious. "Unbutton me," he commanded.

Her hands reached for his belt. He sighed with relief. The strain on his erection had become painful. She wore a long skirt with boots for which he sent up a silent thank-you. Slacks or jeans would have been a whole 'nother ball game.

Once she released him, her hands made their own kind of magic. He shuddered as sensations streaked from his groin to his brain. Did she know what she did to him? Why he had no self-control? How a simple look from her could bring him to his knees?

He snared her gaze with his. She knew. He knew she knew by the impish grin she tried so very hard to hold in. Of course, two could play the game. He pulled on her nipple, rolling the flesh between his fingers and her knees buckled.

She came right back at him as her palm cupped him and began kneading his flesh.

Alexi lifted her skirt. He found a new barrier. Pantyhose? He groaned inwardly. Then his thought processes coalesced. What had he used earlier? His pocketknife.

While one hand fumbled for his keys, the other continued to lift her skirt. He took the knife, opened the blade, pulled the fabric away from her skin, and sliced along one of the seams.

Her eyes became liquid pools of heat. He dropped the keys to the ground, not caring about the noise they made. His fingers tore at the nylon, making the opening wide enough for him to gain full access. He found her core with unerring accuracy. She was so hot, so open, so ready for him.

Alexi wanted her, wanted to be inside her heated flesh. His guts wrenched with need. He spread her legs and lifted her up by her thighs, bracing them both against the wood of the pylons. Her hands clasped his shoulders for balance then wound around his neck as he lowered her, inch by tortuous inch, onto his shaft.

Her legs wound around his back and he lifted her, settling her core around him. They both sighed, the sound total completion. He didn't move at first, didn't dare, even though she began squirming in her need to feel. "Greedy little thing," he whispered.

Her answer was to clench her muscles all around him. Already too far-gone, Alexi groaned. He caught her gaze with his. She had pushed him to the brink. In about two seconds he was going to lose all control, any civilized veneer he thought he might have. When that happened, he was going to be no better than an animal.

"Bring it," she whispered in response.

A floodgate opened. He lifted her hips until she rested just at his tip then he impaled her to the hilt. He could feel no other sensation but the joining of their two bodies, slamming into her so hard the pylons shook.

Between the fire in his blood and the fire in his groin, Alexi was lost. His insides tightened, building an exquisite pressure. Indeed, holding onto that pressure became pleasure mixed with pain.

Her breath hitched. He spread her legs wider. He slammed into her with the force of a ram. He'd warned her. Yet her answer was to urge him on, crying out, even begging him for more.

He leaned his face into her neck. His mouth opened. He bit the soft skin. She screamed. She began to convulse all around him. His entire body focused on each thrust. Between her muscles contracting all around him and her heart reaching into his, Alexi exploded into her body with a mighty roar.

He lost track of time and space for a moment as his seed pumped into her body in a never-ending stream. The power of the Water coursed with it, but dulled in comparison to the realization that hit him. He loved her. As surely as his heart passed through his body into hers. He loved her. She was his rock, his foundation, his other half.

Aftershocks shuddered through him as he kept pulsing in the aftermath. "Wow," he breathed into her neck.

Her shoulders shook in silent laughter. "There are no words."

He looked down and saw his mark on her. "Umm, sorry about that." He lathed the spot with his tongue.

She shivered and he knew he could heat right up again. But they'd pressed their luck enough. "Did I hurt you?"

She seemed dazed. "No."

"Liar."

She tucked her head into his chest. "I never dreamed. I never knew." She shivered and he wasn't sure if the cause was sensation or cold or both. He disengaged from her and began to tuck her back together. "Umm, Alexi?"

He groaned. He'd heard the car approach. His back was to the street but he knew. He heard a window roll down and the static of a police car radio. "Excuse me."

Alexi turned his head. He kept their coats wrapped around them. He hadn't had time to put himself back together yet. "Yes, officer?"

Elena hid her head in his chest. Little coward.

"Aren't you two a little old to be making out on a sidewalk?" The officer sounded exasperated, but Alexi recognized a thread of laughter in his tone.

"Probably." Alexi sighed with relief. A few minutes earlier would have been a different story.

The man shook his head. "Do me a favor, will you? Go home or get a room. Okay?"

Alexi grinned. "You bet, officer."

The car pulled away and Alexi burst out laughing. The movement caused him to rub up against her which instantly created a response. "You're incorrigible."

"You're beautiful."

He tilted her chin up to his face. A kiss was not always just a kiss. He let his newfound knowledge melt into her being. Her breath caught. He so loved the way she did that. A little hitch of surprise. Of expectation. An I-can't-believe-you-really-want-me-that-much kind of hitch.

"I love you," she confessed.

The words soared through him. How had he gotten so lucky? In spite of all their trials, he'd found her. His mate. The one being he would love for all his life and beyond. "I know."

She reared back. "Just, I know?"

Alexi prided himself on being an actor. But this was one facade he couldn't hang onto. He cupped her face between his hands. "I don't know how it happened. I don't know why you do. I don't deserve you. But I love you. With every fiber of my being. I love you." He kissed her again to seal them together for all time.

"Alexi?" she asked, finally tearing her mouth from his. "I don't want the officer to return. Do you think you could, umm...?"

He laughed and pulled his pants up. Once his clothing was back together again, they started walking towards Tara's townhouse. "You asked me to believe. Right now I feel I can win any battle, any war."

"I know. I feel the same way."

He stopped and got down on one knee. "I know this is putting, well, the horse is so far out of the barn we might never catch him. But—," he took both of her hands in his and swallowed hard. "Will you marry me?"

Her gaze turned liquid. "We don't exactly have a marriage ceremony," he continued. "It's a mating ceremony."

Her countenance melted. "Yes, Alexi."

He rose with a shaky laugh. "Good, because I wouldn't want our child to go without my name."

"Our child?" she echoed.

He roared. "Honey. If we didn't just make one, I'm shooting blanks."

Alexi was still laughing as they reached the townhouse. He rang the doorbell, but no one answered. Since no one did, he tried the doorknob. It rotated, unlocked. Alarm flew through him. He looked at Elena, saw her fear, and they both raced inside, skidding to a stop at the scene before them.

Nicholai reclined in an upright position. Tara sat on the bed beside him. The baby rested in his lap. His brother pinned him with a stern gaze, but his lips twitched with suppressed merriment. "Uh, excuse me, Alexi. But exactly who's been f—ing around here?"

Chapter Twenty-Two

When Alexi remained speechless, Elena knew he was in trouble. She squeezed his hand as tight as she could.

He coughed and swallowed several times. "Tears are not always bad, my love."

Her own eyes welled when she met Tara's grateful gaze. She heard Alexi take in a ragged breath and let the air out in a heartfelt sigh. She studied her patient with a keen eye. Nicholai had not come out of his sleep unscathed. There were lines in his face no one would be able to remove and his mouth, although smiling, told tales of a grim darkness.

How alike yet how different they were. The same gray eyes. The same wave to their black hair. The same facial features. Alexi, though much more serious than when she first met him, still carried that hint of disdain, that devil-may-care attitude. Yet he showed his emotions easier, wiping at his eyes and his tears of joy. Nicholai, she perceived to be much more serious, yet steadier. Or perhaps the correct description was steadfast.

"I owe you all an apology," Nicholai said at last. "What I did was unforgivable."

Elena protested. "What you did, brother-in-law, was human."

He made a face at that remark then chuckled, the laughter aimed at only himself. "Indeed. And I'm finding statements like those much more palatable than I used to. I'm grateful that I'm alive. Thank you."

She bowed her head and said, "This was a collaborative effort, Nicholai. I did very little."

"Then I thank you all. I kept searching. Searching." His voice trailed off. She watched him run his finger over his daughter's cheek.

"We don't have much time," she reminded them all. "Dmitri and Charles are on their way. Plans must be made."

"Dmitri? And Charles?" Nicholai exclaimed. He shook his head. "There is much I have to catch up on, I see."

They tried to be brief. They tried to soften the blow of losing Noble Pride.

"Don't flay yourself, Nico," Alexi said when they were finished.

"I should have been here."

"You could not have stopped any of this from happening," Elena told him.

He looked down at her hand entwined with Alexi's. "I see no mating scar."

"We haven't had time," Alexi replied. "Besides, I asked. Elena has accepted. We don't need a ceremony."

Nicholai chuckled and Tara joined him. "I guess not."

Alexi took the reins as if he were born to them and began talking things out. "As I see it, we don't have too many options."

Tara started to protest. Elena could see she was concerned about Nicholai's condition. But Nicholai reached out to stop her. He shook his head and she sat down beside him. "Let's hear them."

"By whatever miracle, Morgan brought us that flask," Alexi continued. "We have no idea where he got it; I don't think we want to know. He would probably end up broken if we tried to find out."

"Dmitri and Charles must have been convincing if they are still alive," Elena added. "Yet this poses another problem. Do we give them the rest of the Water?"

"What if that's all there is?" Tara asked, giving voice to everyone's thoughts.

"That's not our only problem, although you both seem to accept the inevitable," Elena continued. "Sylvana and Jeri have been wronged by the Ancient one. More of the Water combined with the Lorraine leaf may just save them."

"The needs of the many—," Alexi started to quote while staring straight at his brother.

Who stared right back. "Outweigh the needs of the few. Or the one." Nicholai pinned her with his gaze. "We must destroy the Ancient one first."

"We don't know if the Water will work," Alexi cried. "We don't know if we'll be able to use the Water before the Ancient one taints it."

Elena was the first one to realize something was wrong. She whirled to find Ariel, Stefano, and several Nobles standing in Tara's bedroom.

"You should remember to lock your doors," Stefano commented in a dry tone.

The lady Ariel was not the same woman as before. She stood in front of Elena as the leader of her people. Elena could find no softening in her gaze.

"You'll have to forgive the intrusion. I could not help but overhear. The choices are no longer yours to make. Alexi, you are charged with obstructing the will of the High Council. Seize him."

Her gaze rested a moment on Nicholai. "As much as I'm overjoyed to see you well, I must do what I must do. Your brother disobeyed a direct order. Our entire race is now in jeopardy."

"The threat to you and to the Nobility would not have changed no matter what we did."

"That is for the people to decide." Ariel stared at the casket for a long time. She motioned to Stefano who opened the messenger bag then carefully slid the casket inside.

Alexi.

He turned, flanked now by two of the Nobles that had accompanied Ariel. He gave her his signature grin. "Don't worry, Elena. I'm a magician, remember?"

She clasped her hands together until they hurt. This was one time when she wasn't sure he'd be able to escape.

****

Alexi stood alone in the center of the great Hall surrounded by the cream of the Nobility. Each House stood according to rank, the highest, most pure Houses closest to him. He refused to be the least bit daunted. Instead, he closed his eyes and imagined himself on center stage. He could hear hearts beating in anticipation, some faster than others. A comforting thought. Not everyone wanted him dead.

Sergei stood in the place of his House, an honored member of his family. He nodded, his face grim, his gaze full of pride. Imagine that, he thought to himself. Sergei, proud of him.

Beside him stood his heart—Elena. She had followed immediately, unwilling to let them crucify him without a fight. Her presence calmed him. She believed in him, believed in his heart, believed in both their hearts.

Even now he couldn't get over her love for him. Every time the emotion washed through him, cleansing his soul, he knew the aftermath of amazement. He would never understand why, would probably spend years doubting it. But her presence was here in this room, defending his honor. Poor woman, she had no idea what kind of bargain she'd made.

Yes, I do.

He would have smiled if the situation had been

less grave. Still her unwavering faith, her innocence in the face of evil, became the steel rod that set his shoulders high and proud, that lifted his chin, that put a half smile on his face which seemed to infuriated many.

A hush fell over the room as Ariel and Stefano entered. Funny how they stuck to ceremony even now. A roll call ensued, House by House, to make sure all were represented.

"Alexi Valentin," Ariel began. "You stand charged with obstructing the will of the High Council."

Alexi didn't answer. Stefano reached over to tap Ariel on the shoulder and whisper something in her ear. "Stefano has reminded me that not all of you are aware of the danger we find ourselves in at the moment. Nor do you all know how this came about. He has asked me to explain." She did, being as brief and to the point as possible.

"Alexi, you were charged with finding the Water, Han-Sing, or both. How did the Water end up at your brother's townhouse?"

"I don't know. It was at my brother's house when I arrived."

Alexi blocked his thoughts as someone tried to read them. Not nice, he thought to himself. An invasion of privacy he was not likely to forget. They still knew nothing about the flakes he'd found in the lakebed.

"You're asking this entire gathering to believe it simply appeared?"

"Yes." He watched Ariel shake her head in derision. "Hey, listen. You can believe me or not believe me at this point. I'm still gonna stick to the story because it's the truth."

"Then what did you do?"

Alexi was about to speak when he got pre-empted by his better half. "He didn't do anything,"

Elena cried out. "I took the Water and saved his brother's life. As I am charged by my people and my faith to do. I'm a healer."

Alexi's heart swelled with pride as he watched Elena step forward. She pulled her broken body to its full height and threw her shoulders back, her face shimmering with anger. He knew how much pain she was in this close to New York, knew what the effort cost her. "I am not of your people. And yet I am as Ariel has explained. But first and foremost, throughout the centuries of our existence, my race has healed the wounds of the world. I did what I am charged by my very life to do. I saved Nicholai."

"Unfair," someone cried out.

"The House of Valentin has no claim to the Water any more than the rest of us," cried another.

Everyone started talking at once. Stefano slammed his hand down on the table once and all sound ceased. Alexi was impressed. He wondered how the man would fare with a classroom full of five-year-olds. Of course, in his humble opinion, he was in a room with a bunch of five-year-olds.

Dmitri stepped into the center of the room. Alexi swung around in surprise. They must have flown up the Parkway to get here.

"If I may speak?" Ariel nodded. "Though my life and that of Charles Rhys-Jones is in great jeopardy, I hold no ill will or grudge towards Alexi Valentin's actions. I would have done the same."

"Me, too," Charles added.

"That is because Nicholai is your friend," a voice cried out.

"He ain't mine," Charles chimed in. "You'd all best remember that." They did. "You'd all best understand your enemy, too. We're in deep stuff here. And we've got a time limit. Forty-eight hours."

Alexi leaned back and smiled. Elena had once told him he'd be the one to pull them together. Not exactly how she may have envisioned things, but what the hell. It worked for him. "Listen to me, all of you. We are in mortal danger. The Ancient one expects to receive the Water tomorrow night. He can't be sure there is more, neither can we. I wasn't lying. I don't know where the Water came from."

Elena moved to stand beside him. She started to remove the pouch and his gaze flew to hers. She shook her head, telling him not to worry. He shrugged and let her go. "My lady, Alexi is no traitor. To you, this Council, or his people."

"How so, Elena?"

Did she know how proud he was of her at that moment? Alexi's heart swelled. "He risked his life to find these." She opened the pouch and shook out the flakes he'd recovered from the lakebed. Now that they were outside of the pouch, everyone could feel their power. "Your race is dying. My race is dying. We spoke of the joining of the two. Perhaps the answer lies there. Perhaps it does not. No matter what, I give them to you."

"Elena, no," he protested. "We may never find more."

We do not need to, Alexi. Open your mind. What do you see?

Alexi's jaw dropped. He'd been joking before, not really serious. *Are you sure?*

She laughed. Quite sure.

Alexi reached inside her, could feel the changes in her body, already adjusting to her condition. Of course something like this was bound to happen to him at the most important moment in his life.

Our lives, she corrected.

Pregnant. He simply could not get over it. She carried his child, children, whatever. Overwhelmed, he didn't respond at first. Then his natural character kicked in. *I'm going to have to make love to you in public more often.*

Elena had to cough to cover the laughter bubbling inside her. His answer was pure Alexi. She stood holding their very survival in her hand and in her womb.

"The Water belongs to all," someone cried out.

"Each House must have its share."

Elena shook her head in disgust. She was about to speak when Alexi held up his hand for silence. Hadn't she told him he would be the one to bring them together?

"Then you will all die, House by House. We must join forces, and work with each other. What are you waiting for? An I-told-you-so? By then it will be too late. We have one last chance to save ourselves. Can't you think outside the box? Just this once? And forget your own selfish interests?"

"Easy for you to say," another cry sounded through the room. "You got what you wanted."

Elena felt the knife that plunged into Alexi's heart as surely as it did her own.

"What I wanted?" he repeated, his incredulity reverberating throughout the Hall. "My brother nearly died for you, you piece of—." He caught himself just in time. Losing his temper wasn't going to help the situation. "This woman is giving up the foundation of her existence for you in these stones. An innocent, a friend, remains blind for no other reason than her friendship. And my niece will never be one of us, razed at birth by this monster. And you tell me I have everything I want?"

The silence that spread through the Hall came from embarrassment.

"My lady," Elena spoke up. "We spoke of this once before. The key to our success is the combination of our two races. Put the Water with the pieces of the meteorite that we found. Just allow me a small amount to cure those who were damaged by this evil."

Ariel took a deep breath. Elena read her fear. So must Alexi for he added, "No one can force you to work together. But if you want to save yourselves, you'll never do it alone. Sun-Tsu said it best. *Divide and conquer. Stand alone and you will each fall, one by one.*"

Alexi was right and they all knew it. "What must we do?" Ariel asked. Elena glanced over at Sergei to see a father's pride on the man's face. He nodded to her as if he'd known all along Alexi had the ability to lead. "We must combine the Water with the stones then go on the offensive. Attack him where he lives, the house in Smithville. Make the place uninhabitable. Then hound him. Make every place he tries to rest uninhabitable. Force him into the open. Then destroy him."

"I say we keep the Water so we can save ourselves." Elena heard a fair number in the crowd agree.

"If you do," came a voice from the back. A hushed whisper ran through the crowd. "This is what you will get."

A space opened and Nicholai moved slowly towards the dais. Tara supported him, but who supported her? Elena would never know. She never wanted to see such pain on two faces ever again.

"Sylvana," Elena cried, her heart sinking to her feet. She turned to Ariel, the fury of the god's flying from her gaze. "Give me the flask. Now!"

Ariel looked at Nicholai, then Tara, then at the child. She nodded. Elena ran to Nicholai. She felt life in the babe though the spark was nearly gone. The flakes still rested in her hand. She opened the flask and everyone in the room stepped back from the force of the Water.

Elena took one of the flakes and placed it in her other hand. She then returned the rest of the flakes to the pouch. Then she put the flake in her palm and dribbled a tiny amount of the Water onto the stone.

Her arm went numb immediately. She held the appendage as steady as she could then wet her finger. "Tara. Sister. Be brave. Open her mouth."

Tara complied and Elena put some of the mixture on Sylvana's lips. The baby's mouth moved in a natural sucking motion so Elena repeated the process until barely any of the Water remained. "Alexi," she whispered her tone hoarse. "Take the stone, but do not put it in the pouch with the others. It's changed now."

All standing near looked down at her hand. The stone, originally as blue as the sky on a midsummer's day, had turned as green as an emerald valley in the sun. All of a sudden, Sylvana took a hitched breath. She opened her eyes. Their color went from the smoky gray of her father to the green of the stone then back to gray again.

Elena had no chance to wonder. The numbness that had started in her arm had spread to her chest and now seemed to stop her entire body. She tried to reach out. She tried to speak. Nothing came out. She collapsed and the world went dark.

Chapter Twenty-Three

"Oh, God, no," Alexi cried, kneeling beside Elena's prone body. He lifted her head and cradled her in his lap. She was so cold, the arm that held the Water like ice. "The baby. The baby."

Sergei kneeled beside him. Nicholai stood on the other. "The baby is fine now," his brother tried to reassure. "Sylvana lives."

Alexi's gaze flew from his brother to his mentor. "No," he cried. "You don't understand."

Elena, he screamed within his mind. *Come to me.*

He rocked back and forth praying she would find him. "Understand what?" Nicholai asked gently.

"Elena," Alexi sobbed. "Me."

Tara was the first to put two and two together. "I believe he is trying to tell us Elena is pregnant." She put a comforting hand on his shoulder. He looked up at her, all the misery inside him swimming in his gaze. "Alexi. Let's get her off this stone floor."

He released Elena with reluctance. They lifted her as if she were royalty. As soon as they set her down again on the dais, Alexi clutched her arm to his chest. So cold. "I know you can hear me, Elena." He bent down closer to her ear. "I love you. You are now part of my heart; you are part of my soul. You can't leave me, do you hear? I won't let you go."

Alexi looked up to see the same tears he shed on his brother's face. "Hear me, all of you." Nicholai's voice boomed out over the now silent Hall. "This woman shames us. She has done nothing but give of herself, her faith, her abilities, and now she has put her life and the life of her unborn child in danger. For us. For our race. For our very survival."

Alexi wiped his eyes and stood. "No more," he cried. "As God is my witness, no more. No more bickering. No more vendettas. No more backbiting. No more treachery. No more hatred. If we win the day, no more Houses. Only one House. One family. One race. The Nobility."

No one spoke. Then Ariel nodded. "Alexi is right. We stand on the brink of extinction. Either we all join forces or we die as the Ancient one wishes. I, for one, would rather go down fighting my enemy, than my brother."

"More of us are enemies than brothers," a voice cried out. "And have been for centuries."

"Change," Ariel snapped back.

"You expect us to simply shake hands and forget?"

"Yes!" she commanded. "And this Council charges each and every one of you with keeping the peace."

"We face a great danger," Nicholai added. "Greater than petty differences. We were able to win a battle with the Ancient one before, not the war. He means business this time."

Alexi watched Nicholai hand Sylvana to Tara and bow to Ariel. "With your permission?" Ariel nodded. "The Ancient one makes his home just outside of Atlantic City. Gather your people. As many as you can. We must take the Water, and the war, to him. We will fight for our right to exist."

A roar went up in the Hall that shook the rafters. Ariel continued. "It is the charge of this Council that if we win the day, we stand as equals from this day forward. No more ranks, no one more powerful than the next. The Council will sit as it always has, ready to judge fairly, negotiate disputes, and reconcile differences. What say you?"

Another roar shook the Hall. *You see, my darling?* Alexi told Elena. *We're not quite as dumb as we seem. Slow, but eventually we get where we need to be.*

Ariel raised her hand for quiet. "Han-Sing is missing. I do not feel his loss nor do I feel his life essence. There's no telling if he is alive or if he is dead. The Council cannot function with just two. Therefore, I ask that Nicholai Valentin be appointed to the High Council."

This time the roar of approval shook the very foundation. But Nicholai didn't answer. His gaze knifed to Alexi's. "This is what you have always wanted, brother."

"The price is too high."

Alexi brought Elena's cold lifeless hand to his cheek. "I've learned so much from her, Nico." Alexi kissed the soft flesh then swallowed his tears. "I've learned how not to run away from a fight and to fight for what I believe in. I've learned that we are all meant for different purposes. Elena did what she did because she was meant to do it, healing is her purpose. The High Council is yours. It's your destiny, Nico. You have the power, now, to keep them honest, knit them back together, and get them to toe the line. You have the ability to make a difference, create one race, keep it that way." Alexi chuckled and the tears flowed again. "Besides, she'd be screaming mad if you didn't."

Nicholai reached out and pulled him into his embrace. "I love you, Alexi."

"I love you, too, Nico."

They slapped each other on the back and let go.

"I accept the duty given to me," Nicholai called out. To Alexi he said, "As long as you are by my side."

Alexi choked. Fresh tears welled. He fought

them back. Holding onto Elena's arm, he noticed it was still cold but not like ice anymore, but still cold enough to put a chill inside his heart. *God, please. Don't let her die. Don't let either of them die.*

****

At first she thought she was dreaming. Then Elena realized she had no idea where she was. Spread before her stood a harsh and unforgiving landscape. Then she knew this was where Nicholai had spent his days as he slept. She wondered if she would have to endure the same fate.

The urge to move compelled her. She resisted. She recognized the urge as part of the trap. Her hand flew to her belly in alarm. The child grew. Only, she laughed to herself, Alexi was right. There were now two who resided within her womb.

From here there was no meaning, the sensation that of being in free-fall. No beginning, no end, just there. But that could not be. Elena had a better understanding of metaphysics than Nicholai or Alexi. She knew there had to be some ground in reality or she could not be where she was. Using her mind, she bent time and space, and the harsh scene before her melted away.

Cold. So cold. She lay trapped in a solid layer of ice. She could not breathe, could not move, all she could do was see. The sun would shine above her, her only friend, a weak and wavy orb. Then darkness would fall and the cold would grow colder.

Trapped. The word resounded in her. No escape. No hope of freedom. Only the wish to see the Sun again. And the prayer for release. Crying, howling, begging for release from this terrible prison.

Elena knew she'd stepped into the Ancient one's memories. She had never felt so alone, so isolated, or so hopeless in her entire life. She knew, now, why he had changed. And why he would remain beyond redemption. But he could not remain beyond her tears of pity.

The scene changed. Fear. Shadows. Death. Elena drew in a harsh, rattled breath. She hid in a basement of some kind, wearing rags. Dirty, unkempt, not caring, she was utterly miserable, wishing only for another cigarette. Han-Sing. She had found him, hiding, on the run and trying desperately to save his own life.

Elena tried to reach out, to reassure him, and let him know they were trying to find him. Then she realized she was a ghost, on the outside looking in. But if she had that ability, it meant she could try to gather information, no? A cruel reality caught her. She could change the channels but had no mastery over their destination.

The scene changed again. This time she saw a picture of a great celebration in the back of Nicholai's home in the desert. He and Tara were locked in a tender embrace. Elena smiled. She was able to go both forward and back in time. This must have been a picture from their wedding day.

Now the scene chilled her soul. She stood in front of the house in Smithville. She knew the loss of life and light from the plants that had been strangled at their very roots, and by the animals that dared not tread too near. She stood before the antithesis of all she was, all she believed in. Elena represented life. The Ancient one, death. She would fight him with every breath she took until he was defeated.

A teardrop fell onto the back of her hand. Then another.

Her heart broke as she recognized Alexi's pain. She wanted to reach out to him, touch him, soothe him. But she was so tired.

Alexi. Don't cry. I'm all right.
****

She moved. He saw her. Her finger twitched.

"Elena? Oh God, Elena, please. Speak to me. Nod your head. Squeeze my hand. Let me know you're alive."

Her eyes popped open scaring him half to death. "Sweetheart?"

She didn't answer. She drew in a deep breath and let the air out in a whoosh. Her eyes reminded him of those zombie movies he'd seen as a kid. "Come on, my love. You're almost there. Follow the sound of my voice."

She breathed in again and he knew the instant she regained this world. She smiled. "Alexi."

Alexi bent his head to her chest and sobbed in relief. Her hand stroked his hair, each touch helping to wash away the bitter aftertaste of his fear. "I was so worried when you wouldn't return. I kept thinking you would end up like Nicholai."

"Hush," she whispered. His head slid a bit lower to rest on her belly. "The babies are fine. Can you ever forgive me for placing them in jeopardy?"

"Forgive you?" His hold on her tightened. "Thank you, God. Thank you. Thank you," he whispered over and over again. The plural of the word didn't hit him for several minutes. "Babies?" he echoed, lifting his head to stare at her in amazement. "You did say -ies, didn't you? As in more than one?"

She nodded. "I think you were shooting just fine."

Laughter rumbled up through his chest. Never mind, he'd explain the connotation later. He slid up the bed and kissed her with all his pent up joy bursting out. She tore her mouth away. "Alexi, love, at least let me breathe."

He tried to look contrite and failed. "Sorry. I'm just so happy." He sighed and put his head on her chest again. Of course that put him dangerously close to a place he dared not tread. Not now. Not until she was well and whole again.

"Alexi? My love? Where am I?"

He chuckled. She'd been out for hours. "Ariel was kind enough to let me use her home since it was closest to the Hall."

"Oh. Where is everyone?"

"On their way to taint the Ancient one's home with the Water. If he has to start running, he may make a mistake."

"They won't get him to move."

Alexi frowned. "I don't understand. Surely using the Water will make his home uninhabitable."

"True. But that will not be enough. I was able to see pieces of the future while I roamed."

"You know what's going to happen? If we're going to survive?" Hope shot through him.

"Not exactly." His heart sank. "But I did find Han-Sing. He's still alive. Hiding."

"Does he have the rest of the Water?"

"I don't think so. But I believe he knows who does. After all, that has been his job, has it not?"

She was right. "So where is he?"

"Close. Too close to danger. He's hiding in a church right near Tara's home."

Alexi frowned. "That's why the Ancient one still lives nearby."

"I would venture a guess and say that Atlantic City holds its own attraction for him. But there had to be more of a reason."

"Which is?"

"I don't know. Han-Sing got himself trapped somehow. I could feel his fear. As if he'd made a blunder of some kind and knew he would have to pay for it."

"Like leading the Ancient one to the Water?"

"Yes."

"Then we have to warn the others."

She shook her head. "No, absolutely not."

"Why?"

"Because we need to keep the man busy, keep his mind occupied on something else while we go rescue Han-Sing."

"Shouldn't we at least tell Tara and Nicholai?"

"Yes. Tell them to wait for us at their house." She looked around in alarm then sighed with relief. "I thought you'd given the pouch to Ariel."

"I was afraid I might need to use the stones to find you."

"You could never lose me."

But he could lose himself inside her. She knew the moment his thoughts turned in that direction because she gave him a wicked smile. A wicked smile? His prim and proper gnome?

Alexi landed flat on his back on the bed without knowing how he got there. Ariel had lent him a nightshirt to make Elena more comfortable. She straddled his chest and ripped the garment over her head. Her knees pinned his arms to the bed. All he could do was salivate as her breasts bobbed up and down in front of him.

"Don't rip the shirt," he cried. "It's the only one I have."

She made a face at him but took the time to undo the buttons. Her hands slid all over his chest and ribs. He shivered, his lower extremities coming to life with quick precision.

"One kiss," he begged. "Come on. Just one kiss. Please?"

She laughed and lowered her breast to his mouth. She gave him one quick taste then let him suckle the other. But only for a moment. Then she slid lower to straddle his thighs. "Take one arm off that bed and I leave," she growled.

Alexi couldn't have answered even if he wanted to. This was an Elena he never knew existed.

She made short work of his belt and lowered the

zipper, outlining the point in his boxers with her mouth. Dissatisfied with that, she pulled down the material allowing him to spring free.

This new Elena wasted no time. She swallowed him whole. Oh man, not only did she swallow him, she engulfed him, sucking and pulling with all her might. He rose. He swelled. He grew until he could grow no more.

All of a sudden she released him. Somehow she divested herself of her underwear because the next thing he knew, he was plunging into a furnace. She began riding him, lifting all the way up to the tip of his shaft then sitting back down with a force that slapped their thighs together.

"Elena, please," he begged. "At least let me play with them."

"All right," she strangled out.

His hand began to knead her breasts, rolling her nipples between his fingers. Then he lifted his torso so he could suck on them. But he couldn't hold that position forever, even in the shape he was in. He collapsed back onto the bed. "Elena," he choked out. "There is another step we can take. One beyond a simple mating."

She stilled her movements and gave him a quizzical look. A fire burned in her gaze filled with passion and love. "The easiest way to describe it is that we can touch souls, become one."

"Like Tara and Nicholai?"

"Yes. But once we do, there's no going back. You saw what happened to Tara as Nicholai faded. She did too. We would be tied together forever."

"Show me how," she replied without hesitation.

"Are you sure?"

"I love you." Simple, straightforward, Elena. She would never cease to amaze him.

"Lay on top of me. Full length." She complied although the position was not conducive to movement. He rolled them both over so that he took the commanding position. He flexed his hips. She groaned.

"Spread your legs as wide as they will go."

When she complied, he settled his hips into her and thrust as far as he could go. He wrapped his hands around the outside of her thighs, pulled out, and thrust again. As he did, his hands held her core in place and the base of his shaft ground into her. She cried out.

He had no balance except where they were joined, but he wanted to kiss her. They were going to be together everywhere, head to toe. She accepted his weight, opened to his kiss, took the length of him into her until they were truly one.

He reared back with his hips and plunged deep inside again. Then he opened his mind, urging her to open hers. At first he saw nothing but light. Then he found himself in front of a golden gate. He thrust again. Her breath caught. Behind the gate she gave him another one of those wicked smiles and he knew he was going to come to love those things.

He reached out his hand but stopped just before the gate. A frisson, not of fear or apprehension, but of nervousness, ran through him. He so did not want to disappoint her.

Her answer was to swing the gate open.

Alexi thrust again. He began a rhythm between them as old as time. She lifted her knees to give him even more access. He groaned and slid in and out of her moist cavern faster and faster. She mewled. But in his mind, all he knew was the tender kiss they shared behind the gate.

He thrust deeply, harder and faster. She started making really wild sounds in the back of her throat. He answered with his own. They climbed and climbed. Radiant light streamed out between the two of them. Behind the gate, inside their own private

Garden of Eden, they reached out until they found the pinnacle of release. Her breath hitched. He screamed out her name. She followed a moment later with his. The light burst all around them. Their souls touched. And in that moment they became one for all time.

Alexi blacked out. He wasn't sure exactly how long he remained unconscious, only that he looked up to see her smiling down at him. Already she was inside his head, her feelings, her being a woman. "I had no idea," he breathed.

She nodded. "I'm more attuned to nature, but you're right. I could not have understood. Men are," she paused a moment, "interesting creatures."

"So are women," he agreed.

"Don't ever lose your spirit, Alexi. I don't ever want to take you out of, well, you."

He laughed. "That would be a feat indeed."

He nuzzled her neck, flashes of what she felt mixing with what he felt. "Just do me one favor," he continued. She arched a brow at him. "Help me explain to Ariel about messing up her sheets when we see her later, okay?"

She swatted his shoulder then couldn't help herself. She burst out laughing.

Chapter Twenty-Four

Elena never realized the Island could be so dark. There should have been a peace surrounding them, a natural quiet, the kind she knew at home. Instead, discord seemed to underlie all they saw and heard. Even the gulls were silent. "I'm starting to get the creeps."

She had known he would feel the eeriness as she did. "Strange. This is not natural."

As they drove down the Boulevard, she noted the closed up buildings. The summer season was not far off, she imagined. As they drove, Elena noted a huge church and an even bigger parking lot, remarking to herself how big it was on such a small island. "Alexi," she cried. "Stop the car."

He slammed on the brakes. "What? What is it?"

"Back up." He threw her a look, which she ignored. She would know, now, if he was angry and he wasn't. Besides, there was no one on the street, certainly not at this time of night.

"Care to explain?" he asked, his arms crossed over his chest once he stopped the car.

"The sign. Do you see the sign?"

"Yes, love, and I can read. It says, 'St. Francis Roman Catholic Church. And your point is?"

Men, she thought with disgust.

Yes, dear, he answered.

"Does the name ring a bell?"

He winced. "I don't know. I admit it. I'm thick."

"Call Nicholai. Ask them to meet us here. I have a hunch."

"That Han is hiding here," he finished for her.

"Yes."

No more than ten minutes later, Nicholai and Tara pulled up next to them. The men pulled into a darkened corner of the lot so their cars would not be noticed right away, then they both got out and began walking ahead. "I'm happy for you, Elena."

"You know?"

Tara smiled. "Aside from being connected, you're glowing. It suits you." She slowed her steps. "I...I never thanked you for Syl's life."

"Then you know there can be no need for thanks between us." Tara reached out to hug her.

When she let go Tara added, "I'm not sure if the Water has changed her or not. She no longer feels human, yet she doesn't feel like a Noble either."

Elena reached out and gave Tara's shoulder a squeeze. "Then she will be who she is, Tara. And she may have a purpose none of us can foresee."

"As will the children you carry."

"You know that as well?"

Tara smiled. "Like I told you..." She didn't need to finish. Elena understood.

The church was locked. After scouting around, the men found that the recreation center was locked as well. Elena tried to find some clue as to Han's whereabouts from her dream then simply guessed. "Let's try the church basement first."

Nicholai went back to his car and returned with a steel rod. "From my tire jack," he explained. They found some steps that went down to a door, and using their unusual strength, pried the lock open. The door opened into a hallway.

"This way," she told them.

All of a sudden they heard a cry, some scuffling, then silence. Elena broke into a run, followed by the others. They found Han-Sing in a seated position, his back resting against a metal cot. A knife protruded from his chest. "Oh, no," she cried, kneeling beside him. She didn't remember this from her dream. The room looked the same, but she didn't remember Han being mortally wounded. "We need to get him on the bed."

She reached for her pouch, but a tobacco stained hand stopped her. "No, child. I'm done for."

He took a rattled breath. "Please," she begged. "I can heal you."

He shook his head. "I have been waiting for this to happen for a very long time. Now the wait is over." He sighed. "I'm just glad I will not go alone."

Nicholai knelt beside him. "Han. It's Nicholai. The Water. You must tell us. The secret can't go to the grave with you."

"No. Then you sign your death warrants right here."

Nicholai flicked her a glance. She shook her head. She wouldn't be able to save him now. He had bled too much internally. "Han, please. This is not about you or me anymore. It's about the Nobility. Our survival."

A long silence ensued. Then he whispered, "St. Francis."

"Dammit," Alexi cried. "You pulled that one on us before. They're decoys. Tell us the truth. Please."

The elder man took one last deep breath then his head slumped to his chest. Elena closed his eyes with her fingers and motioned for Nicholai and Alexi to lift him onto the cot. She took a cross that he'd been clutching in his fist, placed it between both hands then folded them onto his chest. She said a quick prayer. "He was a good man," she said, lifting up to her feet.

"Yes, he was," Nicholai agreed, when they were finished.

"Let's find a light switch," Alexi added. "See if we can find any other clues."

"I wonder," Nicholai said. "If this is not the way

things are meant to be. Perhaps we should not continue the search."

Tara protested. "Then we're doomed, Nico. We don't have too many options any more."

"Even less now," Alexi added, his disgust evident. He felt he'd been played with and Elena couldn't blame him.

Seeing both sides was a blessing and a curse. "While I walked the paths you tread, Nicholai, I also saw pieces of the future. I can't be sure of the truth of the scenes anymore as I did not see Han-Sing's demise. But I can tell you what I didn't see. I didn't see our destruction. We must keep fighting."

Alexi kept searching the room, ranging farther and farther from her. "Hey, there's another door over here." He opened the door, reached inside, then a light went on. She blinked at the brightness. As her eyes adjusted, she saw a man standing in the doorway. He was holding a gun. "Gunner Mannheim," Tara breathed.

He shook his head. "No. He is dead, as you well know. But you have forgotten the first rule of the Nobility. Twins. I'm his twin brother, Dietrich."

****

This place really creeped him out to begin with, but at night? Charles shivered in the cool, damp air. He felt better now that they'd used the Water to cleanse the place, but still, the evil inside would never truly be eradicated.

Charles tapped Dmitri on the shoulder. "This sucks."

Dmitri turned to him, annoyance etched into his stern features. "What would you have me do about it?"

"I don't know. Maybe answer a question."

Charles listened for Dimitri's exasperated sigh then grinned. "What question?"

"Are you really gay?"

"Charles...," the man replied, then he let out a snort of laughter. "I told you, I had to be convincing."

"Man, I am so impressed. You should be an actor. No, really. I'm not kidding. I really mean it. You even had *me* going."

"And you are a theatrical expert?" Dmitri asked with disdain.

Charles figured he wasn't so he dropped the subject. He rubbed his hands together and blew on them lightly. "How long do you think we've been here?"

"I'm not positive. Longer than an hour, less than two. Why?"

"He's not coming."

Dimitri's face stiffened in surprise. "What do you mean?"

"If he hasn't shown up by now, he won't."

"Are you certain?"

"Gut call. It's telling me something else is going on."

Dimitri reached out and grabbed one of his arms in alarm. "Explain."

"The man's not afraid of us. Sure, he's gonna be pissed as all get out when he finds he can't come back here, but he's not stupid either. Eventually, we'll get him to make that mistake we're looking for, but he's going to finish his plans first. If I lose, you lose too. You get that?"

"A stalemate," Dimitri whispered, letting go. "We must warn Ariel."

Charles grabbed onto Dimitri's shirt before he could rise from their hiding place. "Wait. Believe it or not, this kinda works."

"What do you mean?"

"He knows we're here and it's got his attention. He's probably devising some kind of counter attack right now."

"So?"

"So that buys time. And my guess is the key lies with the Valentins. Somewhere on that island they live on."

"You could be very wrong."

"So, if I am, we waste an hour's ride there and back on the Parkway. By that time, everyone else will have figured out he's not coming too. No harm done."

Dimitri nodded slowly. "You have a point. We could go on a wild goose chase, but the risk is minimal. I will call Nicholai."

Charles shook his head. "Not yet. Not until we get there. We'll surprise him."

****

Alexi refused to budge. "Let them go."

The man simply laughed. "I will kill you."

"You'll only get one shot," Nicholai growled. "Then you'd better make your peace with whatever god you pray to."

Dietrich considered that point. "You are correct. Therefore, I'll make my one shot count." He reached out and snared Elena, putting the barrel of the gun up under her chin.

"Harm one hair on her head," Alexi snarled, "and I'll tear your limbs off your body and let you bleed to death."

Dietrich looked taken aback for a moment then he laughed. "What you describe is physically impossible."

"Try me."

"Give me the information that I require and I'll let her go."

Alexi shared a look with Nicholai. They both knew Dietrich was lying. "Can't help you."

The man really laughed this time. "Your friends don't care for you or your life," he told Elena. "Some friends."

"No, I mean really," Alexi continued.

Dietrich frowned. "Explain."

"You screwed up. Han died before he could tell us."

The man blanched. His grip tightened on Elena, causing her to cry out in pain. "Hurt her again, and I don't care. You're dead." Dietrich let go a little and Alexi saw he was processing. "You know, your boss is going to be really pissed off when he finds out you failed."

Alexi could all but taste Dietrich's fear. He looked over at Nicholai who nodded for him to keep talking, keep going. Nicholai had already been able to shift to the man's side. If he could get a little closer, his brother would have a fairly clear shot at the gunman.

"He panicked. I only wanted him to talk. He threw himself on the knife."

"Han swore an oath to die before giving up any information."

"Then I'll bring you all back with me and my master will get what he needs out of you."

"Back where?" Alexi taunted. Out of the corner of his eye he watched Nicholai inch closer and closer. "We've destroyed your leader's home. We're attacking him, not the other way around."

Dietrich swallowed hard. A thrill of hope shot through Alexi. "You have no place to go," he continued. "Besides you're dead when you see him anyway. He hates failure."

"No. No. I'm his favored one. He will understand."

Alexi laughed. "You've seen what he's done to those who've disappointed him. You know the price they paid."

Dietrich's eyes darted left and right. He had no idea how to get out of his predicament. "She comes with me. He will forgive me."

Elena. When I tell you, go completely limp.

I don't have to. When you are ready, he will drop the gun.

How?

You have the ability to project an image into his mind. Make it a nasty one. I'll enhance the projection.

He had to swallow to hide his grin. He'd forgotten. Smoke and mirrors. He was a magician. "You really believe that?" he asked Dietrich.

Alexi looked over at Nicholai. He was ready. He looked at Elena. She was ready. He closed his eyes and sent a picture of the Ancient one tearing strips of Dietrich's flesh off his bones. The man screamed and let go of Elena as she'd promised. Nicholai leaped, knocked the gun out of his hand, and they both crashed to the floor. Dietrich thrashed around and moaned but Nicholai had no hold of him. His brother stared up at both of them. "What the hell did you do to him?"

"Gave him a picture of his flesh being torn off his bones."

"I added the sensation of it being stripped away," Elena added.

Nicholai blanched. "Remind me not to piss the two of you off."

Tara laughed. "You're a formidable pair. But Nico is right. Just make sure you don't get mad if we screw up your wedding present or something like that."

Their combined laughter was a healing balm. Dietrich curled into a fetal position and continued to whimper. "How long will it last?"

"Not too long," Elena replied. "But long enough for us to try to figure out what Han meant before he died."

Tara let out a little cry of surprise. Alexi frowned, totally puzzled. Elena simply smiled. "Nico," she said in wonder. "We have to go home."

"At a time like this?" he asked, beyond

exasperated.

Confused, Alexi asked, "What gives?"

"Ever since Elena gave Syl the Water, she won't take a bottle any more."

"Oh," he said, not sure if he should laugh or be mortified. Then he realized he was going to be in the same boat soon.

"A few moments won't matter," Elena added. "Alexi and I'll stay, see what we can find. We'll meet you at your home."

All of a sudden Nicholai's cell went off. Alexi jumped, and Tara cried out, pulling her shirt away from her chest. "Dimitri and Charles are on their way," Nicholai informed them after he hung up. "I told them to meet you in the parking lot, then you can all come to the house together."

"What about Han?" Alexi asked.

"We should let Dietrich deal with the police. But if we do, it may open up too many questions," Nicholai answered. "Elena, can you seal the wound?"

"Yes." They walked over to the body. Alexi began the death chant of the Nobility. Nicholai and Tara joined him as she pulled the knife out, took a Lorraine leaf from her pouch, then placed it on the wound. It sealed immediately.

Once the chant was finished, Alexi helped Nicholai wrap Han's body in the bed sheets. Blood had soaked into the mattress. They would have to dispose of that too.

The men carried the body first, then the mattress out to Nicholai's SUV. "Thank goodness you don't own a sports car."

"As soon as I get home, I'll have Sergei dispose of this then take Han back to the Hall. He died a hero. He should be remembered that way. By that time, you will have joined us."

Nicholai and Tara drove away just as Dimitri and Charles pulled up. Alexi explained what happened. Dimitri insisted on trying to get some information out of Dietrich and Charles went with him. As soon as they were alone, Alexi hauled her into his arms. "Thank God you're all right."

Chapter Twenty-Five

"That was a nasty trick we pulled back there."

Elena released a heartfelt sigh of relief. "Close," she muttered to herself. "But not close enough."

"I don't understand," Alexi replied.

Elena reveled in the lean hardness of his body, his scent, the feel of him but she couldn't get comfortable. Something was bothering her, telling her she needed to know something. But what? "I can't place what is wrong, only that I know something is."

She pushed away from him, ignoring his pout. "And I can't think when you hold me."

"Good," he replied, pulling her back. "Don't."

"Alexi—," she warned. He kissed her and let go. Too easily. And that was when the answer struck her. "That's it," she cried.

"What is?"

"Too easy. This entire situation. The Ancient one hasn't confronted us, not since he went after Sylvana. I expected more from him. Much more."

Alexi rubbed the back of his neck with his hand. "Because he's waiting for us to lead him to the Water," he said. "As we thought before."

"No, my love. I think we were wrong. He already knows where it is but can't get at it."

Elena stretched, trying to ease some of the pain in her limbs. Pain and critical thinking didn't mix too well. Alexi pulled her back into his arms and took most of the ache away. "Thank you." She smiled as he gave her an I-told-you-so face. "But I still can't think when you hold me."

"Suit yourself," he grumbled. She would have laughed had the situation been less grave. Men could be such children at times.

Elena decided to walk in an effort to keep from stiffening up again. She began heading through the parking lot towards the front of the church and she was glad when Alexi followed. He didn't say anything for which she was grateful. She kept going over all that had happened to them and kept coming up with a bunch of unconnected threads. She couldn't find anything to knit them together with—yet. "Do you, do you think we will be able to come back to this Island. I like it here."

"We have to have a future first," he replied, his tone grave.

"I know." She made a circle, intent on returning to the car when she looked up. "Alexi!" she cried.

He was beside her in a flash. "What? Are you all right?"

"Yes, yes. Over there." She pointed to the front of the church. "Han said St. Francis. Could it be this simple?"

Alexi shrugged. "Don't ask me. But if he hid the clue in a statue once, he could certainly do it again. Let's go find out."

They walked over to the statue. "Well, there are no cupped hands like the last one."

"Because that was Our Lady of Lourdes."

"Yeah. Right."

The statue was right up against some shrubbery and searching around it proved to be a chore. "Be patient, my love. Your eyesight is much better than mine in the dark. Just look for some kind of crack or opening."

"I don't see anything."

"Take your time." Elena shifted her weight from side to side, barely able to stand still. The thrill of discovery raced through her. She knew they would find a clue; they just had to.

"What's this?"

Elena peeked in front of him. The back of the statue had an indentation. Inside rested an old bird's nest. She was about to put the nest back undisturbed when that inner voice began talking to her again. She removed most of the twigs and brushed away the grass and dirt. "There, it's gone. Can you make anything out?"

Alexi squeezed in even further behind the statue. "No. Wait." She watched him brush more debris away. "I wish I had some light."

Elena walked around to the other side of the statue and pulled on some branches to let in the moonlight. Now that he had more room, Alexi knelt down to get a better look. "That should help."

"Oh, my God," Alexi whispered.

He rose and came out from behind the statue. He was obviously shaken. "What is it?"

At first he didn't speak. He seemed to be trying to figure something out. Then he answered. "Someone carved a picture into the back of the statue."

"A picture?" she asked, rather puzzled.

"Yes," he replied, and she could hear the concern in his voice. "Small but extremely distinct." He swallowed hard. "The Pendragon signet."

****

Alexi could tell Elena didn't get it. At first, neither had he. It was why they were targets and probably had been all along. Maybe even from the very beginning. "I don't understand, Alexi. What has Tara got to do with all this?"

"Yes," another voice chimed in. "I, too, would like an explanation."

Dimitri. "Where's Charles?" Alexi asked, a bit perturbed that he hadn't heard the man approach.

"He said he wanted to have some fun. I saw no

harm, but saw no reason to watch either."

Dimitri had always been fastidious, but Alexi doubted Charles would get any information out of Dietrich. They'd left the poor bastard in pretty bad shape. He began thinking out loud. "When you make a dam out of logs there's always a lynchpin, a key that will cause the dam to break apart if removed. Tara was the lynchpin. All of the events that were set in motion happened when she found the casket inside the Ancient one's home and touched it. I don't think he counted on Nicholai and Tara becoming mates, but he did count on her finding out who she was and, especially, who Morgan was."

Dimitri frowned. "I apologize, but why is Morgan so important."

"He was the one who originally gave the Ancient one the casket. Now the way I figure it, the Ancient one could never be sure where Morgan got it from. He couldn't try to get into Morgan's head. He might damage him so bad Morgan would never recover. So he used Tara to try to get Morgan to open up."

"Then the secret will stay locked inside him," Elena remarked. "What a perfect keeper for the Water."

"Better than Fort Knox," Alexi replied, the implications of his statement hitting him. Because if Morgan really was the keeper of the Water, they wouldn't be able to get their hands on it either. "Stalemate."

"Not exactly," Dimitri said. All of a sudden, Elena cried out. Alexi turned to find him holding her, a gun pointed right at her temple. "Don't even think it Alexi," he cautioned.

Terror clawed its way through his belly. "Dimitri?"

He gave Alexi a sad shrug. "I have a small problem. One that has given me the greatest pleasure, yet the greatest pain of my life. I made a deal."

"Dimitri, listen," Alexi began. "You can re-neg. We'll protect you. I promise. Don't do this. I beg of you."

"I'm already a traitor, Alexi. There is no need to beg."

"Nor is there a need to harm me," Elena added. "I won't fight you. But I'll beg also. Don't take this road. Please. It will only lead to self-destruction."

"Been there. Done that."

"And Nicholai?" Alexi asked.

A flash of pain raced through the man's face. "We have been friends our entire lives. I do not wish to harm either of you. But I have a bargain to fulfill."

He wanted Dimitri to swim in his guilt so he waited before commenting, "I get the funny feeling Charles isn't playing with Dietrich."

Dimitri smiled. "Dietrich is dead. Charles is out cold. We'll use your car. Then I'll call the police. It will keep Charles occupied for quite some time. Now move."

"Where are we going?"

"The Retreat." He kept a firm hand on Elena's arm and Alexi saw no opening as they walked. "And by the way, if you don't talk, I'll know you're communicating with each other. I only need one of you, not both. So don't forget, a long silence will mean her death."

"If you hurt her," Alexi growled. "There won't be enough room in Hell for you to hide in."

"There isn't now." Dimitri made Elena move faster and she stumbled.

Alexi nearly jumped the man. Only a flash of anger, and a quick shake of her head, saved Dimitri. "Dammit man, can't you go a bit slower? She can't walk."

"A thousand pardons," came Dimitri's snide reply. But he did slow down.

Alexi saw now why Elena had said things were too easy. Every inch of their progress had been monitored from the inside. The Ancient one had no need to show himself. Not with an informer like Dimitri.

Alexi figured he had to try one more time. "Dimitri, please listen to me. I don't believe you really want to hurt anyone, certainly not us. Let her go. I'll be your hostage."

"Much as I admit your offer makes sense, right now I prefer to have a back up."

"I'm begging you. Please. Let her go."

All of a sudden the man realized Alexi had another motive. "Why?"

Alexi swallowed hard knowing what he was risking. "She carries my babies."

A knife of pain streaked through Dimitri's gaze followed by sad resignation. "I am truly sorry."

"Dimitri. Please. You don't need her."

"Get…in…the…car."

"It doesn't have to be this way," he pleaded.

"Get in the car. Now." Alexi clenched his fists as Dimitri nudged Elena with the barrel of the gun.

"Touch her again and I'll—."

"You'll what?" Dimitri's smile was Alexi's answer.

"Mark my words, Dimitri Konin. Harm one hair on her head and you'll die before the Sun crests the horizon."

****

Charles awoke, spitting mad. He sat up and the room spun. He held his head between his hands, waiting for the pounding to diminish. Once it did, he looked over. Dietrich was dead.

Gotta warn Alexi, he thought. His hand went to his belt. No phone. Great. He rolled over onto his knees and felt around. No sooner did he find the damned thing than he heard sirens wailing in the distance.

Damn. No time to call. He stuffed the phone into the pocket of his jeans. Time to exit...stage left.

He rose, staggered, and cursed as a jackhammer ripped through his brain. But he made his way down the hallway and staggered up the stairs. He peeked over the concrete stairwell. The police were just pulling into the parking lot.

Double damn. He peeked again. Wait a minute. They were congregating at the front of the church. Like they were waiting for something.

With care, Charles slipped around the concrete wall and inched his way along the brick wall to the back of the church. He glanced around the corner. No one had pulled around back yet. Putting the pedal to the metal, he sprinted through the shadows, across the macadam, and stopped in the darkness of the recreation center next door to the church.

Too much parking lot, he cursed, his head pounding out of his skull. He wanted to run again but had to wait until the pain subsided. There was a certain someone who was gonna pay for his pain, he vowed. But so far he dared not complain. His luck had held. They hadn't discovered the body yet or all hell would've broken loose.

Crossing through the shadows, he ran through a large expanse of lawn and driveway to the corner of a house. His next sprint took him to the back of the house next door.

A light came on nearly scaring him half to death. He had to wait a moment to realize he'd tripped a motion detector. The increase in his blood pressure caused his head to explode and he held the abused organ between his hands, willing the pain to recede. He followed the line of the shore, slipping from house to house until he was several blocks away.

His first call was to Alexi. He didn't pick up.

Trying to figure out why was simply too much for his brain to handle so he hung up and dialed again. This time a voice answered. "Nicholai? It's Charles. Houston, we have a problem."

****

Elena was not nearly as worried for herself or her babies as she was for Alexi. He had the Valentin charm but also the Valentin temper. She worried he would lose control which would really put them in dire straits.

The Retreat, Dimitri had said. She knew the connotation of the word and her heart fell. If this was a retirement place for nuns, as she thought it might be, there would be elderly women residing there. Defenseless elderly women. Nuns who could get very hurt by a stray bullet.

"What if Morgan's not there?" Alexi asked. "He marches to the beat of a different drummer."

She watched Dimitri shrug. "We become guests for a while."

"They have no stake in this and you know it," Alexi cried. "Since when did you decide that killing and maiming innocents was more important than saving them?"

"At the age of thirteen, if you must know."

Elena understood immediately. "I believe that is the age you knew you were different, is it not?"

Alexi remained silent for many moments. "Ahh, jeez, Dimitri. You mean to tell me you sold your soul because you're gay?"

"It's not as simple as that."

"Yes, it is!" Alexi exploded.

"What would you know of it?" the man asked, and in that question she heard the pain of a lifetime. "Always hiding your feelings for fear of being ostracized. Shunned by your family; those very same people who profess to love you, until of course, they're faced with reality. Afraid that one wrong word, one wrong step, one small gesture will be the one that puts a neon sign over your head. Look at me. I'm gay. I'm gay."

"I know that two wrongs don't make a right," Alexi commiserated.

"You know nothing," came Dimitri's bitter reply.

"What you're doing now," Alexi continued, "is ten times worse than what you feel you've been through. His kind of promise will never give you happiness. It can't. It comes from evil."

"Dimitri," Elena added, trying terribly hard not to let any pity bleed into her tone. "I'm an empath. I'm at one with the world around me. It's not too late. You can still redeem yourself. There is a piece of you. Inside." She pointed at her chest. "That he has not corrupted yet. Find that part of you. Hold onto it. I beg of you."

Dimitri shook his head, a touch of wonder in his voice. "Why should you care?"

"Because I do. Because I do not believe that evil of any kind can beat goodness."

"That's the dumbest answer I've ever heard. Power wins. Power protects. Besides, I have the gun."

"Guns are meaningless among us and you know it," she replied. "But you still have to have the courage to use such a weapon. I don't believe you can."

Dimitri simply smiled. "We'll all have to wait and see, now won't we?" To Alexi he added, "Pull up in front, Alexi. Go inside. Tell them something's happened to Tara and you need to find Morgan right away. If he's not here, find out where he is or when he's coming back. In the meantime I'm going to have a really interesting philosophical discussion with your mate. Who just happens to have a really good heart but the sense of a flea. What she thought she saw inside me died a long, long, time ago."

He stopped just for a moment to pull a phone out of his pocket. "And Alexi? No tricks. This is a walkie-talkie phone. I have the other one. Try anything and I'll kill her."

Chapter Twenty-Six

"Do you really expect me to believe such nonsense?" Nicholai asked him. "About a man who has been my friend my entire life?"

"Normally, Valentin, I wouldn't give a crap about what you believe. I would probably tell you what you could do with yourself too. But I don't like being cold-cocked by anyone. So just do me a favor. Lend me your car. Mine's in the parking lot back at that church and there are probably a dozen cops crawling over it right about now."

He watched Tara walk into the room. She looked frightened. At least someone in the place had some sense. "I overheard. I'm really starting to worry. Alexi and Elena should have been here by now."

"Let me try Alexi's cell," Nicholai tried to reassure. Himself or his mate or both? "That's odd," he added, hanging up. "It went right to voice mail."

"I'm telling you, we have a big time problem here," Charles reiterated. "Dimitri's gone traitor on us."

"Can you connect with him, Nico?" Tara asked.

He watched the other man try. "He's blocking my attempts."

"You know Alexi would only search for so long before giving up. He's got to be in trouble to be incommunicado this long."

"All right, Charles. You've made your point," Nicholai answered. "Now tell me again. Real slow. Exactly what happened."

He did, wondering if things could get any crazier. Here he was, a friend and ally to his sworn enemy while Nicholai's lifelong friend had betrayed them. "We must alert Ariel," Nicholai decided.

"We don't have time," Charles argued. "Just give me a set of keys. Please."

Nicholai arched a brow at him. "Charles, try to think things through for a moment, will you? Just this once. And listen. Where are you going to go? Not back to the church, right? That leaves you with a rather short list of destinations."

Okay. The man had a point. "It's a small island. I'll find them."

"They may be detained by the police," Tara interjected.

"Then Alexi would have at least answered a private summons," Charles answered. There. That made them even in the point-making contest.

"Think, Charles. Please. We need more information. Did Dimitri say anything that might give us a clue?"

Charles frowned. "I don't know." His head tried to split open again as he thought back to their conversation. "Do you think I could have maybe some aspirin or something? And something to wash them down with? My head won't quit hurting."

"I'm sorry, Charles," Tara replied. She left the room and returned a moment later with some pills and something stronger than water to take them with.

He lifted his glass. "Thanks." Probably not the smartest thing to do, but that was never his strong suit to begin with. He took a long pull on the drink after taking the pills and enjoyed the slow burn right down to his belly. "Not much of anything registered 'cause I was in shock, same as you were." He took another sip this time to savor the bite of the whiskey in his hand. "He did say something about not judging a book by its cover."

"He would," Nicholai agreed. "Dimitri would

want to soften the blow. Or at least give cause to his actions."

"Oh, no," Tara cried. "I don't think that's what he meant at all."

"Huh?" Charles asked, a bit befuddled by her words.

"It's Morgan. The Ancient one knows he gave us the Water. Dimitri wasn't only talking about himself."

"But then," Nicholai thought out loud. "The Ancient one has known Morgan's purpose all along."

"Hey, would one of you explain please? I'm confused."

"Morgan's mind is terribly fragile," Tara answered. "He can't be probed. He'd become a vegetable."

"The Ancient one is using us to track down the Water for him," Nicholai continued.

That was just wonderful. "I'll bet Dimitri's out looking for Morgan right now. And he probably has Alexi and Elena with him."

A loud thumping stopped his next question, the one where he was going to ask what they planned to do. Charles didn't have long to wait to find out. A moment later, the object of their discussion stood right in front of him.

****

"Good evening, Sister. I'm sorry to bother you at this terribly late hour."

"Normally, Mr. Valentin, I would not have opened the door. But for you, I'll always make an exception."

At first it didn't dawn on him. Then he realized she thought he was Nicholai. "Sorry. You have me confused with Nicholai. I'm his twin brother, Alexi."

"Oh, I beg your pardon." She sounded quite surprised. "I would bet you drove your mother crazy."

He smiled. "We did. And I would love to tell you some stories, but I came here to find Morgan. It's very urgent that I speak with him. I would have called, but you just can't contact him that way. He doesn't quite get phones."

The Sister smiled. "I know."

Alexi put his finger to his lips. He pointed to the phone. Stay with me, he asked silently. She nodded. He made a writing motion with his hands. "Is he here?"

Very quietly, which was impressive, she handed him a small pad and pen. Then he rolled his finger in a circle near his mouth to tell her she needed to keep talking. "I haven't seen him since dinner, but then I usually don't. He could be anywhere. He likes to take walks along the beach."

"Then he could be gone for hours."

"Then again, he could turn up in a moment. That's Morgan. Let me see. I think Sister Bernadette is still up. She's our night owl. I'll bet she's brewing a pot of tea right now. Would you like a cup?"

"No, no thank you, Sister. If you could just find out for me that would be great. Tara sent me to find him. Some kind of family emergency. And my brother would have come, but he didn't want to leave her right now."

As he spoke, Alexi wrote a note that said: *Please call this number. Tell whoever answers that Alexi needs help right away. At Tara's home.*

He handed her the note and she scanned it quickly. She nodded. "I understand. I'll be back in a jiffy." She was gone less than a minute. "You're in luck. Sister Bernadette said that Morgan is already on his way to his sister's home. He must know about the problem already."

That was the understatement of the century. "Thank you, Sister. Thank you very much."

As he walked out of the Retreat, he said into the

phone, "Did you get that?"

"I heard," came the partially static-filled reply. "Move. I have to hurry. I want to be able to surprise your brother. Even with that kind of advantage, he's a formidable foe."

****

Asking Morgan anything was probably the most frustrating exercise in futility Nicholai ever experienced. "Try again, Tara." He remembered the time Morgan helped them, the one time Nicholai had seen the man whole. So much life in his gaze, so much beauty in his face. Not that there wasn't now. But that moment gave him a taste of the real Morgan.

"Morgan? It's Tara."

He blinked. Then he smiled. "Tara."

"If anything, Nico, he seems worse than ever. He used to be able to hold a thought, take a direction."

"What about the signet? It worked by accident before."

"Do we dare?"

"I don't know that we have a choice," he replied.

Tara slid her signet ring into the palm of her hand. She reached up to touch Morgan's temples, just as Nicholai's cell phone went off. It was Charles. He'd taken the keys anyway and had started his search of the island. "We have to get out of here. Now. Move. Dimitri's on his way over here. Charles just passed him on the road."

"Did he see Charles?"

"He doesn't think so." Alarm raced through his mate's face. "Easy, sweet. We just have to hide."

The both had the same thought. "The old pier by the store."

Nicholai nodded. They threw on jackets and put the baby in a hooded one-piece suit. As soon as Morgan saw Sylvana, he wanted to hold her.

"Let him take her or we'll never get out."

He watched Morgan hold his daughter as if she were a priceless treasure. Which, of course, she was.

"Baby," Morgan told them.

"Yes, Morgan," Tara reassured. "Now come with us. Okay?"

Nicholai shook his head. Life was just plain strange sometimes.

****

Alexi pulled up in front of Nicholai's home. They all got out of the car. Dimitri seemed preoccupied. "You will wait by the car. Your mate and I will go up."

Alexi shrugged. He caught Elena's gaze as she went by, telling her not to worry. She gave him a quick smile. He felt her try to communicate with him but shook his head. Now was not the time. Not yet.

He wasn't surprised when they came down a short time later. Dimitri didn't look happy at all. A huge thrill of relief washed through Alexi. "He's not here."

No sooner did the words come out of his mouth than the man's cell phone rang. Dimitri hadn't taken the thing off speaker, so they all heard who was on the other end of the line. "You made a bad deal, old friend."

"Not quite. I still have your brother and his mate."

"Except that we do things my way now. Release Alexi."

"And have the two of you floating around?" Dimitri snorted. "I think not."

"Then you get no trade."

Alexi watched the man think that one over. "Okay. We do it your way. Where?"

"Look across the parking lot. The amusement park. It's wide open. No tricks. Morgan for Elena. But you let Alexi go. Now."

"Always playing the big brother, eh Nicholai?"

"You have no right to speak to me like that ever again, Dimitri."

Alexi almost felt sorry for the man as his face turned to stone. Almost. "You're right. And you have yourself a deal." Dimitri slammed the phone together.

Alexi walked over to Elena. Dimitri still had a death grip on her arm. He reached out and cupped her cheek with his palm. She closed her eyes and melted into him. *I love you.*

He turned and walked away. A couple of minutes later Nicholai connected with him and told him where they were hiding. He ran to meet them as fast as he could. "Dammit, Nico. What are you doing? We can't make a trade."

"We have no choice. We have to draw the Ancient one out into the open."

Alexi understood Nicholai's reasoning in a flash. "To destroy him. But how?"

Nicholai outlined his plan. "Good," Alexi replied. "But I have an even better idea."

After Alexi finished speaking, his brother nodded and smiled. "I always knew two Valentins were better than one."

"I can't tell you how glad I am to have you here fighting beside me," Alexi replied. "You, too, Tara."

Nicholai shook his head. "I'm sorry, Tara. Not this time. You have to take care of Syl." She started to protest but stopped, resignation etching into her features. She was making a choice Alexi knew he wouldn't want to have to make. "Should something happen—," Nicholai began. That set Tara off big time. Nicholai had to calm her down by kissing the hell out of her. She had to hate this passive road. After all, she was the one who actually came close to destroying the Ancient one the first time around. "Go to Jeri's. Wait there. If we don't come back, call Ariel. She and the rest of the Nobility will protect you."

Alexi's heart broke for his sister-in-law. He could tell she was beside herself but trying to hold it in, for both of them. "Remember," Nicholai reminded her.

She smiled through her tears. "With love, we will win."

****

Elena wondered if she weren't in some sort of spaghetti Western movie. She and Dimitri stood in the middle of the huge parking lot of the amusement pier. She couldn't help but stare at the pylon wall where she conceived the twins she now carried. Would they have a chance to make more babies? Would the ones she carried have the chance to be born and live their lives in peace?

Alexi, Nicholai, and Morgan approached from the opposite side. They walked slowly and every now and then one of them would have to stop and speak to Morgan. His reticence was palpable. Not that she could blame him.

"That's far enough," Dimitri called out.

They stopped. Dimitri grabbed her arm again and began hauling her towards them. "I can walk."

"No tricks. We play this straight."

She nodded and he let go which helped her balance as she walked. She knew Alexi and Nicholai weren't going to give her up this easily. So did Dimitri. He continued to move but each step seemed to take forever.

When they were about twenty-five yards apart, Dimitri stopped. "Just Morgan and Elena from here."

"He won't move," Alexi countered. "You saw the trouble we had getting this far. Let me walk with him."

Dimitri didn't have much choice. "All right."

Alexi and Morgan started moving towards her.

She looked at Dimitri. He had one last chance at redemption. He shook his head and let go. Elena started walking towards her mate.

"Oh, I do so love it when a plan comes together."

Alexi stopped as Morgan tried to bolt. Elena watched as Alexi had to actually restrain the man. "Morgan. Take it easy. It's Okay. It's all right. Calm down."

"No. Bad man. Very bad man."

Elena reached out with her mind to soothe Morgan. They seemed to be able to connect on a very basic level because Morgan started to quiet down.

"I would like to thank you all for performing your duties in such a flawless fashion," the Ancient one announced.

"Screw you, you miserable excuse for a living being," Alexi answered.

"Now, now. Name calling is not permitted." Alexi doubled over in pain.

"Alexi," she cried, rushing towards him. Dimitri reached out and stopped her.

"Listen," he said to the Ancient one. "I don't have to stay and watch this. I did what you asked. Give me what I want and I'm out of here."

The Ancient one, so terrible in his cold beauty, shook his head. "Weak stomach," he muttered. Then he lifted his hand. A bolt of light flew out of his palm and directly into Dimitri's chest. A moment later all hell broke loose.

Chapter Twenty-Seven

Mad didn't even come close, Alexi thought as he launched himself through the air. That bolt of light nearly hit his mate. He was going to put an end to this son of a bitch once and for all.

Alexi reached into his pocket for the flask of Water Morgan had brought. What the Ancient one didn't know, and neither had Alexi, was that Morgan had brought two flasks of the Water, not just one.

What the Ancient one also didn't know was that the reason the holders for the Chalice and the Water were made out of wood, was because wood acted as a natural insulator to the power. So did anything made out of wood. No one could feel he had the flask because it was wrapped in paper.

But they did as soon as Alexi pulled the flask out of his pocket.

Alexi knocked the Ancient one down to the ground and pounced on top of him. While he grappled with the man, he heard a car motor roar to life. Tires peeled. Another mistake the Ancient one had made. The lone car in the back of the lot wasn't unoccupied. Neither the Ancient one nor Dimitri had paid attention. Charles was still alive and not in the hands of the police.

Following their plan, Charles flung the door open and Nicholai shoved Morgan into the car. Then Charles hit the gas. Alexi knew they were successful by the smell of burnt rubber as the car fishtailed and screeched out of parking lot.

The Ancient one screamed in anger at being thwarted. He took hold of Alexi's neck with one hand, trying to choke the life out of him. Alexi sat on his chest, one hand clawing at the steel band cutting off his air supply, the other trying to pour the Water down the Ancient one's throat. And that was when Alexi realized *he'd* made a fatal error. The cap was still on the flask.

He would have to get away long enough to loosen it. Alexi pulled at the fingers around his neck. All of a sudden, he heard a squeak. Then another. His gaze flew to the flask. The cap was moving and *he* wasn't turning the metal.

****

Elena was positive she would not have had the strength to move the cap if her life depended upon it. But Alexi's life depended now on her abilities and that gave her all the impetus she needed.

She focused on the cap first although she was certain that had the situation been less dire, she would have gone after the fingers choking her mate first. Each turn of the cap drained her and she wondered why. Then she realized the babies were already changing her body, sapping the additional energy she needed for this particular task.

Still, she refused to give in. Reaching deep inside, Elena moved the cap around again and again, and again. Then using the strength she had left, she flipped the top off the flask.

Elena could feel Alexi fading. *Hold on, my love.* She collapsed onto her knees and her hands clasped together naturally as if she were going to pray. Well, she was, wasn't she?

All of a sudden, Elena knew she was not alone. Nicholai joined her. Tara. Ariel. The entire Nobility came together in her mind and her heart. She was amazed by the power hidden within.

Finger by finger, she tore the appendages off Alexi's neck. Then, holding them free, she focused on the hand holding Alexi's wrist. The Ancient one began to weaken. So did she. The rest was up to her mate.

Alexi tore his other hand out of the Ancient one's grasp. "You have hurt us for the last time, you miserable son of a bitch."

The Ancient one laughed and the grip on his throat closed with ten times the force of before. But the opening was just enough. As was the opening of the Ancient one's mouth. "Here. See how you like this drink." Saying that, Alexi poured the Water down the Ancient one's throat."

"That won't hurt me." the man laughed. He sputtered, forced to swallow or choke.

Alexi reared back, breaking the Ancient one's grip, and staggered to his feet. "Oh, no?"

Alarm filled the man's gaze. As Alexi watched, the Ancient one stopped moving. Limb by limb, starting at the extremities and working inwards until only his eyes darted back and forth. In terror. "You forgot something else, you spawn of the devil," Alexi told him, rubbing his neck with his hand. "There was more than one meteorite. We found pieces of another one. Combined with the pure Water of Change, we figured it would kill you. But this is better. As it was in the beginning, so it will be again. Knowing all that goes on around you but unable to move."

A scream reverberated in his mind and he held his ears even though he heard no real sound. As he looked around, he saw Nicholai do the same. And that was when he found Elena collapsed on the ground.

Alexi ran to her and kneeled beside her. She was alive. Thank God. "Elena? Oh, sweetheart, please. Wake up. We've won."

He bent down, hauled her into his arms, and kissed her. Her lips twitched beneath his so he went for broke. Then next thing he knew, her tongue was dancing with his. He couldn't help himself. He started laughing with relief. So did she. Then Nicholai joined them.

A moan drew their attention. Dimitri, Alexi thought. Elena struggled out of his arms and made her way over to where the man lay. She kneeled down and reached into her pouch, ready to try to save him. Dimitri stayed her hand. "No. I deserve my fate."

"No one deserves death," she replied, her tone gentle.

"I'm too far gone." He choked and tried to swallow. "Nicholai. I'm sorry. So sorry. Of all the pain I have caused, losing your respect and friendship has hurt the most."

"It doesn't matter as long as you understand. Fight now. Fight for your life. Let Elena help you."

Sadness filled him as Elena looked up at him first, then at his brother. She shook her head. Dimitri took one last hitched breath then sighed. "I forgive you my friend," Nicholai told him.

Alexi wanted to hate the man but couldn't. He helped Nicholai arrange the body and joined his brother in the death chant of their people. Once they were done, he helped his mate to her feet. They began walking towards their nemesis who remained unmoving. "Do you think he will stay that way?"

Elena could only wonder. "Oh, my," she whispered. "They're coming."

"Who's coming?" Alexi asked.

A moment later, cars began filing into the parking lot. Ariel had gotten their message and sensed where they were as she drove past. Last but not least, Charles followed with Morgan.

Everyone got out and they all gathered around the prone bodies. She could feel the woman's rage as she stood over their enemy; feel her sorrow as she looked down at Dimitri's now peaceful countenance.

Ariel then turned to her. Before Elena could bow in greeting, Ariel paid homage to her. She bowed low and long before rising. "Hear me, all of you," Ariel called out as she rose. "This woman will be forever remembered by our people as the savior of our race and the creator of a new one."

They would have shouted their approval, but they were in a public place in the middle of the night. Instead, Elena heard the roar as it ran through her mind. She would have smiled but for the problem they now faced. "My lady," she said quietly. "We still have a problem."

"Not anymore," Ariel replied. Morgan came forward holding a casket even more beautiful than the one that held the Chalice. He took out another flask of the true Water of Change. "I'll need the leaves you created."

Elena blanched. "In my head, I know what needs to be done. But in my heart, I can't help you. I ask your forgiveness. I can't be a party to this."

"Still, it has to be done," Alexi told her, pride shining in his gaze as she held onto the courage of her being. She was a healer and could never take part in a killing. He took her pouch and pulled two leaves out, handing them to Ariel with great care. "Let us leave first, please." Then Alexi turned to his brother. "Nico?"

"I must stay. I'll be along in a few minutes."

"Give them to me," Charles chimed in. "I won't have any trouble at all finishing the job."

Elena turned to him. "Have a care, Charles. Do not do this with a glad heart. What goes around comes around."

"Yeah, and this bastard is getting just what he deserves."

Elena started to walk across the parking lot with her arm wrapped tight around her mate. Then she stopped. "Much evil has been done. I would like to heal some of it." She turned back. "My lady? Would I be able to have a tiny amount of Water? For Jeri and Sylvana?"

Ariel bowed again. "You are a lesson to us all. Understand, though, that we must destroy the Ancient one for the future of our race. No other reason."

Elena nodded. "I do."

Ariel motioned for a small portion of the Water to be placed in the flask Alexi had used. "Let us hope the only use we have for this water is to heal in the future."

Elena bowed. "I wish for that as well."

They got into Alexi's car and were just about to leave when Elena felt a sigh rustle all about her. A great weight lifted from her shoulders. She reached out and clasped Alexi's hand in hers. "He's gone."

"For now," her mate replied. And Elena could only pray that it would be forever.

Chapter Twenty-Eight

Elena sat back and stretched. Alexi came up behind her and began kneading the tension out of her shoulders. She hated waiting. Not knowing was worse.

She had taken her last leaf, wet it with the Water until it really glowed green, then placed it on Jeri's eyes, one at a time. Then she took the used leaf and touched it to Sylvana's lips. Elena believed that this would make Syl into a true Noble. The baby began to make a sucking motion so Elena had to believe some of the Water made its way inside.

Now they waited.

Sylvana began crying and Tara rose to feed her. "Ouch," she heard Tara cry out. Tara looked up at Elena and smiled through her tears. "She's getting ferocious."

That was a good sign, though none of them could tell if she was a Noble or not. She seemed to be, they all felt she was, and that was good enough for Elena. Besides, the babies she carried would not be True Nobles either. She hoped they would be the best of both races.

A couple of hours passed. Elena sensed the Sun was about to rise. So did everyone else. Tara, Nicholai, Alexi, even Sergei tried to cram outside onto Jeri's small deck.

Jeri awoke just as the great orb tipped the horizon. Elena breathed a sigh of relief as the woman recognized her right away. "Thank you, God."

"I can see. I can see," Jeri shouted. Everyone

came running inside from their morning feed, took one look, and hugs started flying around the room. "Thank you. Thank you, thank you."

Eventually, Elena motioned to Alexi. "I'm exhausted, but I'm too wired to sleep. And there is one more task I need to perform." She whispered in his ear and he threw his head back, roaring with laughter. When everyone turned, she simply smiled and shrugged, leaving some puzzled faces around the room. "They'll probably give us a penthouse or something like that for the night," Alexi told her. "Any ideas on how to use it?"

Elena simply arched her brow at him.

****

The phone rang, dragging him out of a sound sleep. Charles cursed and rolled over. Damned thing, he thought, intent on burying it somewhere. Then he reached out. He might as well answer it. "Hello?"

"Is this Charles Rhys-Jones?"

"Yes." Befuddled, Charles tried to shake the sleep from his head. "Who is this?"

"My name is Sarah Mitchell. I'm an account manager at Chase Bank."

"Look, I don't know what you're selling, but I don't want any."

"No. Please. Don't hang up. I'm not selling anything."

"Okay. Don't sell me anything. Good-bye." He hung up. The phone rang again, just as he was getting nice and comfortable.

"Sir. Please. Wait. Don't hang up. My boss will kill me."

He was about to say too bad when Elena's parting words popped into his head. *Aww, what the hell.* "All right. I won't hang up. You do your spiel and I'll leave the phone off the hook."

"I'm sorry, but that's not why I'm calling."

"Then just why *are* you calling?"

"We need you to come down to the bank as soon as possible. Preferably with a passport, a current driver's license, and a social security number to prove your identity."

"What? Why?"

"Sir, someone who would prefer to remain anonymous just opened an account in your name. Now let me make sure I have this right. Yes. One million, one hundred, and seventeen thousand dollars."

Charles started laughing. He laughed until his sides hurt. "You still there?" he asked when he could finally draw a breath, wiping at his eyes.

"Yes, sir. And there was a message I was to give you. I was told to tell you, I always pay my debts. Then I was to tell you the words Atlantic City."

He started laughing again. He couldn't stop. When he finally did, the woman continued. "Now this is the one I don't understand," she told him.

"What's that?"

"Bottle caps aren't the only thing I can move."

Epilogue

Alexi stood next to his brother unable to stop shaking. "Relax," Nicholai told him.

"That's easy for you to say. You've done this before."

"And you've been on center stage most your adult life."

"Opening night jitters, I guess."

Nicholai cracked up. "Now that is truly putting the cart before the horse. Relax. It's only a ceremony. And rather late to boot."

"I can't help it. I'm scared Nico. What if I—." He never got his next words out of his mouth. Elena looked stunning. She wore the traditional wedding dress of their people with the tie-crossed front, no back, and my goodness. He'd never realized she had such gorgeous curves. The dress fit tight as a glove.

Nicholai nudged him with his elbow and Alexi stopped gaping. Even old Jacques was smiling. But Alexi had eyes only for his mate. When she reached his side, he thought his heart would burst from the love he felt for her. He knew she felt the same. Her eyes were shining and her gaze told him all he needed to know.

Sergei and the rest of the people stood before them. "I, Alexi Mikhail, Head of the House of Valentin, ask the people a question. Will you accept Elena Kyrinova as my lifemate? For all eternity?"

A shout went up as people began clamoring for her. Alexi's heart swelled.

Sergei's voice rang through the air. "Elena Kyrinova, you are not of Noble Blood, but you come to us as a favored of the people."

A joyous shout rang out through the crowd and they began chanting their name for her, The Lady of the Lake.

"Do you swear fealty to the House of Valentin for all time?"

"I do."

"Will you bond with Alexi Mikhail for all eternity?"

"I will."

Alexi held out his right hand and pulled back the sleeve of his wedding tunic. Sergei directed Elena to do the same with hers. Using a golden rope, he tied their wrists together. Chanting in the ancient tongue, he told them they were bound, now and forever. Then the rope was removed. Using tongs, he held out a fiery circle of gold, fashioned in the crest of the House on both sides. Alexi nodded to his mate. *Be strong, my love. It will hurt but a moment.* Alexi positioned his wrist on one end, Elena on the other. Then they pressed their wrists together.

Alexi felt no pain as his lips captured Elena's. There was only the warmth of her love and the love of the people surrounding them. As he removed his wrist he held onto hers, kissing the wound. She did the same. Then he held their arms aloft for all to see.

A great roar of approval rose from the crowd. Now was the time for great celebration. But first he had to find his bride. For as soon as he had let go, she was whisked away by Nicholai, then Sergei, then a host of others. Just when he was about to pout, he found they were standing in front of one another.

"I wish we were alone right now."

"We could be if you choose. But you can wait, can't you?"

He nuzzled her neck. "Care to ask that question again?"

"All right," she laughed. "I give in. But not for long. Then I expect my magician to make magic with me."

"Forever and always, my love."

A word about the author...

Linda J. Parisi found her calling when, as a scientist, she discovered romance. Her idea of the perfect hero is a cross between Frank Langella's Dracula and his Zorro: tall, dark, handsome, and untamable. Her heroines will never give up or give in, so the sparks continue to fly through her books until her characters reach their happy ending. The road might not be easy but the fun is in the travel.

She's been a member of New Jersey Romance Writers and Romance Writers of America since 1993 and is now a member of Liberty States Fiction Writers. During the day she's a research scientist and project manager for a diagnostic technologies company. But at night? At night, she gets to play with vampires.

Thank you for purchasing
this Wild Rose Press publication.
For other wonderful stories of romance,
please visit our on-line bookstore at
www.thewildrosepress.com.

For questions or more information
contact us at
info@thewildrosepress.com.

The Wild Rose Press
www.TheWildRosePress.com